New Dawn

Diane Pike

Published by Diane Pike
Publishing partner: Paragon Publishing, Rothersthorpe
First published 2023

ISBN 978-1-78792-013-2

Book design, layout and production management by Into Print

www.intoprint.net
+44 (0)1604 832149

PART ONE

'New Dawn' is dedicated to my amazingly brilliant and creative editor, Paula Holmes, and to all my author friends and beta readers, who inspired and encouraged me to write my first ever YA Sci Fi novel.

Chapter 1

SP8

Cara was here, racing through space along Galactica Corridor Five. She beamed with delight as she sat at the control panel of Space Pod 8, her mind running on with the purr of its incredible acceleration. "This is what I call a challenge," the young officer cadet exclaimed. "At last, I'm in command and working on something important. My future has begun!" she said aloud as her heart raced with a thrill.

She watched the whole galaxy stretch before her and into infinity. Silent comets sped away from her across the vast darkness, burning up and avoiding distant planets before they collided or crashed into them.

When she'd launched from New Dawn Space Station, the chief AI, Guylo, had calculated the distance and speed needed for her flight. Speed Pods were one of the fastest forms of space travel, and Cara was delighted as she flew through the purple gas rings of Planet Zedimus at a breathtaking rate, and meteorites of all shapes and sizes struck the outer surface of the space pod. The chunks thudding into it created a raucous clamour that eventually ruptured into a mad, wild clattering.

"Cara, do you copy?"

The voice startled her. "Cara, this is Valina. Do you copy?"

"*Er*—Yes. Copy," Cara responded vaguely.

"We've been expecting you to make contact. Copy."

Cara frowned and gave a nervous giggle. "Oh, yes. Sorry, copy. I mean, yes, ok. Copy."

"Cara, you must turn on your VCS. Copy."

"What did you say? Copy," Cara replied. She could hear the agitation in the First Officer's voice but figured that was because it was hard to keep track of the space pod without clear communications. She knew that sometimes slight interference problems occurred when a pod flew through meteoric storms such as these.

"What is wrong with you, Cara? Your Visual Communication System. YOU NEED TO TURN IT ON!" Valina yelled.

"Ah, yes!" At last, Cara remembered what to search for. She identified the key and tapped it. Immediately, a holograph of Valina appeared in the air. "That's better!" Cara grinned. "Now we don't have to go on with that silly 'copy this' and 'copy that' nonsense, do we?"

Valina didn't smile back, and Cara thought about how grim-faced she seemed. "Cara. Are you sure you can pilot a space pod?" Valina asked solemnly.

Cara glanced at the floor as the colour rose in her cheeks. She was flustered rather than upset by Valina's question. After a pause, she answered, using her high-pitched, shifty voice. "Yes, of course, I can handle a pod. Why do you ask?"

"When we tried registering your exact position, it was difficult because your speed and flight path were erratic. That's why we needed urgent contact with you." Valina's image glared at Cara. "You didn't realise that you flew off course and almost drifted into a violent cosmic storm – did you?"

Cara looked at the controls and studied the data for a few seconds. Then, satisfied that all looked normal, she answered sharply, "Well, everything is how it should be now."

Calmly, Valina raised her brow in a questioning manner. "Tell me, Cara, did you successfully obtain your Flying Pass?"

When Cara didn't answer, Valina sighed heavily and loudly. "If you operated a space pod like you've been flying this one, there's no way you could have passed your flying exam. So you weren't successful, were you, Cara?"

Cara flushed and said stiffly, "I'll have you know, Valina, I achieved outstanding results for the *simulated* space pod exam. But the trouble was that I had a terrible fever on the day of the proper flight test. I felt far too ill to fly." There was an awkward silence until Cara cleared her throat and said, "You needn't worry. I'll accomplish it next month when we report back to HQ."

Valina shook her head slowly and sighed again. "So, this *is* the first time you've ever operated and piloted a real space pod, right? I must say, Cara, I find that knowledge extremely disturbing."

Valina's holograph faded to a dim outline as the Pod travelled farther and farther away across the galaxy's outer regions. Soon SP8 would be out of reach of New Dawn Space Station's VCS scanner.

"Ok, ok, yes. It is the first time," Cara admitted with a sigh of resignation. She held up a hand. "But Valina, please let me carry out this mission!"

Reluctantly, Valina agreed. "At the moment, a huge amount of cosmic dust floats around you, weakening your VCS signal. So it seems there's no option but to let you go on. For the moment, that is. But, unfortunately, our holographs are becoming increasingly feeble, and I'm afraid they won't last much longer. So that means you'll soon be on your own."

Valina continued in a voice that was now only an echo. Cara noticed Valina's image was hazy, and her shape was hardly distinguishable. "It's a good job that we swapped you over onto autopilot. You might be ok if you can remember the basics of piloting a space pod."

"Oh, thank you, Valina! I won't let you down. And I'm sorry about accidentally helping the thief! I am, honestly. I couldn't help it. I—"

But Cara didn't have a chance to finish her sentence because Valina's holograph had disappeared. So instead, she gazed wide-eyed at the incredible control system and fantastic technology of the speed pod. Cara smiled and didn't feel particularly sorry about anything. That accident allowed her to be where she was now, in command of a ship in deep space.

My first real mission, she thought with a slight, self-satisfied grin. *So, why should I be sorry?*

CHAPTER 2

A Clumsy Accident

Earlier that morning on New Dawn Space Station.

Cara's day started quiet and routine. A dull morning, as usual. Mundane and ordinary. After sitting for over two hours studying a screen filled with nothing but meteors shooting through space, Officer Cadet Cara Davis had gradually slid into a mindless stupor, far away from the task she should have concentrated on. She closed her eyes and imagined herself an explorer on some strange planet's surface or suspicious asteroid. She imagined it so vividly that she flexed her leg (as if to leap over a deep crater) and kicked the panel at her feet. Then, startled back to reality, Cara kicked the panel again, this time in a small fit of temper.

This sucks! She thought. *I might as well be back in London with Grandma and Pops. I'd hoped to do something interesting and exciting when I joined the Galaxy Patrol Force.* Cara wanted desperately to show her folks back home how capable she was. But right then, it was like someone had altered the gravitational pull – even her eyelids felt heavy, and she yawned again.

Cara noticed Valina – who, as First Officer was in charge while their captain was away – giving her a side glance with furrowed brows. Immediately, she retaliated. "What? I can't help it! I'm so bored," she grumbled. "Who wants to gawk at a screen for hours, staring at meteoric bombardments with gigantic lumps of rock colliding and crashing into each other? Not me, that's for sure." Cara shrugged, rechecking the screen. "Anyway, this phase is at least two million miles away, striking a distant galaxy now."

A shower of meteorites fled across the vast darkness of outer space like a fiery blizzard. The bombardments were hundreds of thousands of miles away. Cara, seated at her data screen, had peered endlessly at it through unseeing brown eyes. Finally, she let out a long, complaining grunt and thumped her leg. "I need to work on the more challenging, exciting stuff. This is rubbish! I didn't join the Galaxy Patrol Force to watch trashy bits of rock fly across the sky all day," she complained.

"For heaven's sake, Cara, we can't keep putting up with your constant whinging," Valina responded sharply, glaring across the control deck. "If you're that bored, I'll suggest to Captain Lydian that she adds more duties to your rota."

Cara narrow-eyed Valina, but it didn't stop her. "I'm trying to authorise additional duties for all twenty-five robotic crew. So, if you don't mind, *Cara*, the rest of us wish to continue our work in peace."

When Valina rolled her eyes at her, Cara huffed and gazed back at her screen, which still showed hundreds of fiery comets speeding downwards and across the galaxy.

"According to the astronomy forecast, the bombardment should die down directly," Valina said. She came over to peer at Cara's screen. "In the meantime, Cara, you must maintain a tight view of it."

"And on any other objects that might venture towards our space station," a gentle voice stated from the ceiling. Cara looked up and saw Debian, another officer cadet whose gravitational pull differed from her crew mates. Debian, a Quistic, had levitation powers that enabled her to float.

"Remember the oath you took, Cara. As officer cadets of the Galaxy Patrol Force, we have sworn an oath to protect the galaxy from harm. Our duties entail monitoring all ecosystems, creatures, and beings. The Patrol force assigns us to protect them – "

Cara thought, *Who will protect* me *from people who keep reciting the manual at me?* She stopped listening as she watched the Quistic drift down from the ceiling. Debian's fluorescent skin gleamed, and the cabin lights lit up her brilliant orange hair that stretched down her back in a tightly twisted plait. Cara always thought how beautiful it was, compared to her own short, black hair.

"So," Debian finally concluded, "We must be vigilant at all times for the sake of the Galaxy. How can that much responsibility ever be dull?"

Cara saw her crew mates exchange a look. She felt they didn't really understand her and probably never would. She thought *I'm only an Earthling – no special powers*, remembering her dad's favourite humble-brag line. Whenever he'd achieved something unique, that was what he'd say. He'd said it last in his final message to her. She still wanted to cry whenever she thought of that. Or of the doomed planet where both her parents had died minutes after they'd sent the message.

Cara didn't need any fuss and never cried in front of crewmates. Still, she felt a sob rising in her throat. Rather than let herself cry, she breathed deeply, yawned and stretched to her full length, sweeping her long arms up as she exhaled.

"What the *skag* was that?" she said in a muffled cry when she heard a distinctive unhealthy crunch and struggled to smother another yawn.

"Oh goodness me, Cara!" Debian gasped, "Now see what you've done!"

Cara looked back at the screen she'd been staring at and found it was gone. Vanished. She looked with an empty gaze, for there was now nothing there. Only the interior of the control deck was visible to them. The other two gave her a fixed look of disbelief.

Debian levitated to study the remains of the splintered sensor panel. "You've turned off all the external surveillance cameras with your fist when you stretched like that." She touched the power button two or three times, but it wouldn't react. "You've broken it!"

Cara sized up the damage, screwed up her nose and sighed in a neutral tone, "Oh yeah! So, I have. Sorry!"

She guessed the New Dawn Space Station crew members were getting used to the idea that she was incompetent. And why not? Captain Lydian constantly reminds her to stand straight, stop gazing around, and smarten up. *"If you want to survive the Patrol Force, Cara Davis, you can start by paying attention to your surroundings! It might very well be your arm next time! Now go mend your uniform sleeve and think about that while you do!"* And so on.

Now scowling and pressing a hand to her forehead, Valina said unusually irritatedly, "I'm afraid, Cara, that Captain Lydian would consider you idiotic to yawn and stretch like that."

Cara swallowed hard at Valina's remark. It was true, and the Captain had already warned her that she had just six more weeks to make all-round improvements or face dismissal from her duties as an Officer Cadet on New Dawn Space Station.

She snatched at an excuse in an attempt to soften the situation. "But it's only the screen that's gone. Right? I'm positive the *autosave* is still on. So, the data won't disappear, and it will still pick up anything that might come toward us."

Debian dropped gently back to the floor. "That's all very well, but with no screen, how can we see what's approaching us?"

Valina turned away, moved back to her console again and said stiffly, "It would still operate as normal, Cara, if you had concentrated on your duties." She flicked her hand in the air. "You'd best go to the control lab immediately and repair it before it loses total power. And no more yawning and stretching. You've craved more interesting work. Well, now you have it."

Cara's anger returned. In two strides, hands-on-hips, she confronted Valina. "I didn't mean mending stuff!" She folded her arms and glared. "It was an accident! I didn't *intend* to smash the panel, Valina!"

Valina kept working, pointedly ignoring Cara.

Cara paused for a moment before launching her next tirade. "Nothing exciting ever happens in these outer sectors of the galaxy!" she said in a raised tone. "And you know what? It's even duller around here when Captain Lydian's away, and we have *bossy* Valina pushing us around."

At that, Valina turned and glared threateningly at Cara. "Somebody needs to put you in your place, Cadet. Like it or not, I am in charge." She narrowed her eyes and then made a disgusted, dismissive gesture. "You are such a headache sometimes, Cara." Turning back to her work, Valina said, "You have your orders, Cadet. *Go.*"

Instead of heading up to the lab, Cara turned her back on the First Officer and left the control deck without another word.

She stopped just down the corridor, as always, at the large portal with a view outside the space station. She leaned on the handrail and, as she got closer to the glass, saw her reflection, illuminated by the bright lights in the corridor. Specks of light caught her face and lit up her smooth, light milk chocolate complexion. Cara considered herself reasonably good-looking, if a little ordinary. She was tall, athletic, and strong. She tried to smile reassuringly at her reflection, but all she could see were sad, brown eyes looking back at her.

Cara leaned in closer to the window and looked past her reflection, gazing across the vast void of space. She felt very, very far from anywhere and homesick. Something was missing in her life. Adventure, for one thing. But also friendship. She never thought that she fit in with her crew mates. She never felt accepted. *Or acceptable,* she thought. *I can't seem to do anything right.*

Thoughts of failure brought her grandmother's voice to mind this time. Grandma, who had a lot of patience, said to her unusually anxious, *"Cara dear, if you're not careful, you're going to lose another job! So maybe try paying more attention to your work and less time daydreaming about space nonsense."*

I know it's because of what happened to Mom and Dad that Grandma was so against me joining the Galaxy Patrol, she thought. So *I need to prove myself to her so she won't worry.* And she'd start by not getting kicked out of the GPS by the Captain.

Deep down, Cara was fond of her fellow crew mates and admired Captain Lydian. Whether they knew it or not, she always tried to impress them. Although somehow, it never quite worked out. Cara – *only an Earthling with no special powers* – could never quite meet their expectations.

Now with one weak punch, she'd taken down all external surveillance on the New Dawn Station. But, if she could fix it quickly (with some help from the AI), then it would all be just a temporary, short-term, minor inconvenience – surely that was all?

Cara hoped this inconvenience didn't turn out like the last time she'd messed things up and sent the entire crew to redo a week's worth of work. *How did I know the database needed an encryption code before I deleted it?* She thought. She still got glares and grumbles from Valina and Debian from that incident.

"This time, I'll make the repairs so fast that—" she said aloud but got no further because a shrill *screech* of an alarm going off on the control deck made her jerk back as her hands flew to her ears. Cara was abruptly catapulted out of her doldrums by the sound.

She ran toward the control deck thinking, *Well, at least this isn't my fault, right?*

Chapter 3

A Visitor

Cara immediately knew what the alarm meant, and to prove it, she announced, "Something has either hit or breached the station!" as she ran to activate a portal and mute the alarm.

"True," Valina said, "But unfortunately, since you demolished the external surveillance controls and haven't yet repaired them, we can't *see* anything."

After activating the portal, Cara mounted the metal stairs and sped along the gantry that led to the control lab. An odd sight caught her eye as she approached one of the internal circuit monitors, so she hit the transmission band on her wrist. "Guylo! What's going on?" she asked the AI.

Guylo responded, "Company. We have some company."

At once, Cara shot back down the steps two at a time and returned to the control deck.

"Valina! Debian!" she yelled with excitement. "Something's going on. A Zeg-Mar spacecraft is docking. It just showed up on the gantry ICM."

Cara stared into another ICM. She gasped louder than intended when she saw Guylo had let a sizeable two-legged creature enter the space station. "Who the *skag* is that?" she exclaimed.

"Guylo, who is it you are allowing into the terminal? I have not permitted entrance," Valina called.

Guylo's sure and steady drawl permeated the control deck. "His name is Mr Golbat Gorn. He is a Galactic Council Advisor and diplomat. There is no need for alarm, Valina. The visitor has passed all security checks."

No sooner had Guylo announced the visitor than the door slid open, and the tall, two-legged alien entered, carrying a square metal canister. Cara was unfamiliar with this type of creature and couldn't help staring at his gloomy face and evil-looking eyes. She guessed he was of the reptilian race, for he had a most offensive and unfriendly manner about him. His attempt at a winning smile revealed vicious yellow teeth pointed at their tips. The teeth made him appear monstrous as he placed the canister on the floor while he stood, rubbing his hands together and bowing to the three cadets.

Cara saw Valina study him sheepishly, and the skin of her cheeks became a darker blue than the rest of her. Her voice trembled a little as she spoke. "I'm sorry, sir, but if you hoped to see Captain Lydian, she is away at Conference," she said.

Gorn was a powerful, barrel-chested being. His drab face was vulgar, made up of chunky green-grey scales that formed lizard-like features. Cara noticed how his heavy brow concealed dark, narrow eyes that scanned the control deck, eying everything and everyone in his sight. He replied to Valina with a grunt from his bulbous snout. "I know full well where Captain Lydian is, and it doesn't matter."

He wore green garments, the like of which Cara had never seen before. The green robes extended over his short tunic and down to his knees, where black trousers tucked neatly into high boots. "I come from Patrol Headquarters. I am Captain Lydian's advisor, and she requests I take all the Kwaidem Crystals and Imperium Domes stored on New Dawn Space Station," Gorn announced.

Around his thick waist, he had a broad belt that a Law Enforcer might wear. Etched into the belt were rows of patterns in golds and purples, and Cara supposed it might stand for his influential position. To this, he had fixed a hand weapon. His slit eyes rested on her and her crew mates as they stood timorously together in a protective group. At first, no one spoke, but then Gorn straightened, and it seemed to Cara that he'd suddenly grown inches taller. He stuck out his jaw and said irritably, "I must deliver the crystals and domes to our expert scientists, who will calculate their power. These scientists will use them to create stronger Power Transmitters."

With a clawed hand, he gestured, "So tell me, who is in command here while Captain Lydian is away?"

Cara wasn't sure how to react, and by the expression on their faces, Valina and Debian were having the same problem. For a short time, the three cadets remained silent until Valina took a faltering step forward and lifted the delicate features of her beautiful face. "Er, I am," she said, clearing her throat. "I'm First Officer Cadet Valina Skarn. But I can't give them to you, Mr Gorn, unless I receive direct orders from Captain Lydian."

Valina moved away from the reptilian and towards the communication console. "Until I speak to the Captain, I don't know where she keeps them. They're not my responsibility," she lied.

Cara noticed that Valina's ears twitched and caused the spiral earring that all Listrocs wore to spin. Over time, she had learnt that their ears twitched whenever a Listroc felt uneasy. Cara knew at once Valina was anxious. So, thinking it would be helpful, she rushed to Valina's side and tapped her arm. "I can tell you where they are, Valina. The Kwaidem Crystals and the Imperium Domes are all kept in the Protection Vault on the lower deck," she gushed.

With a frown, Valina gave her a sharp-side glance and an almost imperceptible head shake. Cara was keen to be *helpful* and get this Gorn creature off New Dawn, and she thought Valina was acting weird because she felt anxious. However, Cara had noticed no immediate danger and shot one of her beaming smiles at him. "I can show you if you like," she cheerfully announced as she headed over to him.

With speed, Debian floated straight in front of Cara and faced her. "Wait, Cara! It needs a code to activate the door to the Protection Vault."

"— And," Valina cut in, "Captain Lydian has never informed us of it. She is the only one on board with authority to deal with such powerful items."

Gorn pressed his clawed fingers together, bowed his head and in a low, gravelly voice, said, "I consider myself to have much patience, but at the moment, I'm finding some difficulty." Then, with his claws fisted and dropped at his sides, he said, "Yes indeed! At the moment, it is like trying to explain things to a group of very stubborn children."

Then he gave each of them a menacing stare. "I do not think you are wise to annoy Captain Lydian with your stubborn resistance." He stepped closer and glared. "It's obvious she knows I can manage this situation. There was—" He paused briefly, thinking what to say. "An arrangement made."

He lifted his scaly hand, and Cara and the other two cadets cringed in unison. Then, walking off a few paces, he turned back and leered at them. "Mm, well! Do not trouble yourselves. I have the code stored here in this Code Reader and now know exactly where to find the Protection Vault," the stranger answered. He produced a small handheld device from his belt that he waved about. He made a hideous grin and, to Cara, said, "Let me see! The lower deck, you say?"

Chapter 4
Thief

Cara wasn't as wary of Mr Gorn as the others and thought being polite might get rid of him quicker. "Yes, sir, the items you require are all in the Stability Chamber, just beneath us," she said helpfully.

His shifty eyes locked onto Cara, and he said lowly, "In that case, please be good enough to show me where to go. I need to leave as promptly as possible. I'm to contact an acquaintance in the next atmospheric zone, and I don't wish to get caught in the solar storm."

Cara watched Valina put an arm around herself and rub the hollow of her neck. She felt rather sorry for their leader. But it was quite a responsibility to be second in command, and Cara was glad it was not her task to sort this out. She saw Valina glance across at Debian, probably for support.

"Didn't Captain Lydian send a message, sir?" Valina ventured to ask, suddenly appearing more anxious and on edge, her one spiral earring twirling.

For a moment, Cara took her eyes off Valina and observed Golbat Gorn more closely. To her dismay, she noticed his raptor eyes glow red, and a dribble of thick green saliva dripped from the reptilian's hideous mouth. He leaned uncomfortably close to Valina, surveying her like a predator ready to swoop down on its prey, and said with a snarl, "I have given you the message. I am here to carry out the Captain's instructions."

Valina caught her breath and froze. But at that moment, Cara thought Debian must have found the courage from somewhere because she suddenly hovered unexpectedly above his beastly head and face.

"My colleague means, sir, that it's better if Captain Lydian herself informs us. A holograph perhaps, or an audio message?" she said.

Cara wiped a hand across her face. By now, she also began to doubt the alien's veracity as his impatience and anger increased.

He stretched his head until his ugly face practically touched Debian's. "I do not hold myself answerable to a pack of cadets! Now you are getting above yourselves!" he stormed.

Cara thought that was funny since, at that moment, it was Debian hovering above Gorn. But then she heard a faint whimper as Debian quickly floated away. Gorn continued to scowl at everybody. Until finally, his voice dropped from rage to a threatening murmur. "My orders are from Captain Lydian, and as your A.I. told you, I am her advisor and a diplomat. I am also your Commander's advisor."

Cara heard a quiet gasp at this latest information. She felt that something wasn't right, and it was a shock to learn that Commander Predaton's business directly involved Mr Golbat Gorn. After all, Commander Predaton was one of the most senior officers in the force. Cara had never met the Commander personally, but they had all seen him on the big screen when he addressed the officer cadets at the start of their training.

"So, let that be sufficient for you," Gorn continued with another growl. "You will allow me to press on with the business your Captain requires me to carry out."

He stepped towards the elevator door, opened it, and passed through. The instant it sealed, Cara dashed to an interior surveillance monitor to view his actions. The others followed her, and together they watched him attach the code reader device to a panel on the vault door. Within a few moments, the panel responded by sliding free.

He took out each Kwaidem Crystal until all four had disappeared into the transport canister. Next, he removed the two Imperium Domes and opened them to peer at the contents. When satisfied, he placed those in the canister, too.

Cara, Valina, and Debian all looked on helplessly. "Do you think he's telling the truth? Why is he taking them?" Debian murmured.

"And more to the point, where is he *really* taking them?" Valina added.

Then, Cara saw him close the vault and transit canister with the code reader. "He's coming back," she cried, and all three shot away from the screen and the door. By the time Gorn re-entered, Cara had thought his mood had softened, and she noticed his eyes were no longer red.

"There, that finishes the business. I apologise for interrupting your duties today," Gorn said in the same growly voice and bowed graciously to them. Then with a most wicked and triumphant grin, he rasped, "I can assure you, young officers, that all is well. And now, I bid you a good day."

Cara and her crew mates stood gaping at each other as they heard Guylo go through the protocol for all departing spacecraft. But, of course, they couldn't watch Gorn's spacecraft leave because Cara hadn't repaired the exterior camera screen.

"He's a thief," Cara exclaimed with a sudden shift in her opinion of him. "I'm sure of it. I knew the moment I looked at that reptilian's terrible face; and those eyes that peer in all directions so that you can't tell whether he's looking at you," she said, pulling at the corners of her eyes to make them the same shape as Gorn's.

Valina bit down on her lip and frowned at Cara. "Well, you've soon changed your mind, seeing how willing you were to assist him. But yes, I'm certain you're right, Cara." She groaned, taking two or three frantic paces around the floor. "He's escaped with the most powerful energy sources ever known to live beings." She brandished her hand as she paced. "Those Kwaidem Crystals and Imperium Domes make Power Transmitters. They can supply energy to thousands of planets for hundreds of years." Valina paused and took a breath. "Not only that, it could devastate the universe if they fall into the wrong hands. Some horrible tyrant might use those same crystals and domes to create deadly weapons."

"Yeah, tell us something we don't know already," Cara said in a weary tone.

"He's worse than a thief," Debian whispered in a broken voice.

Cara glanced at Valina and then watched her go to Debian and touch the small cadet's shoulder. "Worse than a thief? What do you mean, Debian?"

As if recalling unpleasant thoughts, Cara saw Debian peer down at the floor with a painful expression, and her lips quivered along with her voice. "Gorn is from Planet Glydor, whose inhabitants are a barbarous race of reptilians called Chortons," she said.

"What makes you so sure about that?" Cara broke in, wondering why Debian was becoming so upset.

Debian lifted her face and looked at her. "Many years ago, they were at war with us. I was just nine years old when they invaded and plundered our planet. I remember fleeing from our home with my brother and parents as their troops marched into our town. They seized many of our people and enslaved them."

"Well, at least *you* escaped," Cara replied cheerfully, trying to lighten the mood. But, unfortunately, Cara realised her comment seemed to have the opposite effect as Debian's eyes filled with tears.

"My parents, myself and my brother did, but my uncle Hyto, my father's brother, did not." She dabbed away a tear and continued. "He, his wife, and their three children were all taken prisoner before we could save them. We never heard from them again," Debian said, making a tiny sob that sounded more like a hiccup. "We don't know what became of them."

Cara stood by, saddened at the thought of Debian's lost family members. "I'm sorry, Deb," she said softly.

Valina put her arm around Debian's trembling shoulders, "Oh, Debian, I'm sure the sight of Gorn must have terrified you when he came on board."

Debian was a Quistic, and Cara was always amazed that Quistics are never noticeably aged. She always thought Debian looked about the same age as herself, eighteen, nineteen maybe. But her jaw dropped when Debian told her she was three hundred and nine years old.

Cara felt bad for Debian now but was practical enough to feel it might help if she pointed out: "It's very sad. But it did happen three hundred years ago," she said, "and right now we have to do something about Gorn."

Valina gave Cara a disapproving glance. "How long ago it was is completely beside the point, Cara. It would be hard to forget something so horrible, no matter how long ago it happened. I'm sure you would never forget it." Valina's voice softened, "Gorn's visit must have brought back the most terrible memories for Debian."

Despite Valina's objections, Debian did brighten at Cara's reminder. "Fortunately, we had friends and allies in our Galaxy who eventually defeated the likes of Golbat Gorn." Then, in a calmer voice and with a weak smile, she said, "A few years later, many worlds united, including the planet Glydor, and formed the Galaxy Planet Union."

"Why not just say G.P.U. like everyone else?" Cara asked, not for the first time. She liked Debian, but her overly formal way of speaking was too much sometimes.

Valina screwed up her eyes and said, "Whatever, Cara. Let Debian finish."

"Well, the *G.P.U.* is supposed to work together to bring everlasting peace to our worlds and planets, but with the likes of Golbat Gorn still around, who knows what might happen?" Debian finished.

Valina still looked uneasy. "Exactly. How do we know we can trust someone like Gorn, who belongs to such a cruel race of people?"

Cara sat down and put her hand on her face as she realised the seriousness of the situation. "Captain Lydian might never see those crystals and domes again," she said. "Then it will be all our fault for allowing him to take them."

"But what could we have done?" cried Debian, anxious again. "If we had tried to stop him, he might have attacked us. I'm sure he would have killed us!"

CHAPTER 5
Speed Pod

Cara couldn't sit still any longer. She paced up and down New Dawn's control deck, feeling guilty about disclosing the location of the Kwaidem Crystals and Imperium Domes. The young cadet wracked her brain to find a solution. Still, knowing Valina was a Listroc and therefore highly intelligent in all things, Cara couldn't quite understand why – as First Officer – she hadn't figured out a way to stop Gorn. Usually, Valina could work out solutions to the most difficult of problems. Maybe it was fear that had prevented her from acting.

Cara remembered when she and Valina, an Earth immigrant from an outer galaxy, first met. They'd been seatmates in a crowded shuttle-tube rocket, travelling to the Universal Galaxy Academy to begin training as Galaxy Patrol Officer Cadets. That day, proudly wearing her new UGA Cadet uniform, Cara longed for conversation with other Cadets.

Unfortunately, her seatmate responded, "Valina," when Cara introduced herself, but otherwise did not respond to any other attempt at conversation. It was the closest Cara had ever been to a Listroc, and she had many questions.

However, Valina only studied her tablet for the rest of the journey. She kept as still as a statue – a lovely creature with a soft blue lustre to her skin and no head of hair. Cara thought perhaps she *was* a statue since she hardly seemed to breathe.

Poor Valina, Cara thought, remembering how she'd continued to pepper the living statue with random questions for a while. But, since she'd needed to talk, Cara wasn't troubled that Valina ignored her and spent the rest of the trip sharing her hopes and fears about the UGA.

But she'd actually listened to me, Cara remembered with amusement. At the end of the flight, as they stood to exit, Valina looked up at Cara and said, "Your grandmother may be right about you being a flibbertigibbet. As an Officer Cadet, you might want to work on your self-discipline and impulse control."

Since then, Cara had often watched Valina sit like a statue, studying some new, unknown technology or equipment. Then, with unbelievable speed, her Listroc friend understood whatever it was and knew exactly how to use it.

How can I ever live up to that? However, a thought came to her, and she knew it was true. *I have to make up for what I've done. I have to get the power transmitters back from Golbat Gorn!*

After all, Cara was glad Valina had not devised a way to stop Gorn. Because now she could prove her worth to her crewmates and assuage the guilt she felt for unwittingly helping Gorn.

She asked herself, *Who would someone like Gorn fear?* And she thought about that as Valina and Debian worked on repairing the things she'd accidentally broken. The answer was simple, and she soon saw how to do it.

"I've got a plan!" she shouted. "It's brilliant, and there's not a moment to lose, so you two had better listen to me right now!" she said, taking the stairs to the control lab two at a time.

Valina stopped what she was doing at her workstation and eyed Cara cautiously. Debian only shook her head and kept working. Unperturbed, Cara told them only the basics of her plan. *No time now for details*, she thought.

"Listen, you guys, I'm going to take off in the Space Pod and trap that villain," Cara announced. "We all know our Pod is faster than the spacecraft Gorn arrived in, right?"

Debian and Valina exchanged that *'Cara's about to make a mess of things,'* look again. Finally, in her gentlest voice, Debian said, "Cara, I think maybe we should all discuss the details of this *brilliant plan* of yours before you do anything rash."

"Well, I'm sure you won't enjoy facing Captain Lydian to tell her that an evil reptilian invaded us and stole all the rare and valuable power transmitters, will you?" Cara replied with a frown. She paused, hoping that what she said next would sound convincing. "I mean, I can't imagine our Captain simply smiling at us when she finds out that we trembled like timid vermin instead of stopping Gorn."

Valina sighed heavily and entreated, "Even if you get to Gorn, Cara, what will you gain? How will you get the Power Transmitters away from him?"

"It'll be faster to show you," Cara said. "Wait here." She ran across the gantry, leaving her crew mates staring after her.

Cara worked in the control lab for the next few minutes. Not to fix the surveillance system she had smashed but for other, more exciting reasons. Going straight to the mainstream computer complex, she sat down and patiently entered hundreds of searches. It took only a little while to find what she was looking for. The girl was aware of time passing and Gorn getting a better head start with every passing second.

Valina and Debian were undoubtedly curious about what she was up to and probably assumed she was causing trouble again. She knew both considered every idea she had was crazy, so nothing new there!

The minutes ticked on. Cara entered personal data and used the 3D printers to complete everything. It had already taken her over twenty-five minutes to get this far, and she still had to collect something from surveillance. She expected Debian or Valina to come and find out what she was doing any minute now.

At last, she was ready. They'd finished the repairs and were no longer in the gantry. As quietly as she could, Cara returned to the control deck. She stood silently for a moment, watching them, wondering how long they would take to notice her. Then, at last, Cara grinned and stamped the boot she'd made on the floor once, with some force. It made a metallic ring, startling both her crew mates.

Cara heard Debian gasp at what she saw standing at the entrance. She saw how afraid the Quistic was to see a tall, daunting figure dressed in a black tight-fitting space suit, cloaked and high booted, and wearing a black helmet over the head. Most intimidating was the blacked-out visor. It hid her face entirely, so neither cadet recognised who stood there. Cara's plan was working already. Behind the visor, Cara's smile was wide. *It's working!* She thought.

In a trembling voice, Debian began, "Oh, who . . . ?"

Valina yelled, "Guylo! Intruder! Security to Control D—"

Valina's commands were cut short by the harsh, powerful voice that yelled at the two terrified cadets. "Hand over all the Kwaidem crystals and Imperium domes stored on this station! I want those Power Transmitters NOW!"

It's perfect! The voice enhancement feature really works! To complete the performance, she aimed the nozzle of the fake laser gun at them. *It looks so realistic,* Cara thought, admiring her work.

Her crewmates stood frozen on the spot with horrified looks on their faces. Cara chuckled in a shriek she thought they'd recognise. She peered through the visor from one wide pair of eyes to the other. "Oh, I've tricked you two, haven't I? Isn't it brilliant?"

Valina began a call to security again, and Cara realised her friends were still hearing the loud, angry voice. So she switched off the voice enhancement and said, "You see? It's foolproof," she laughed.

Cara pushed back the dark visor and, lowering the laser gun, tucked the weapon into her belt. With deep, sparkling eyes, she leaned in and lowered her voice, "He'll be as terrified as you two and I'll be back with that canister before you know it!" She raised her arms slightly and turned slowly on the spot. "Don't you think I look fantastic in this disguise? No one will ever recognise me."

Debian looked Cara up and down. "But wherever did you get it? You look like one of those space pirates the Galactica Police Squad captured last month," she said.

"You mean the Radicans," Valina said in a harsh tone.

Cara grinned. "Correct, Valina. I discovered an image of one of the Radican pirates on the mainstream computer and uploaded it to the 3D printer. I entered all my dimensions, and here I am! As you can see, the suit has turned out perfectly." Cara gave them another spin. "Fits me like a mitt – wouldn't you say?"

Valina stared at Cara's belt. "And the laser gun? How did you come by that, Cara?"

"Guylo, let me borrow one from surveillance, and I scanned and copied it to the 3D printer, too. Don't worry; it probably doesn't work," she assured them.

Debian's brow creased in a stern frown, "I should hope not, Cara, seeing how you pointed it at us just now!"

But Cara was intent on her mission. "Who would dare say I'm just a young patrol cadet now? As that wretch called me. Oh, boy! I will give that Golbat Gorn the fright of his life. I'll threaten to open fire and order him to hand over the crystals and domes!" Cara bragged.

"But Cara, surely you won't dare try to bring off anything like that. What would Captain Lydian say?" exclaimed Valina.

In a warning tone, Cara leaned in towards them. She said, "Captain Lydian will say plenty if she discovers that we've let a thief steal the Power Transmitters. Particularly as we didn't attempt to stop him," she reminded them again.

She took two strides toward the door and swung around to meet her audience. With a lofty salute, she declared, "I shall fly along the Galactica Corridor to hook up with Gorn's spacecraft. I will intercept that spacecraft and invade its docking bay." She carried on like some famous actor in a movie. "After I'm onboard Gorn's spacecraft, I will point the model laser weapon at him and force the villain to hand the Power Transmitters back to me!"

Valina shook her head with wide eyes at Cara, "You mean to make him suspect that you're a genuine space pirate, a Radican, come to loot the Transmitters?" Valina said in an astonished voice.

"Yes, that's my intention. Now I must leave at once." Cara announced dramatically. She tossed her cape back and hurried toward New Dawn's shuttle launch. At the last moment, she turned, paused, and peered at Valina and Debian. They stood dumbfounded at what Cara was about to undertake. Then, with a broad grin, she flipped the voice enhancement on, closed the visor, and yelled in the loud, growling pirate voice, "Wish me luck!"

Valina hurried after her. "Wait, Cara! If you're determined to do this, and I can see you are, take your cadet uniform with you. You never know. You might need to change back into it."

"Yes." Debian agreed. "If the Galactica Police Squad detain you dressed in that pirate suit, you'll be in trouble. They will arrest you and take you straight to planet Canton."

Cara stopped in her tracks at Debian's comment. "To where? Why, what's on Canton?"

Debian hovered nearer. "Canton is one humongous prison. If they seize you, you'll have much explaining to do."

"Don't leave, Cara!" Valina tried to persuade her.

Cara didn't need any advice from her fellow cadets. She ignored Valina's authority as First Officer and, for an instant, looked from one pleading face to another. Then, finally, she opened her visor again and said in her own voice, "Don't worry about me. I'll return with the Power Transmitters the devilish Gorn stole from us. Trust me, ladies, Captain Lydian will never even know they went missing." She ran back up the stairs to retrieve her uniform, then back down the corridor to the shuttle bay.

With high zeal and a swipe of her hand, Cara snapped shut the black visor and darted to where a Speed Pod awaited. As she raced by, an interior monitor showing the control deck caught her eye. It amused her that Valina and Debian still stood in the same numb state as when she left.

As she watched them, Cara heard Valina groan, "Oh, I dread to think how all this will turn out. I hope Cara is successful. Otherwise, I can't imagine the trouble we'll all be in."

Cara chuckled and whispered, "Don't worry, guys, I've got everything in hand. Just leave it all to me!"

Chapter 6

Cara's Mission

Back on the SP8

"I won't fail," Cara said, although Valina's hologram was gone. She stared at where it had been for a second or two before returning her full attention to her mission.

The control panel of Space Pod 8 informed Cara about their speed, location, and potential hazards ahead. Cara said, "Thank you, SP8," as if it were a living being. "Let's take the quickest route possible." Strangely, the pod responded as though it completely understood her, adjusting its speed and direction ever so slightly. *Excellent*, she thought.

After a second, Cara smiled, laughing at herself a little. "Oh, it's probably because Valina put you on autopilot, right?"

SP8 continued to high tail along GC5. Great lumps of frozen meteor rock flew away from the pod's power thrusters. Then, through the view screen, Cara saw a bright streak of burning stars as they rose towards a giant blue planet that seemed to loom monstrously close. Her whole body tensed at its nearness and its threatening immensity. She finally relaxed as the ship moved away from the daunting blue world.

Cara checked the tracking monitor for any sign of Golbat Gorn's spacecraft. She scanned as far as the controls would allow, but seeing no flying objects ahead confused her.

"Where's that thief gone?" Cara wondered aloud. Considering the urgency of her mission, she thought it best to try contacting New Dawn again for some help. And, to her ease, it wasn't too long before she got a response.

"Come in, Cara! Yes, I'm pleased to say we're receiving you with a clear audio signal and tracking your position. Copy?" Debian replied distinctly.

Cara was delighted to hear Debian's friendly voice, "Yes, copy! Loud and clear," she said, then explained her problem. "Debian, I expected to identify

Gorn's spacecraft ahead of me, but there's no sign of it. And I know there's no alternative route other than GC5, right?"

"Copy that," Debian said. "You're right, Cara. Straying from GC5 into unexplored zones of the universe is extremely dangerous."

Cara paused for a few seconds, thinking about how poisonous gasses from mysterious planets sometimes engulfed entire spacecraft and their crews. Vicious aliens and space pirates were said to attack unlucky ships caught in solar storms. Nobody knew for sure because those ships always disappeared, forever. Cara figured there was no way Golbat Gorn, however malicious he was, would have strayed from GC5. Yet, there was no sign of his spacecraft anywhere ahead.

"Cara, do you read me? Copy." It was Valina again. "Have you realised there is another craft following you? At this moment, it's about fifty thousand miles away," Valina said.

Startled by the news, Cara scanned the external surveillance screen again as Valina spoke. "It's definitely getting nearer to SP8. Guylo has more advanced technology for tracking, so he's attempting to discover its identity. Copy!" Valina said.

"Ok!" Cara replied as she re-programmed her tracking device to see if something followed her. Guylo was right, and she saw the dot-like image of a craft coming up behind but travelling much slower than the pod. At that moment, it was not closing up too much distance.

"Cara, this is Guylo! Do you copy?"

"Yes, Guylo. Copy!" Cara answered and thought to herself wearily; *Here we go again! Copy this, copy that! I just wish they'd get on and say what they mean.*

"Cara, I have identified the craft following you. I can confirm it is the Zeg-Mar5 that Golbat Gorn is travelling in. Copy."

Cara started in amazement. "What? How can that be? I'm following *him*, aren't I?"

"Apparently not." Valina broke in.

"We put you on autopilot and steered you away from that hazardous solar storm. But, unfortunately, the storm's magnetic forces must have propelled you at such an extreme speed you overtook Gorn's craft. And now you are ahead of him instead of behind him."

Cara went silent, struggling to figure out how it had happened – trying to remember how and when she had overtaken Gorn. There was no communication between them for a short time until, once again, Valina broke the silence.

"Cara, Cara – can you still hear me?"

"Yes, but I can't recall the moment I overtook him. I would have seen it on my screen. I just…"

"Listen!" Valina cut in, "The reason you don't remember is that the magnetic forces from the solar storm were so potent they caused you to pass out."

Cara fidgeted nervously in her seat. "Then. Gorn must have realised I was following him."

"No, he couldn't have detected you. Flying at over twenty thousand miles an hour, you were invisible to Gorn's tracking device. Fortunately for you (and us), we have Guylo's highly advanced technology. That reminds me, Cara. You haven't given clearance for your AI to activate. You need to do it immediately! Do you know how to do that, Cara? Copy."

Cara wasn't paying attention, and she'd been so intent on her quest that she hadn't given SP8's AI a single thought, let alone activate it. Her heart raced faster with excitement. "Then Gorn's still unaware I'm around?" she exclaimed.

"No," Valina answered warily.

At once, Cara revised her plan, still determined to steal the power transmitters from Gorn. "So, for now," she said, speaking mostly to herself. "I need somewhere to hide and wait for Gorn to catch up with me."

"Cara, you must listen! I've checked the readings on your transmitter gauge. You have plenty of thrusts to return to New Dawn Space Station from where you are. Copy?" It was Debian who, by her tone, sounded to Cara that she was genuinely concerned for her fellow cadet's safety.

"Thanks, Deb, but I'm not returning yet. I'm determined to wait for Gorn's ship to come past." She checked her tracking screen and saw that Gorn was still thousands of miles away. However, since the speed of SP8 had reduced, the Zeg-Mar5 was at last steadily gaining on her position.

"Cara, do you read me? Copy," Valina asked.

Cara rolled her eyes and gave a long, exasperated breath. "Yes, Valina. Copeeeee!" she replied in contempt.

"Cara, we're reporting a vast gas mountain, expanding by the second and incredibly near your location. The gas itself," Valina continued, "won't harm the pod. But, a huge atomic explosion will occur if a new star forms inside the gas. If that happens, Cara, I can assure you, it will be fatal."

Cara adjusted the scanner and, at once, picked up the image of the gas mountain. Valina's voice went on. "You can stay on GC5 to return to the space station, but you must give the gas mountain a wide berth."

Cara stiffened. She stared with wide eyes and raised eyebrows at the growing size of the gas mountain but remained silent. Valina's voice was stern and assertive. "Now, listen to me, Cara! Your situation has become profoundly dangerous, and, as First Officer, I order you to return to base at once. Do you understand? At once, I say! Copy?"

Cara felt the sting of sweat on her brow but still didn't reply. Instead, she entered SP8's position into the navigation instruments and could see the exact location of the colossal gas mountain looming ever closer. Then, an idea came to her, and she clenched one fist and grinned stupidly.

This time it was Debian who interrupted. "Cara, we are now altering the course for your return journey to New Dawn. Once you have activated the reverse thrust engines, they will fire in ten seconds. We cannot activate them on autopilot from the space station."

A bead of sweat dribbled into Cara's eye, and she almost held her breath, trying to remember which button she needed to push. Perhaps it was a particular key she had to tap? The AI might know, but she hadn't learned how to activate it. She'd leave that for later.

Anyway, it wasn't the 'reverse thrust' control button or key she was seeking. No. Cara craved complete control of her space pod, and it annoyed her that Valina and Debian always seemed to think she couldn't do anything right. "I'm an Earthling and smarter than they think," she whispered. "I have the training to fix things *right now*."

She identified the button she was looking for and pushed it. In a split second, the pod juddered, lurching forward violently. It hurled Cara painfully to the floor, and its suddenness left her stunned and disoriented.

In which direction was her space pod travelling? How fast? Which way up were they? Cara hadn't the slightest idea at all of what was happening. She thought she had selected and pressed the *abort-autopilot* button. The machine, however, still maintained a mind of its own, and its behaviour now frightened her.

Cara lay on her stomach, eyes screwed up tight, gasping for breath through clenched teeth. She knew she needed to do something but could not make any changes. She opened her eyes and tried to focus on the base of the pilot seat. The uncontrolled dipping and spinning motion made her feel queasy as she dragged herself towards it. At last, she reached out, grabbed on, and hauled herself towards the control panel.

Tumbling into the seat, she strapped herself in and exhaled a long sigh when she discovered that they were, in fact, the right way up. Her eyes shifted frantically from one section to another as many instruments went crazy, and lights flickered on and off. All the disorder, every system offline or malfunctioning, terrified Cara. *What have I done? I have to get it all under control!*

"It's my fault; I know it! But, once again, I didn't think about consequences," she cried, in a frenzy now as she haphazardly flicked switches… read screens… pressed keys until she was shocked to find that the first switch had not only cut off the autopilot but also shut down all external communication. After that, she'd get no more help from her crew mates.

She put her head in her hands as she considered her plight. *So now I'm left,* she thought, *to traverse the dark unknown, vastness of space, entirely alone.*

CHAPTER 7

Cara Has Company

As she came to her senses, Cara relaxed, amazed that the space pod had somehow rebooted itself and maintained a steady course. She tried to breathe evenly until calm enough to assess her circumstances and control herself and SP8. Cara didn't want to crack up and fail. Nor did she want to give up on the best opportunity to prove she was a skilled officer cadet worthy of respect.

So, she settled at the control panel, concentrated, and worked out her exact position on the navigation system. "Well done!" she said. Cara always talked to herself when she was alone. It eased the discomfort of fear or loneliness. But, unfortunately for Cara, the communication equipment wasn't functioning, so who was there to call? She'd tried many attempts to contact New Dawn, but nothing worked.

"I think it's time we proceed with the next part of my plan," she said into the surroundings. Then, checking the control panel, she added, "I seem to have you steady now."

"Yes, you have, Cara!" came a statement from nowhere. "How shall we proceed?"

She gasped, then strained her neck to peer behind the seat. "Who's there?" Cara was more puzzled than afraid and was not about to give way to jumpiness again. She glanced around the pod. "Who spoke to me?"

"It was me. I agree that I'm steady now. Thank you, Cara, for that. Now how to proceed?"

For a moment, Cara sat in silence while trying to find an explanation for what was happening. Was SP8's AI talking to her? She had to admit the mystery voice gave her an unpleasant shiver, making her anxious again. Valina had told Cara to activate the AI, but Cara had left that task for later.

"Who are you? Identify yourself!"

"I'm SP8 of New Dawn," a gentle male voice replied.

Cara's brow creased in disbelief, "SP8? That's …" she trailed off.

"Your space pod. Correct!" the voice interrupted.

Cara stared at the controls while the voice continued.

"You interfered too much with the systems when you switched controls *ON* and *OFF*, then *ON* and *OFF* again. As a result, there was poor pilot control, poor navigation techniques, and so on. Finally, the system determined there was no pilot and alerted me, Barnie, the SP8's AI. I auto-activated. You were here – and *yet* didn't even bother to speak to me," the AI whined.

Cara opened her mouth in an attempt to talk but was immediately interrupted again.

"It has taken me all this time to gain voice recognition, but now that I have it, you can ask me anything, and I will help you."

Cara's tone rose. "Well. Okay! I forgot to activate you. Anyway, how'd you— ?"

But Cara could barely get a word in. The Barnie voice filled the air and carried on.

"I squeezed a tiny audio wave towards New Dawn Space Station. It was a very weak one, but Guylo is *so* powerful he connected with me at once and sent a unique encrypted code that enabled me to function.

"My full name is **BINARY ARTIFICIAL REASONING, NANO-INTELLIGENCE AND ENERGY**. At your service!"

"Well, that's great!" Cara started, "I must admit, I could do with some assist—"

"I am your virtual artificial intelligence assistant, Cara! That's VAI for short, if you want to know."

Cara blew out her cheeks and exhaled. "An AI that doesn't let me get a word in," she said under her breath.

"And as a Virtual AI, I have that extra function to download solid 3D matter. Additionally, I am the ship's Virtual Medic. Are you hurt, Cara? You hit the floor extremely hard. Do you need a medical dressing for the cut on your head? A pain blocker?"

Cara put a hand to her forehead, where it smarted and touched a sticky patch near her hairline. "Oh," she said, "I guess I hit my head."

"You should keep your helmet on, Cara. Health and safety procedures, and all that stuff. I'll send a dressing to you."

She looked and saw blood smeared on her fingertips, and at once, a small wound dressing appeared on the armrest of her seat. "Put the medicated dressing on your wound, Cara, and instruct me on what we need to do next," Barnie said.

Cara wanted to *instruct* her AI to give his audio function a good rest but thought better of it. She knew *exactly* what she intended to do next. "Well, Barnie, it feels good to have a real grasp of the job at last. And to have someone or, in your case, *something* that makes sure they carry out the business to my orders," Cara said, applying the dressing to her head and relaxing a little.

Cara was in command. " First, we're going to hide inside that gas mountain and wait for the Zeg-Mar5 that's approaching. Do you see it? Track his position and keep me notified. We'll give him a lovely surprise visit when he's near us."

Barnie's warning came in a clear, rational reply: "That will be dangerous. We could get lost in the gas and never be able to get out. A new star might explode and…."

"I know all that, thank you, Barnie, but we must surprise Gorn," Cara said impatiently. "We can't risk detection; the gas will hide us."

Excitement crackled through Cara like the lightning she'd seen coming from the gas mountain. Gradually, they approached the boundary where the gas mountain started, and a strange pink light glowed all around. "Steer us through, Barnie!" she commanded.

"I will need to analyse the gas as we go through. I am also detecting vortices that could knock us off course. Do you wish to proceed, Cara?" Barnie asked.

"Proceed!" Cara replied in a hot-headed fashion.

The iridescent pink veil pressed against all sides of SP8 as they moved further into the vapour so that Cara felt as if they were underwater. Everything was a thick pink dimness through the misty glass panes of the pod, and she could detect a peculiar odour. She sneezed as a dusty smell filtered into her nostrils, leaving a sharp, stinging sensation in her mouth. Grasping her water flask, she took two or three gulps, but it had little effect on soothing her throat.

Barnie found the edge again, where the gas had started a boundary between the gas mountain and the GC5. "We can keep behind this gas barrier, and nobody will see us. Turn off our exterior lights," she commanded. And there, in the gloom, they waited.

Cara's heart pounded as the Space Pod hovered between Galactic Corridor 5 and the veils of bright pink vapour. It was hard not to contemplate the potential threat of a fatal atomic explosion. The air pressure in the cabin seemed to change suddenly, and though Cara's head ached, she thought it was probably from the bump she'd suffered earlier. The stinging sensation at the back of her throat worsened from the strong acrid odour inside the pod. It was causing her stomach to churn and turn to nausea.

But whatever the cause, she knew the gas hid them well from Gorn's advancing spacecraft, and she had no intention of emerging until it caught up.

"Gorn's craft will be level with us in five minutes," Barnie reported.

"Very well," Cara mumbled, wishing the five minutes were only five seconds. She was desperate now to get out of their oppressive hiding place.

Barnie's screeching reached new heights without warning: "HYDROGEN! HELIUM! METHANE! GAS, CARA! GAS!" he yelled.

It was impossible to see anything outside through the pink cloud. Not knowing what was happening, Cara's anxiety grew so that the five minutes she waited for Gorn soon became an eternity. Scrunching up her eyes, she watched the approaching image of the Zeg-Mar5 on the navigation panel. What else could she do? She certainly wasn't giving up.

Cara suddenly realised, however, that she was inhaling and exhaling in rasps and gasps as she tried to give Barnie her following command. "When . . . Gorn's spacecraft . . . is level . . . with us, we'll . . . emerge from the vapour . . . and follow him." Then, after a brief coughing fit, she said, "Start the count-down at sixty seconds!"

When Barnie started the countdown, Cara thought she might throw up. *Are some of those gases getting in?* She wondered, but Barnie's count was already down to thirty seconds. She found her Radican helmet, placed it over her head and snapped the visor closed.

"Ten, nine, eight, seven…" But that was as far as Barnie got. A mighty jolt shoved the space pod backwards and deeper into the dense, pink mountain gas. Suddenly, an alarm like a siren blasted out, and a warning light above Cara's head flashed 'DANGER'.

"What's going on?" she tried to shout and could barely hear Barnie above the din, but what she heard scared her.

"We've hit an atmospheric vortex of high-pressured gasses! Wind speeds are hitting us at one thousand three hundred miles per hour."

They travelled through a great dark spot paired with bright-coloured clouds of yellow and white. The white clouds brought a significant drop in temperature, and it reminded Cara of wintery Christmases on Earth with her grandparents. However, the temperature here was far from merry, and she shivered inside her Radican costume.

Barnie's voice was more precise now. "Turbulence inside the gas mountain.

It is a sign a new star is growing. We need to steer clear in the event of an atomic blast. Firing thrusts now!"

They flew towards the boundary through the dangerous gasses and, to Cara's relief, emerged from its gloomy shadows into the vast open dark and the light of the friendly stars. But there was no sign of Gorn or his spacecraft. Cara held her breath and swallowed the bile in her throat. Her shivering had stopped; now, she was sweating with fear inside her helmet. "Have we come out to a different place? Where are we?" she yelled over the continuing and unsettling noise of the warning system.

After Barnie shut off the grating jangles, his calm and reassuring voice again replaced it. "We are in orbit around planet Z 53a. Do you want me to recalculate our position?"

Still unsure about where they were, Cara urged Barnie to proceed. "Yes, yes, and locate where Gorn is! I must carry out this mission and take back the Power Transmitters."

Such was Barnie's technology that they were soon stalking Gorn again in his Zeg-Mar5. Her nausea and headache had abated, and Cara watched the tracking screen as it showed a decreased distance between the two spacecraft. Her eyes were bright, and her heart thumped with wild excitement. In her black suit, she was confident that she looked convincing. "What a joke, Barnie! I'm a Radican Pirate and about to rob a robber!"

"Cara, it's not too late to forget about Gorn, and if you wish, I can set a course to return safely to New Dawn Space Station," Barnie suggested.

"Ha! I will not do that. I don't think I could. Besides –" There was a flash and rumble as the pod surged closer to the Zeg-Mar5. "If I'm almost close enough to board Gorn's spacecraft, it's already too late for me to change my mind."

Chapter 8

Fiasco

SP8 approached Gorn's spacecraft, and Cara commanded, "Deploy connectors!"

"Understood." Barnie acknowledged and released two massive metal cables which flew from the pod. "Do you wish me to activate stealth mode, Cara?"

Cara stopped, narrowed her eyes, and shouted sharply, "You didn't tell me this pod has a stealth mode!"

"You didn't ask," Barnie replied.

Cara threw her hands up and let them fall to her sides with a slap. "You mean to say we hid in that dangerous gas mountain when we could have always become invisible?"

"I can do most things, Cara, but reading human minds is not one of them!" Barnie said curtly.

Cara rolled her eyes and let out a long sigh. They were rapidly approaching Gorn's Zeg-Mar5, and she had no time to argue. "Magnetise! And for skag's sake, switch to stealth mode," she commanded.

They latched onto Gorn's spaceship, and the two crafts immediately bolted together. Cara continued giving out directives. "Lock onto the central docking bay!"

The noise of SP8's power thrusts died down, and she felt a slight nudge as it connected with Gorn's ship. But her next problem was how to get aboard without being detected. The SP8 was invisible, but once Cara stepped out, anyone and everyone would see her. The microchip implant in her hand opened most doors of other Galaxy Patrol Force craft, so she hoped it would open the door of the Zeg-Mar's docking bay, too.

SP8's door slid open. Then, tentatively, she placed her palm onto the connecting door and finally, obligingly, and with a gentle hiss, Zeg-Mar's docking bay door also slid open. Cara was in! Her blood coursed faster than usual through her veins, and her nerves began to crackle at what she was about to do.

It seemed, though, that luck wasn't altogether on her side. As Cara entered Gorn's spaceship's entrance, she encountered an unsuspecting, older crew member about to store equipment in a large storage locker. Both of them froze and stared at each other for a split second.

When she saw his eyes widen with astonishment at seeing a Radican pirate on board, it reassured Cara that the shock had rendered him helpless. She realised he was neither fit nor strong enough to make things difficult for her. Caught off-guard and with his arms full of technical instruments, she guessed he could make little effort to defend himself.

Cara raised the little laser gun to his head and confronted him in a gruff, commanding voice. "Hand over all your Power Transmitters – now!" Her confidence grew as she saw the man cower and drop slowly to his knees, letting the instruments fall from his grasp.

"Don't fire!" he gasped, raising both hands in surrender.

Ruthlessly, Cara kept the model laser at his head. "Get up, you idiot and get inside that skagin' locker!" she growled in a growling, menacing voice, thanks to the voice enhancer.

In an instant, and before she let him realise what was happening, Cara shoved the man roughly inside the locker. Then, she smirked with contempt behind her black visor as she sealed the door on him and strode along the gantry towards the control deck. She thought her impersonation of a Radican Pirate was paying off. Full of confidence and pride, she whispered, "Now I'm going to terrify that villainous reptilian thief!"

She rushed through the door onto the control deck and thrust the model laser gun in front of her as she entered. Then, again, she shouted, "Hand over all your Power Transmitters, now! Give up all the Kwaidem Crystals and Imperium Domes you have onboard, or I'll—"

But all her fierce, enhanced speech ended in a startled gasp. Cara became limp with shock, and the little laser weapon clattered harmlessly from her hand – gone, dropped over the gantry rail somewhere. Instead, she stood and stared at the control deck, open-mouthed, confused and utterly taken aback. It was not only the reptilian who sat at the control panel. This spacecraft had another occupant.

"Oh no!" she stammered, forgetting her voice sounded like a fierce pirate. "I – *I* didn't think – I mean, I didn't *know* . . . *you* . . . were *here*... ?" Then, remembering protocol, Cara stopped talking, saying only, "Sir!" as she slowly raised her right hand to her left shoulder in salute.

A tall, powerfully built, grey-haired man slowly rose from his seat. His steely black eyes flashed with shock and rage as he glared up at Cara, who stood motionless on the gantry, waiting for him to return the salute.

It was Commander Predaton.

The Commander was the perfect picture of power in his immaculate grey uniform and highly polished boots. Every member of the Galaxy Patrol Force respected him, and all took orders from him, including Captain Lydian. He was their Supreme Commanding Officer.

Confusion flashed through Cara. *Why was the Commander on the same spaceship as the thief, Golbat Gorn?* She vaguely remembered Gorn saying someone was waiting for him when he rushed to leave New Dawn. But she'd assumed he meant a fellow conspirator; never in a million years did she expect it to be the Commander! Cara felt the breath leave her body as the implication of what was happening sunk in. She tried to work out where it had all gone wrong, but as she stared at the Commander, she realised she'd made a terrible mistake. *Not just me,* she thought. *We all thought he was a thief!* Cara now knew (too late!) that she and her crewmates had misjudged Mr Golbat Gorn.

A security officer dressed in a distinctive red uniform approached and pointed an automatic weapon directly at Cara. He was shorter than she was, but he gripped Cara's arm with such strength she winced in both pain and fury. "Come on, you!" he said in an off-centred tone.

His tight grip seemed unnatural, and Cara could do nothing to prevent herself from being propelled along and down the steps. Finally, a mighty hard shove forced her into the control room's centre, and she stumbled to her knees. Within seconds and with little effort, this vicious officer grabbed her arm again and pulled her to her feet. In other circumstances, Cara's angry response would have landed the wretch a flying kick to the face, but she thought better of it. Such an action would bring her no favours.

The brute swiftly whisked off Cara's visor with a surprising speed. And it was this action that made her suspect he was not a living creature at all.

Now, Cara was in full view. Commander Predaton had a clear picture of her face and snapped an order at another of Gorn's AIs. "Castro. Identify this imposter!"

Castro answered immediately. "Identity: Cara Davis. Space Officer Cadet 407. Stationed on New Dawn station. Under the command of Captain S. Lydian."

Commander Predaton gave Cara a sharp-edged look. "Well, Cadet Davis, what mad trick is this?" he demanded fiercely. "What set you up to such a foolish bit of play-acting, *eh*? I expect Captain Lydian will have plenty to say about this when she finds out."

Cara knew that only too well. She opened her mouth, had the urge to yell at the Commander, to ask what the skag was going on, but couldn't even speak. It felt like her breath had evaporated as Cara deflated with a hot flush of humiliation.

Captain Lydian is going to kick me out, was all she could think. *I'm done.*

CHAPTER 9

Arrested

Though overwhelmed with panic, she could not let the Commander think she had played a stupid and mischievous prank for fun. So she stammered and dared to meet the Commander's glare. " I…I didn't do it as a joke, sir."

"Not as a joke! Then what is the meaning of it?" the Commander yelled.

Never had Cara seen a commanding officer with such rage. A wave of deep red anger spread down his neck, and Cara's speech came out as a nervous, confused account when she tried to explain. "I, I mean, *we* thought it was a thief that had taken all the Power Transmitters from our space station!" she exclaimed hastily.

Her words fell over themselves in confusion. "And- I meant to take them back like a Radican Pirate might have done. But, I couldn't figure out any other way."

Commander Predaton stared at Cara, then turned his back on her and returned to his place. He sank into his seat and gave a low, scornful laugh. "Did you hear that, Gorn? This dim-witted girl took you for a thief."

Gorn grinned and chuckled as he shook his head in disbelief.

The Commander became severe again in a second and glowered as he turned back to glare at Cara. "Look here, girl, you have made a real fool of yourself," he said severely. Then raising his hand towards Gorn said, "This is Mr Golbat Gorn, my excellent friend and a highly respected diplomat who has the authority to conduct important business on behalf of the Galactic Council. He has done so for many years."

Cara sweated beneath her Radican suit. She felt she might faint if the Commander kept tongue-lashing her like this. Predaton blinked a slow, disdainful blink. "You can hardly expect him to account for himself to a team of young officer cadets, now, can you?"

Cara remained silent and looked down at the floor while Commander

Predaton rose and strode towards her, "Not that it's any of your business, but I took the opportunity to travel with Mr Gorn to the Conference. It appears it was lucky I did, considering your stupid prank."

Cara sensed his approach as he closed in and winced when he prodded her shoulder with a powerful finger. "Look at me!"

Her head jerked backwards as if the Commander had hit her in the face. His dead icy stare settled on Cara, and his palpable fury made her catch her breath. There was something not right about the man, and she could tell he enjoyed making her feel afraid. Nevertheless, she obeyed and lifted her gaze to his.

"I hope you are *satisfied*," he glowered.

Cara considered *satisfied* an odd word because she had never felt less so in all her life. In a matter of minutes, he had crushed her verve for adventure. She stood motionless, shattered, and sad, but she dared not lose eye contact with the Commander. In the same instance, she wondered whether she could ever look Golbat Gorn in the face again. Of course, Grandma would say she owed him an apology. But could she even dare to do that?

For the first time, she noticed the Reptilian had not joined in with any of the scoldings she received from the Commander. Now, when he spoke, his voice sounded calm, even gentle.

"And so, what shall we do, sir?" he asked. "We can't waste any more time in this location, but we cannot leave the young cadet here."

Suddenly Cara's heart lightened at the thought of escape, and this time she didn't flinch at the savagery of the Commander's glare when she spoke. "Oh, sir. I'll fly the Space Pod back to New Dawn alone. I'll be ok," Cara assured him.

The Commander only glared at her and shouted. "Quiet! I have not permitted you to speak!" Then, turning to Gorn, he shook his head. "You're correct, Golbat. We can't leave this irresponsible dullard to her own devices. And we don't have time now to turn back."

Commander Predaton clenched a jutting jaw, reflected silently for a few seconds, and then said, "I have it! Lock her in a cargo bay, and she can travel with us to the Golden Dome Conference Centre."

Cara's brows creased, her hands fisted at her sides, and she leaned slightly towards the large, savage man towering above her. "Oh, Commander, sir! Please allow me to fly straight back to New Dawn," she pleaded again, feeling she couldn't bear to be in his fierce presence any longer. "I'll put myself in the hands of my ship's AI. It will not allow me to deviate or do anything stupid.

We'll fly straight back and—"

The Commander, unswerving, cut in with a voice rising almost manically over hers. "NO! Certainly NOT! Request DENIED, you wretched fool! I shall not allow you to do that, and when we reach our destination, we will hand you over to your Captain."

He put his hands behind his back and leaned back on his heels. Then, sticking out his chest, he said with great sway, "You're her problem. We'll let her deal with you."

Gorn, who had said little until then, Cara noticed, rose from his seat and growl-huffed, "With all due respect, Commander, I'm afraid there is a problem with that order."

"What do you mean, Golbat?" Predaton asked, turning to Gorn.

Gorn's lips curled upwards to reveal his lizard teeth. "Commander, if we are to get to our destination safely, she can not remain on board," he growled. "This ship only carries enough fuel to reach its calculated destination."

Cara watched Gorn glance sideways and swivelled his eyes to focus on her. "If *she* stays on board, her weight will amplify during deceleration, and the extra stress will cause the engines to burn up all the fuel before reaching our destination. As a result, the engines will fail, and we'll likely crash. There could be casualties," he explained, rather matter-of-factly, Cara thought.

Once again, not wanting to yield to the Commander's order, Cara's heart jumped at this perfect opportunity to leave. "So, Commander, I must return to New Dawn in the SP8. I cannot stay on board, sir. It'll be too dangerous for everyone."

However, Cara's statement only made her situation worse. The Commander's brows creased, and in a low, stern, and unrelenting voice, he turned on her and said, "No! It's obvious now; that you can't stay onboard this spacecraft. So, in that case, young woman, you will fly your Space Pod close to Zeg-Mar5 and follow us to our destination."

On impulse and in her typical obstinate way, Cara took a stride towards the Commander. "But sir!" she tried to implore, "I—"

Predaton looked like he thought Cara was about to attack him and immediately shouted angrily to the red uniformed security officer, "Lieutenant Cyjay, power-cuff this deadhead and escort her to the docking bay. I will not put up with this idiot a moment longer. Take her away!"

A pair of powerful arms wrenched Cara's hands behind her back, and Cyjay instantly activated two electronic manacles that encircled her wrists and bound them tightly together. Cara gasped. She had never been power-cuffed before, and the tightness made her cry out as their power burned into the flesh of her wrists. Then, when she was no longer a threat to him, Predaton moved in closer. Cara met his cold and foreboding eyes as they stared into hers. "I repeat, as soon as we reach our destination, I shall hand you over to your Captain, and *she* can deal with you. Do I make myself clear?"

Cara looked down at the floor, "Yes, sir," she replied hoarsely in painful dismay, and tears welled.

But the Commander's ranting hadn't finished. "Your idiotic behaviour has delayed us long enough. I'm placing you under vehicle arrest, and you will not leave the ship until your Captain tells you otherwise. Get her out of my sight!"

Cara had no choice when Lieutenant Cyjay stepped up to her. "Move it!" he barked, giving her a sharp prod between the shoulders and marching her back to the docking bay.

The Stealth mode on SP8 had deactivated, and it was visible to everyone again. Cyjay disconnected the power cuffs, moved in close, and thrust the little laser gun into Cara's face with a sneer, "Don't forget your little toy laser gun, cadet girlie!"

As Cara reached out to take the model gun, Cyjay laughed scornfully and dropped it at her feet. "Well, pick it up, Davis. You might need it!" he taunted.

Keeping a close eye on him, Cara slowly bent down and picked up the little laser gun. Cyjay pulled her up roughly by her arm and then pushed her viciously backwards into the pod's doorway. "Now get in there and order your AI to shadow our ship! Remember, you're under vehicle arrest and can't leave. No more dumb tricks or things could get rather unbearable for you. And be-lieve me, I will personally make sure they do."

The docking bay door slid open. Cara entered and watched Lieutenant Cy-jay turn smartly on his heel and leave so fast he – or it, whatever that creature was – became a total blur.

Chapter 10
All for Nothing

ara removed her helmet and slung it with force across the cabin floor onboard SP8. As it clattered to a halt in a corner, she screwed up her face and clenched her hands into tight fists. She closed her eyes tightly to stop crying, but the tears flowed anyway, and she sobbed. She knew she had no one to blame for this predicament except herself – which was the main reason for her tears and anger.

Eventually, Cara sat in the pilot seat, buckled up, ready to follow Golbat Gorn's spacecraft and in a tight broken voice, gave Barnie the order, "Release connectors!"

"Welcome back, Cara. I trust your mission was successful," Barnie said as SP8 drifted away from the Zeg-Mar5. Cara didn't respond to Barnie's untimely greeting. She couldn't! Tears ran sharply, and Cara was grateful to be alone. Even so, she knew she had to face the consequences of her actions. She dreaded facing Captain Lydian most of all.

"Are you upset, Cara? Would you like some calming tea?"

"I'm in real serious trouble, Barnie," she sniffed, rubbing her wrists where the power-cuffs had burnt her skin.

"I'll send you that tea," her AI said. In an instant, the steaming beaker of drink appeared on her armrest. "What else would you like me to do for you?" he asked.

Cara only sank deeper into her doldrums. "How will I tell Valina and Debian what a jerk I've been? I tried to hoodwink Gorn into handing back the Power Transmitters, and the trick backfired," Cara sobbed.

"I am standing by for your next order, Cara," Barnie's untroubled voice trundled on.

Cara ignored him, "I never imagined for an instant that Commander Predaton would be onboard Gorn's spacecraft, too." In her gloom, Cara sank her head into her hands. "Just because Gorn looked sinister and cruel, I was stupid enough to think he must be an evil criminal," she croaked. "And after Debian told us the dreadful tale about her early horrors with the Chortons and the Glydor race, it convinced me the monstrous-looking reptilian could not possibly be what he claimed."

Cara sobbed so hard her words came out in gasps, "Oh, what a skagin' pinhead I am. They should never have allowed me to go after Gorn." In her mind, she was half blaming Debian for convincing her Gorn was evil and Valina for not stopping her. But Cara knew deep down that this fiasco was all her own fault. She was in trouble, with no one to blame or turn to for help.

"Do you wish me to set a course for the return journey to New Dawn Space Station, Cara?" Barnie enquired pleasantly.

Cara desperately struggled to hold her tears in check, but it wasn't easy. Her voice trembled, childlike. "Barnie, I'm *scared*. What will Captain Lydian say and do to me when she discovers my idiotic behaviour?"

At last, she realised her AI was asking her a question, and, with a struggle, she returned to her senses. "What?" Cara asked.

"I asked if I should set a course for the return journey to New Dawn Space Station?" Barnie repeated.

"Yes, of course!" she snapped, wiping her red and swollen eyes. Then, in an instant, she realised what she had said. "*Er*, I mean no! No, Barnie, I can't return. The Commander ordered me to follow Gorn's spacecraft."

"In that case, a shadowing program to follow the Zeg-Mar5?"

Cara hesitated, but she dared not defy the Commander's orders. So, with a long, relenting sigh. "Yes. I suppose so."

"At what distance do you want SP8 to track the spacecraft, Cara?"

Cara squinted at the control panel, and another sob caught her breath. "Oh, as far away as possible," she said miserably, flicking her hand. "I don't care anymore. I really don't!"

Within moments, Barnie had increased power, and the hum of the thrust engines grew to a crescendo, causing the pod to shoot away at a tremendous speed. Cara was aware of the rise in temperature inside the cabin as they moved directly away from Gorn's Zeg-Mar.

Around the white flash of speed, the chill darkness of space expanded vastly, and Cara could still make out the clusters of stars around the galaxy's edges. The heat inside the cabin seeped into the Radican pirate suit, and she wiped away the sweat and tears from her face. Cara was afraid that the Commander might assume she was deciding to slip away, and beyond a doubt, she wished she could.

Just then, she caught a fleeting glimpse of herself on the interior surveillance screen. She sat there, still dressed in the fictitious costume – a Radican Pirate, sad and forlorn. Cara didn't want to see herself like that anymore and looked away from the screen.

Wearily she got out of her seat and thought, *Perhaps I should change back into my uniform.* Cara noticed it was still where she'd dropped it upon first boarding SP8. Regrettably, it was that same shabby uniform with a ripped sleeve and stains on the front of the jacket.

She looked at it, frowning. "Who to be? A shabby Officer Cadet who failed to regain Power Transmitters that turned out not to be stolen after all? Or a phoney Radican whose attempted crime ended in punishment and humiliation?" And now, although she clearly understood it was time to cast aside that fictional Radican and once more become herself, Cara couldn't do it. *So what's the point,* she thought. *I'm a failure no matter what I'm wearing.*

Although she yearned to be back at New Dawn Space Station with her crew mates, Barnie confirmed that neither of them, unfortunately, had contacted the ship while she was onboard the Zeg-Mar5. Cara picked at her fingernails as her agitation grew. "Oh, Barnie, why haven't Valina and Debian called me?" She wrapped her arms around herself and continued, "Do you think they're angry with me, too?"

Barnie didn't respond and let her carry on with her maudlin outpouring. "Maybe they'd rather I just disappear. I'm sure it would relieve Captain Lydian to see me leave the squad," she snivelled.

Cara dropped her chin onto her chest. "I'm the only Human onboard the space station, and I don't seem to fit in. Even the robotic crew don't always properly function when I give them commands," she said.

"You're not the only Human on New Dawn, Cara," Barnie said.

Thinking she hadn't heard him correctly, she looked up and spoke into the air. "What do you mean, Barnie? Valina is a Listroc, Debian is a Quistic, and the rest of the crew are all robotic. So who else is there?"

Barnie continued, "The Captain, of course. Captain Sarah Lydian has the high intelligence and integrity of her Leontyne father and her human mother's physical strength and beauty. She has inherited the best of both parents. Her courage and honesty have made her what she is – a capable and caring leader."

Cara shrugged. "*Huh!* Well, I can tell she cares very little for me by the way she constantly criticises and nags me. I dare say she'll have even more to say when she finds out what I've been up to. She paused for a moment and clenched her jaw as anger replaced self-pity. "Now is when I need to talk to friends like Valina or Debian. Not you, an AI. Not a skagin' robot!"

Barnie made a beeping sound like he was clearing his throat before he said in a precise tone, "May I remind you, Cara, that none of the transmission systems functioned after you terminated the autopilot before we entered the gas mountain."

Cara continued to yell. "I terminated the autopilot because I didn't want to return empty-handed to New Dawn." She pinched the bridge of her nose and closed her eyes. She knew it was a waste of breath arguing with an AI.

It was a lengthy course into the next galaxy, where they held the GPU Conference. Cara longed to see Valina and Debian, even if only through their holographs. She hoped they weren't too far away to transmit those back to the pod. "Barnie, can you restore the transmission systems?" she requested, calmer now.

"Yes, Cara!"

"Restore all transmission systems now!" she commanded. The transmission system came to life immediately, and the pod erupted into a cacophony. It forced Cara to clasp her hands over her ears as many beeps, buzzes, and whistles echoed around the compartment. The terrible noise jarred her nerves.

"For skag's sake, Barnie, turn that din off!" she tried to yell. "Barnie, can you— ?" Cara was still hollering when Barnie turned off the racket. Embarrassed, she took a calming breath and lowered her voice to match the relatively quiet hum of the pod.

"Barnie, can you repair the Visual Communication System, too?" she repeated in her normal voice.

"No, I cannot repair the Visual Communication System, Cara," Barnie answered.

"What do you mean, *no, you cannot?*" Cara retorted in a rising tone, hoping her AI was not malfunctioning.

Barnie continued in a calm, monotone voice. "I cannot repair it because it needs manual work to fix it. For example, the turbulence we encountered in the gas mountain damaged it, along with several webcams. Only a living being or a programmed robot can fix the VCS. It is very delicate work."

Cara huffed before tapping a few commands into the control panel. Nothing resulted in it, and she didn't understand what Barnie meant. "So. Nobody can restore it?" she concluded, folding her arms and slumping into the pilot's seat. Her tears welled again, away from shame this time, onwards into anger.

She'd experienced quite enough of this disappointing, humiliating adventure.

Barnie responded in a brighter tone. "Yes, they can, Cara!"

Predictably, Cara was losing her patience with Barnie and also with everything else that was happening around her. "But Barnie, you just said that we *can't* restore them. Have *you* stopped functioning, too?" she said through gritted teeth.

"No, Cara! I said that *I* could not restore the VCS because it requires manual work that I cannot perform."

Cara shrugged. "Ok, ok!" she said in a crusty tone. "So, who, may I ask, will do the work since I'm the only human onboard?"

"Just so, Cara. Only you are onboard." He went silent as if waiting for her reply.

Cara dropped her shoulders, let her head fall back and rolled her eyes. "Get *on* with it, Barnie!"

"It is you, Cara! *You* must repair the Virtual Communication System and webcams. You!"

With this last remark from Barnie, Cara thought she would go mad! On top of everything else that had happened, now she might be responsible for breaking the only possible communication she had with New Dawn Space Station. She certainly didn't want the responsibility of trying to fix it. What else might she break, ruin, or lose? She pulled herself upright only to let her head fall into her hands. Cara realised she'd landed herself in one huge foul-up and hadn't the slightest idea of how to get out of it.

"Do you wish me to explain and guide you through the repairs, Cara?"

Cara stood, stretched (carefully), then bent her head back to look at the ceiling of the pod, arm raised, elbow crooked around her head. She puffed out a long sigh of frustration. "I don't *know*!" she replied in a broken tone.

After a moment of silent contemplation, she sighed. "All right, yes. There's nothing else to do."

CHAPTER 11
Repair Job

Cara surveyed the SP8's busy, complicated control panel. "This is worse than New Dawn's. Everything's smaller for one thing!" The mention of the station reminded Cara that she'd gotten entirely out of mending all the controls she'd smashed up that morning. *Was that only this morning?* It felt like days ago.

"Well, Grandma," she said, stifling a half-hysterical laugh, "I suppose getting out of making those complicated repairs earlier on New Dawn is one of those silver linings you always told me to look for in times of trouble."

Repairing any important ship's system generally made Cara panic, even on an average dull day. She'd go to great lengths to escape it if she could. But now, the panic made her feel a little giddy. *I'm about to crack,* she thought as she gripped her hair with both hands. *I can't do this!*

"Do you want to add anything to your message to Grandma, Cara? Or shall I send it now?"

She ignored him. Why was he always talking so much?

"Cara?"

"*Fine!*" She shouted. "What*ever*! I can NOT make repairs to the VCS, Barnie." She raked her fingers through her hair and yelled, "You know very well I have little experience of how these things function, let alone how to repair them!"

"Message sent to Grandma," Barnie replied. "Do not worry, Cara. I will instruct you on how to mend the damage. I will talk you through it step by step. Do not become irritated. I do not recommend stress for a Human's well-being. Now let's fetch the tools stored in the ejector bay. I'll tell you which ones you'll need."

Cara let her hands fall, her jaw dropped, and she stared with wide eyes, "*Excuse me?*" she shrieked at the AI.

"The tools. You must fetch them. They're in the ejector bay," Barnie repeated.

Cara frowned in anger. "No! *Excuse me*. I just told you I CANNOT do it!"

"You must—" Barnie began.

"Listen! I'm the one to give the orders around here. Not you, not an AI! A skagin' robot! I heard you the first time, and I told you I can't and I *won't*!"

"Then I cannot help you," Barnie replied flatly.

Cara sighed and closed her eyes tight. She saw precisely where this was heading. Barnie wasn't a human or any other sort of living creature. It was an intelligent machine with a voice, and Cara knew she had no choice but to try and make the repairs. If she refused, she and SP8 would undoubtedly be in serious trouble. The crew on Gorn's spaceship would have no time to rescue her if other things deteriorated. And for all she knew, they wouldn't even try.

There was no alternative. Reluctantly, Cara exhaled a deep breath of frustration. "Ok, Barnie, you win," she conceded. A long, perceivable silence grew in the air between them. Cara stood with pursed lips and hands on hips, waiting. "Well, go on! Talk me through repairing the Visual Communication System then, step by step."

Perhaps she imagined it, but Cara was sure something strange was happening. The sensation of a current of something went rippling transparently through the space. Was Barnie laughing at her? With reluctance, Cara pushed the stupid thought from her mind and started gathering the tools he told her she'd need.

Even though it wasn't easy, Cara followed Barnie's instructions as best she could. She huffed, cursed, and grunted her way through it. Searched for and dropped intricate tools, cursed, sweated, and often screamed at the AI to repeat himself. Yet, thanks to Barnie's easy and precise instructions, Cara completed a successful repair job on the VCS. The delight from this achievement almost made her feel hopeful. "Now, let's see if it functions!" she said in a gush of words as her hand hovered over the control screen.

"Stop! *Wait!*" Barnie yelled. "You will need to do one last test before transmitting externally. I cannot resume automatic responses with the VCS if you don't do the test. So, do you choose to carry out a completion test?"

Cara shrugged and pulled a face. "Yes," she replied. "Start testing!" Although Cara had learned a lot in doing the repair, she didn't relish repeating the entire process. Instead, she wanted Barnie back in automatic control again, if only to take away the stress of everything.

Barnie followed up with more instructions. "Open 'view' on the screen. Then, when the menu drops, tap 'Int'." Cara asked what 'Int' meant, but Barnie didn't answer, so she crossed her fingers when he told her what to do. The screen hung before her at once and displayed images of everything inside the pod. By then, she realised that 'Int' meant 'interior'. The webcam screens, too, were all functioning perfectly. "Continue to direct," she said assertively, recalling that she was in command.

"Tap any image on the screen and then press the 'enter' light," Barnie said. Cara chose an image of the beaker on the armrest. A green transparent light appeared next to the proper beaker, and Cara observed closely as the green light gradually turned into a distinct shape. Two identical beakers sat there in a split second: one real solid and one a virtual-reality beaker. Cara's successful repair work convinced her she would soon see and talk to Valina and Debian's holographs.

Cara had practically forgotten the other trouble, the arrest, and the orders to follow Gorn. Until that is, in the thrill of the moment, she yelled "Yes!" and punched her fist high into the air.

The entire space pod was plunged into total blackness.

Cara gasped, and a sickening dread rose in her gut. The darkness was absolute. She placed a hand in front of her wide-open eyes. Nothing, she could see nothing at all, not even her fingers. "Have I gone blind?" she whispered. Remaining utterly still, struggling to get her bearings, she tentatively raised a hand, hoping to touch something familiar. Next, she threw her hands out in front of her, still feeling nothing. There was nothing there but a void of darkness. Was she floating in some open black hole?

Cara inhaled deeply, trying to calm herself. "I'm definitely not floating in mid-air," she said, "I can feel the floor under my feet." She took a step backwards and felt around. She touched familiar bits of the panel that reminded her of where, with Barnie's help, she had been repairing the VCS. Her voice came out high-pitched, "Barnie, can you hear me? Barnie? Hello? Respond immediately!" But the AI made no noise.

Every light in the SP8 was out. Cara, filled with panic again, thought Barnie, too, was out of operation. "Barnie, answer me. Please!" She felt the rippling sensation again and held her breath while peering with alarm into the blackness. She wouldn't have given such nonsense a thought in normal circumstances, but lately, events had been anything but ordinary. Thinking about it made her feel somewhat spooked. In the pitch dark, she could make out nothing. And her imagination was about to go into overdrive. "Barnie, are you laughing at me again? Barnie? This is serious. You are a machine. Machines don't laugh!"

Cara's panic and fear had caused such irrational thoughts that she had to force her mind to focus on the reality of what was happening. The rippling sounds were nothing more than the AI's technology struggling to reboot, surely? And, considering what had just occurred, she guessed it might take Barnie a while to recover his power and functional ability. Yet, with no immediate response, it seemed like an eternity to Cara as she waited helplessly in the terrible darkness. Her unseeing eyes filled with tears. "What's taking you so long? Barnie! Help me!" She yelled again, "Please!"

Finally, Barnie responded. "Activating emergency lighting now!" As Cara let out the long breath she'd held unaware, small blue lights lit up the outline that led to the pilot's seat. Similar blue lights came on and showed up on both overhead controls and separate sections of the pod. With legs shaking and hands trembling, she cautiously approached the pilot's seat, found and slid into it.

"All emergency lighting functions are now completed," the AI concluded.

Cara noted some controls were still inactive, and she entered various critical operating codes. "What happened?" she asked.

This time, Barnie's response was prompt: "You were successful in your task! You celebrated by punching the air above you in joy. But, unfortunately, the result of that action terminated some essential systems. The primary lighting control system, for one."

Cara froze, then slowly covered her face with both hands. She couldn't believe it. "Not again! Please don't say I've ruined something else!" She swallowed hard, not wanting to ask, "Is there much damage done, Barnie?"

Barnie was swift to answer. "Yes, Cara! You have damaged the Central Power Core and destroyed the main circuits. All incoming and outgoing communication systems are down again. Computer and regulator systems are also malfunctioning – main power internal and external lighting cut. Emergency lighting will cut in precisely two hours," he droned flatly.

There was a brief pause, but Barnie certainly hadn't finished. "Life support systems will cut out within the next two hours. I will also stop functioning. There will be no AI support."

Cara wiped the sweat from her brow, and her heartbeat doubled. This whole horrible experience was like her worse nightmare ever. The only hope she had was waking up from it. Her eyes brimmed with tears again as she tried to calm her thoughts. "Barnie, Can you—?"

"No!" Barnie cut in unexpectedly. Cara thought the AI must have known what she was about to ask. Maybe he could read her mind, after all. "No, I cannot repair them. You must repair the systems again, Cara. Again!" Barnie enforced with an unusually high-pitched screech.

Cara suddenly had a piercing headache. A tingling sensation penetrated all her limbs, and when her fingers went numb, she knew something dangerous was already happening inside the pod.

Barnie spoke to her. "Are you feeling ill, Cara?"

"Yes," she gasped, "are we losing oxygen?" Cara put her hand to the pain at the back of her head.

"Losing oxygen and pressure. It would be best if you acted as quickly as possible while I talk you through restoring the power systems," Barnie continued.

Cara staggered out of her seat, clutching her throat. Her head spun, and she gasped for air, thinking she might pass out before they could do anything. "Barnie, I can't breathe!"

Barnie's voice was faint. It sounded like it was coming from a great distance, but she heard him say, "Releasing emergency oxygen!" A small panel above the pilot seat revealed a light oxygen device. The robot gave her another order, and she was more than glad to obey. "Cara. Allow the remote oxygen device to cover your air passages immediately!"

Her limbs trembled while sweat beads formed across her brow, and Cara was vaguely aware of an object approaching her face. Reflexively, she shot out her hand in a grasp but missed catching it. However, the oxygen device automatically attached itself to her face, and she took in huge gasps of air.

Though she'd regained most of her senses, she dreaded the exceedingly complex task of repairing the power systems that lay ahead. Worse, she'd be racing against time to complete it. "Explain what I need to do to repair the power systems," she ordered breathlessly.

Again, Barnie was as good as his word. Bit by bit and piece by piece, the AI instructed Cara precisely until she had replaced all the extra parts. "You must do one last thing to complete the task. It will still not function if you don't," Barnie told her.

Cara's condition got worse. "You'd best hurry and tell me what that is! My oxygen is running out, and my head's about to split with the pain," she groaned.

"There are two small red clips at the centre of the circuit. Do you see them?"

Through the dim lighting, Cara peered through her blurred vision and focused on the two red-coloured clips. "Yes, I see them."

The AI gave its last instruction. "You must fuse those two clips together with a laser to complete the circuit!"

The entire business of repairing the damaged power systems, concentrating on Barnie's precise instructions, and the lack of oxygen was nothing short of stark horror for Cara. On top of this, the pain in her head had grown noticeably worse. "What sort of laser machine? I can't find one!" she snapped, rummaging around in the equipment locker.

Barnie's reply was daunting. "There isn't one... SP8 does not have a laser machine on board. Only our trained technicians have them when they come aboard for repairs."

A sickly wave of terror overwhelmed her as she stared at the nauseous blue lighting. "Then . . . I'll never complete the repair job? Because we don't have the right equipment?" Cara cried.

After a moment's silence, Barnie answered her. "It is unfortunate. SP8 does not have a laser machine. But you do, Cara!"

"What? What do you mean I have a laser machine? Where?" she gasped.

"In your belt, Cara. You have a small laser machine tucked into your belt," the AI replied.

Trying not to throw up into the oxygen mask, Cara leaned wearily on the locker for support. At first, she couldn't fathom what Barnie was talking about. She struggled for more air and then realised what he had meant. "Oh no! No, you don't understand!" she whimpered, taking the model laser gun from her belt. "This gun," she said breathlessly, holding it up – this laser gun is a fake. I made it with a 3D printer back at the space station. I planned to point it at Golbat Gorn when I caught up with him."

She heard Barnie's voice. "No, Cara," was all she heard, but distantly, as she felt herself fading. There was no point listening to him, but she tried.

She thought she heard Barnie say, "Your recklessness has finally caught up with you, young lady!" *But no*, she thought. *That was probably Grandma or Pops.* Cara tried apologising and asking how they'd got here but couldn't make a sound.

Cara's spirit and will to survive were fading rapidly. *It's so hard . . . to breathe. So, this is the end?* she thought as, in silent tears, she slid helplessly onto the floor of SP8, the little model laser gun held limply in her hand.

PART TWO

CHAPTER 12

Lost

With Guylo in charge and all robotic crew programmed to run a regular daily routine, every Thursday was 24-hour Rec/Rel time on New Dawn Space Station. Living crew members were relieved of all duties and only went into action if an emergency occurred.

Valina usually looked forward to a rousing game of Blindklask during Rec/Rel. Blindklask requires speedy eye-brain coordination. The players' eyes control a glowing globe on a marked-out pitch. While concentrating on the globe, your opponent's brisk focus can snatch the sphere away within a split second. Players wear virtual sight masks and aim to score goals by steering the globe with their eyes into a 'hole' at opposite pitch ends. If the globe touches any of the three marked blind spots on the pitch, then the player in control of the globe becomes blind in one eye. However, they can recover their sight if they score another goal soon after.

Valina and Debian were well-matched as competitors, and usually, the game could go on for several hours. Today, though, Valina couldn't concentrate. After losing several points in a row, she sighed, sat down at the side of the pitch, and took off her virtual sight mask. "It's no good. I'm blinded again already. I can't focus on the game."

"Me either," Debian said, walking towards Valina. "I asked Guylo to notify me – even during our game – if there was any word from Cara. Still nothing. We should have heard from her by now." She tried to smile, "Another game?"

"Might as well, I suppose," Valina agreed with a strained smile.

Valina started the game well, scored a goal and gained the first point. Unfortunately, she lost points for scoring an 'own goal' and touching one of the blind spots.

"Careful, Val!" Debian warned her. "Touch two more, and you're blind."

"I know that, Debian. You're putting me off my game," Valina bit back irritably.

During the game, both girls became blind in one eye. After that, Debian became entirely blind but somehow continued to score another goal split seconds after declaring blindness. As a result, she won three games to one.

Did she achieve that last goal blind? Valina wondered. She found it strange that Debian kept her play in high form even when blinded in one eye. But, on the other hand, Valina always lost points with this handicap. Try as she might to up her game, she could never seem to score against Debian while blinded, even in one eye.

Debian was the overall winner, two games to one. "That was an awful performance. I'm still off my game, I guess. Sorry, Deb," Valina said half-heartedly.

Debian deleted the globe and hovered towards her. "Oh, it doesn't matter, Val. My game wasn't much better."

They looked at each other for a long time, and then Debian said, "What are we going to do about Cara? I can't believe she hasn't contacted us. What's happened to her?"

Valina dropped her gaze and sighed. "I wish I knew. If only she'd make contact. But Guylo says there's just no signal coming from SP8. So he has absolutely nothing to go on."

"Listen, Val," Debian said calmly, "we can't do much about Cara until she communicates with us. So why don't you go and relax in the hot tub? Take the edge off things."

"I'm going to the gym for an hour's workout session instead. It'll take my mind off worrying." Valina answered with a frown. "Join me?"

"No, thanks," Debian answered. "I'm going to the library to read more of the traditional Quistic literature I found. But meet you in the spa for a drink later?" They agreed on a time before heading off in opposite directions.

Later, when Valina entered the spa, there was no sign of Debian, so she sat down to wait. She ordered drinks which the Android server brought a minute later. It was so unusual for Debian to be late for anything that Valina wondered whether she'd fallen into the deep sleep Quistics required every so often. She tapped on the table and browsed through the audio library, choosing some music only to find the sound of it increased her anxiety. She turned it off and fidgeted in her seat a while before finally tapping her wrist communicator and whispering into it.

"Debian, are you there? Are you awake? Are you coming to the spa, or have you changed your mind?" Valina asked.

Debian responded immediately, so it was clear she wasn't asleep. "Valina,

I was about to call you. You'd better come at once to the control room," she said briskly. "There's something you need to see!"

Valina exhaled a puff of exasperation that ended in a half-laugh. "Debian, I thought we were meeting in the spa? Is there something wrong? Guylo didn't contact me."

"Yes, I know, sorry. But remember, I asked Guylo to alert me immediately if he found any signal from Cara. He's found something he thinks might be SP8. He's refining the search. We don't know for certain yet," Debian replied.

As soon as Valina heard Debian mention Cara's name, she got out of her seat, placed the tray of refreshments onto a dumbwaiter portal and sent it up to the control room. She hoped it was nothing terrible if it was something to do with Cara.

A minute later, Valina entered the control room to discover Debian staring at her screen in a silent trance-like state. "What's up, Deb? What's happened?"

Debian peered at the screen and pointed to a pulsating red dot. Her voice was grim. "There. See?"

Valina knew at once what it was, "A distress beacon?"

Debian nodded. "Yeah, so who do you think is possibly having a catastrophe right now?"

Valina took a deep breath, knowing that specific mechanisms activated when a spaceship was in distress. Something was wrong. It meant that nobody – not even the AI – could pilot or repair the ship. *Was that Cara?*

"So, do we know where the signal is coming from? Who's transmitting it?" she asked. *Not SP8, please.*

Debian nibbled at her lip and turned to Valina, "Yes," she nodded. "Guylo has established that it's transmitting from SP8. It's coming from Cara's Space Pod."

At once, Valina tensed and, with a furrowed brow, called out, "Guylo, calculate the location and distance of SP8."

Debian resumed staring at the red dot on the screen, "Whatever can have happened to her?"

Valina pinched the bridge of her nose and tried to think. "I don't know, but it must be something dire. Distress beacons don't activate unless the entire control system has broken down."

Guylo's voice was steady. "Valina! I have readings showing the distance and position of SP8," he said.

Valina turned to look at the flashing beacon, "Go ahead, Guylo!" she responded, and at once, the information appeared on the screen.

"SP8 is just over two light years away and drifting into another galaxy," Guylo informed them.

"Will it be possible to reach her?" Debian asked no one in particular.

"I can confirm," Guylo cut in, "that it will take too long to travel from New Dawn to Cara's location if you intend to rescue Cara. With life support on SP8 down, she'll deplete oxygen reserves in just over two hours. So, you could not be in time to rescue her. It would take too long to reach the SP8 using available modes of travel."

Debian floated away from the screen, turned around to look at Valina and in a voice hardly louder than a whisper, said, "Maybe it's time to inform Captain Lydian."

"No!" Valina snapped.

"About our situation, I mean. Everything seems to keep going from bad to worse."

Valina was adamant, "No! Debian, we can't inform the Captain until I sort this mess out."

"How about we teleport to her?" Debian ventured.

Guylo cut in at once. "Negative! My data shows that neither of you has completed teleport training, including medical screening and inserting a teleport chip into your body."

They were both silent for a moment. Then, Valina said with wide eyes, "Debian, I have an idea!"

"Oh, yes? *Ha*! I remember Cara saying that, too. And see where it's landed us?" Debian said, staring back, waiting for Valina to continue.

"Well, what if we used that Time Travel Capsule, the TTC, to go after Cara?"

"What! Valina, are you *joking*? How is that helpful at a time like this?" Debian said with raised eyebrows. She floated forward to face her crewmate. "We've already lost the power transmitters and allowed a crew member to endanger herself. I don't think the TTC is of any use because — for a start — we haven't trained or learned how to operate it! What's more, we don't even know if it works!"

Valina touched the glinting spiral in her ear for a second, taking a pace away. Then, with fists clenched, she turned back to Debian, "As First Officer, it's time I took full responsibility for the predicament we're all in. I have to sort this out before Captain Lydian returns," she said.

A team of scientists had housed The Time Travel Capsule in one of New Dawn's spare docking bays. Valina remembered when, months ago, Captain

Lydian had shown the machine to the crew, offering only some brief information about it.

"The TTC is still very much in the experimental stage," Captain Lydian had explained to her crew. "Operational trials aren't complete. However, headquarters has arranged for a professor and his team to visit New Dawn later this year. They'll be our guests for a year, maybe longer. While here, they will test the TTC's deep space functionality, which we hope will be its last development phase.

"But until then, it must remain secure and locked away," the Captain had ordered. "It is strictly off limits."

So, they'd sealed it away, and Valina hadn't thought about it until now.

Valina pressed on, regardless of the Captain's off-limits order. "I'm sorry, Debian, but if we want to save Cara, we have no choice. I believe Captain Lydian would do the same to save a crew member. The TTC will get us there in a matter of seconds. If you don't want to come with me, that's fine. I understand. I can't order you to go, and I certainly don't want to endanger you. You stay here with Guylo and take charge of the space station."

They stood silent for a few seconds while Valina searched Debian's eyes and sighed. "Debian, you must understand; I can't leave Cara out there to die. I know she probably doesn't appreciate that I care about her, but I do. She means a lot to me, to our team." There was a sudden change in her tone as she straightened. "And, as First Officer Cadet, I'm completely responsible for her safety," she stressed, turning on her heel and walking away.

At once, Debian closed in and floated to within inches so that Valina smelled the fresh sweetness of her breath. "No, no, Valina! I'll come with you! Who knows what dangers and horrors we might find when we get to Cara? Besides, she may need medical attention, so I must go. I want to help save Cara, too," Debian insisted.

Valina glanced at Debian's hand on her shoulder. The simple gesture made her smile for a second. Then, just as quickly, her face became serious again as she lifted her gaze. "I don't know what dangers and perils might await us, Debian, but I'm certain that the sooner we reach Cara, the better."

"Then let's go, shall we?" Debian said, pulling Valina toward the spare docking bay where the experimental Time Travel Capsule had remained locked away and off-limits. Until now, that is.

Chapter 13

A Risk

"Guylo," Valina commanded as they stood before the Time Travel Capsule. "I need to know how to operate the TTC now. And I need to know quickly."

"I can instruct you now and tell you everything you need to know and be brief about it, Valina," Guylo agreed.

Valina hoped the AI was right, but she was doubtful.

"After some brief and necessary warnings about the Time Travel Capsule. One—"

"Guylo. Stop," Valina shouted. "We've had all the warnings already!"

"I have no record of giving you these warnings, Valina."

"It was the Captain," Debian added. "She informed us about the machine already, Guylo."

"Such as?"

Valina thought back to what Captain Lydian had said. "Well, there've been experimental tests. The data shows a 98.5% success rate." She remembered this because she'd wondered, *What happened to the 1.5% that didn't return?*

"It is still only in phase two of an early experimental state, and long-term data on how it might affect TTC passengers or cargo is unavailable," Debian added helpfully.

Valina thought again about the enormous risk they were taking. She closed her eyes and let Guylo pepper them with warnings. *There's no other choice. It's the only way we can save Cara.* She told herself.

Guylo instructed them on how to open the capsule, working as a team. Valina and Debian stood at the entrance of the docking bay chamber and stared at the inside of the Time Travel Capsule. Its surfaces were smooth, felt solid and had very few controls that Valina could see.

"You must wear Personal Solar Protection Equipment!" Guylo's voice echoed across the bay. "This PSPE should keep you safe. You must wear it at all times." Debian gripped the end and pulled her long orange plait to the front of her. Valina wondered if that was her way of easing anxiety.

"You will travel so fast it will damage your bodies beyond repair if you are not wearing PSPE," Guylo said flatly, and, at this, Valina saw Debian wince and grip her plait even tighter.

Everything depended on Guylo's advanced artificial intelligence to safely get them there and back to New Dawn Space Station. "Guylo, can you assure us you have enough knowledge and information to understand how to launch and control this machine? And, as far as you know, is your data correct and up to date? We are about to entrust you with the most precious things we have. Our *lives*," Valina said with a slight quiver in her voice.

"Pay attention; this is important information!" Guylo announced, recognising no obvious doubts that Valina had. But then why should he care? Guylo was a machine, highly intelligent – but deprived of all emotion. Yet, what he said next was something Valina thought highly unscientific, most unexpected, and nearly sent her into a fit of nervous giggles.

"You must understand the Cinderella Effect," he said in his usual flat tone.

"Cinderella Effect?" Valina asked. Debian snickered, which left Valina trying to keep a straight face.

"I detect a fool-hardy chuckle in your voice and mannerisms, you two. Stop and listen! I'm about to disclose important information," he replied. Valina gave a slight cough, and both cadets straightened their faces. "Thank you! Can I assume you've heard the ancient Earth myth about the human girl who had to return to base before 00.00 hours? And if she failed, the powerful energy crashed, and the beautiful clothes she wore disintegrated."

Debian nudged Valina, pointing to the time, an exaggerated look of fear on her face as she mouthed the word, *Cara*. "Oh, that sounds like a fascinating story. I'm sure we already know it. Right, Valina?"

"Yes, actually," Valina said. Aware of the minutes ticking by, she babbled to convince Guylo they understood. "Cara told me that tale. She said it's ancient. Cinderella was a beautiful young human girl with cruel stepsisters and a wicked stepmother. They were mean to her and wouldn't allow her to attend important social events, you know, like a prom or something. There was magic involved, so she got to go to the prom. But as Guylo said, she had to be back before 00:00 or the magic —" Valina made a *poof* sound and motioned with her hand. "All gone."

"What happened?" Debian asked, wide-eyed. "Did she make it back before midnight?"

"No. She didn't make it back in time and her beautiful clothes…" but Valina didn't finish her sentence. Out of nowhere, a loud blast of hooting pierced the air, and the shock caused the cadets to screw up their shoulders and cover their ears.

"Ok, ok, Guylo! You can stop that now! We're listening! We're listening! Valina yelled. The hooting ceased.

"We've far more important matters to deal with," Valina whispered to Debian. Then she shouted into the air, "Over to you, Guylo!"

"Am I to understand you've finished wasting time and will now allow me to continue the explanation?" his disgruntled voice droned and went on. "As you already know, this Time Travel Capsule is in its initial stages of development. Therefore, it may not fully understand parallel time lengths."

Debian's brow creased, "What's that?"

"There is an internal mechanism that triggers the end of a program. My data tells us the machine has only a short functioning time."

"How long?" Valina cut in.

"When it arrives at its destination, you have precisely two-and-a-half Earth hours left," Guylo warned them.

"Then what happens?" Debian asked quietly.

"It replicates the return journey. If you do not board the machine in time, it will disappear and leave you behind. Stranded!" Guylo announced gravely.

This information was troubling, and Valina swallowed hard, "How will we recognise when it's time to get back inside? Will the capsule give us any warning signal?"

"Yes, but you must give yourselves plenty of time to get back inside the TTC," Guylo replied. Valina saw Debian touch her forehead pensively and thought her crew mate was probably having second thoughts about any rescue mission. "What would we do if the TTC left without us?" She asked.

Valina was still for a few moments staring out at something and said, "Think of it like this, Debian. If the TTC disappears while we're on SP8 with Cara, I'm sure that between us, we have enough knowledge and skill to save Cara, repair any damage and make our way back to New Dawn Space Station in the SP8."

Debian's brow creased. "But—"

Valina interrupted. "It's not going to happen that way."

"*Er*, right," Debian said grim-faced.

At this, Valina waved a hand in dismissal and continued questioning Guylo. "What's the signal? Does an alarm go off when the return program begins?"

"No. You will know the TTC prepares to return when the humming gets louder."

Valina was about to ask what Guylo meant by *the humming,* but the AI continued the instructions.

"Put on your helmets and connect the communicators via the control at the bottom of the headgear," Guylo instructed. Both were dressed in their PSPE and Valina, increasingly edgy, walked with Debian around the capsule. The Time Travel Capsule consisted of solid metal and a glass-like transparent material. The space inside held two fully reclined seats attached to a platform. It was very narrow, with no room for over two passengers.

Valina climbed the short ladder attached to the machine's side. Her hands trembled as she hoisted herself into the tube. "Valina, place yourself on the travel panel in a straight horizontal position with your hands at your sides," Guylo instructed.

Valina faltered as she viewed the *'travel panels'* and thought morbidly that they were more like gurneys without wheels. "Lie down!" the AI ordered. Debian followed. Of course, she didn't need to use the ladder, and soon, both officer cadets lay side by side on the flat travel panels in the strange, long vessel.

"Valina, can you hear me?" Debian murmured in a trembling voice.

"Yes, I can." Valina reassured her and asked, "Are you ok?" She thought Debian still sounded uncertain, so Valina added, "Look, you need to say right now if you've changed your mind about coming with me. It's not too late." But maybe it *was* too late.

"Activating wave bands!" Guylo announced. At once, a loud humming sound began, followed by glowing blue bands of light that encircled the girls' bodies. *Ah! The humming,* Valina thought, remembering Guylo's instructions.

Then, out of the corner of her eye, she saw Debian turn her head to her right and heard her trembling voice. "Valina, I'm worried we might become lost somewhere or get separated from each other. You might go somewhere, and I might end up somewhere else!" The blue light bands grew brighter around them while the humming got louder. It was now so loud it made Valina's sensitive hearing buzz, and she found breathing was becoming difficult.

Debian started on at her again. "What will happen if we're trapped somewhere and can't return to our own time?"

Through gritted teeth, Valina answered sharply, "Then don't come, Debian! I'll order Guylo to stop the launch! We haven't any more time to discuss what might be. Cara needs help!"

At Valina's sudden cutting tone, Debian closed her eyes. "Ok," she whispered passively.

"Raising power to maximum time thrust! Guylo informed. A transparent shield slid from one end of the capsule above their heads and enclosed them. Metal bands shot over their wrists and ankles, holding the girls in place. Valina disliked that trapped feeling and twitched her wrists to free them, but it was too late.

"Ejection into the new time thrust in thirty seconds!" Above the loud volume of humming, Guylo's voice was barely discernible. Valina wondered if the pain in Debian's ears was as excruciating as it was in her own, and all at once, she had the nauseous sensation of falling. She heard Debian gasp and call out, "Valina, I'm dropping into a pit … Guylo, can you— ?"

A tremendous white flash filled the space, and Debian was no longer beside her. Instead, all Valina could hear from a distance was Debian's screams of terror, yelling, "Guylo! *Guylo*! Let me out!"

Another white flash followed, and Valina saw no more.

CHAPTER 14
Found

Valina woke up thinking she was in her New Dawn Space Station bunk bed. She opened her eyes and closed them again just as quickly. Why was it so dark? When she tried to stretch, she felt tight bands around her arms and legs spring open to release pressure.

The TTC, she remembered. *We've arrived. Somewhere.* Tentatively, she reached out and touched a shoulder. "Debian, is that you? Are you there?"

But what if it wasn't Debian?

Valina switched on her helmet beam and clambered out of the Time Travel Capsule. She turned her head to the side, and Valina's light beam lit up other things. Then, standing at the side of the TTC, she peered in to make sure it was Debian in there. Of course, it was, but she looked terrible.

"Are you ok? You don't look too good. The tint of your skin is paler than usual. If you're going to throw up, don't forget to activate your body fluid ejector first. You don't want to hover with all that sloshing around in your gear, do you?"

Debian sat up, "Where am I? I mean, where are we?"

"In Cara's Space Pod, I hope," Valina replied. "Here, give me your hand, and I'll help you. Unfortunately, there's no ladder to climb down, but you don't need one, do you?"

When Debian didn't move, Valina took her arm, but try as she might, she failed to pull her up into a standing position. Debian looked around. "Do you find it extremely dark here?"

"Don't worry, switch on your helmet beam! You'll become more confident when you can see what you're familiar with," Valina assured her crew mate.

Debian sat up and remarked with a sigh as she glanced fleetingly around without switching on her beam, "I can see we're in a Space Pod."

Valina's usual patience was wearing thin, for Debian still did not get out of the TTC. "Well, come on! If you can see that well in the dark, we must get on and search around for Cara. You heard what Guylo said about the time limit on this thing. It might suddenly disappear when we least expect it. If so, I don't know what will happen."

Still, Debian didn't budge, and Valina lost her patience. "What in the moon's name is the matter with you? Come on, switch on your light, and get out!"

A quiet sob and two or three muffled sniffs came through Valina's earpiece. Her voice softened. "Debian! Are you upset? Please don't be frightened; we'll do this together. We'll find Cara first, help her sort everything out, and leave as soon as possible," Valina coaxed. Her brow creased. "I should have ordered you to stay on New Dawn. I guess I'm not assertive enough yet!"

Debian sobbed again, croaking, "It's not what you think, Valina. You're right, I am afraid, but it's not about being in this situation."

Valina tilted her head. "I don't know what you mean. Tell me as we go, so we can get on and look for Cara!"

"I can't move!" Debian groaned.

Valina shot her a look of concern. "What? But you've just this second sat up. What bit of you can't you move?"

"No, I mean, I can't hover. I've lost my levitating power. My body seems too heavy, and I can't lift myself into the air."

Valina shook her head inside her helmet. "But how can that be? What could cause your levitation power to disappear like that?"

Debian put a gloved hand on her helmet and turned her head. "It must be something to do with travelling through time," she moaned. "It's certainly something I've never done before. This time travel machine must have affected the gravitational pull."

Speaking of *time,* Valina was conscious of how it was rapidly ticking away. "Can you move your legs? Can you try standing up?"

The small officer cadet pushed herself into a standing position with some effort. "My legs have become like lumps of lead. Can you help me down? Maybe there's something wrong with the gravity level here," she said.

Valina checked the reading on her wrist control. "Nope! The gravity reading is normal, and it's not affecting me. *Ooof!*"

Debian climbed out of the TTC with effort, only to land with all her weight on Valina. For some moments, both lay sprawled on the floor.

"You'd better stay here, by the machine, while I investigate," Valina huffed as she shoved Debian to one side and stood up.

"No, wait! Please don't leave me here. If you help me onto my feet, I'll try to shuffle along," Debian said, sounding short of breath.

Once more, Valina consulted her wrist control pad. "Well, we need to move faster if we're to find Cara and get back to the machine in time." She turned to Debian, concerned. "Can you breathe properly? You don't sound good."

She didn't wait for an answer. The personal oxygen supply had activated, and Valina breathed easily inside her suit. She figured Debian did, too. However, the monitor on Valina's control pad told a different story outside of their suits. She brought Debian's attention to the digital gauge on her sleeve. "Look! The gauge shows there's not much oxygen left in this space pod. So, we must hurry if we're to find and save Cara in time!"

Debian raised her gloved thumb as a sign she understood, and they moved in slow motion away from the TTC. Valina shone her light beam ahead, which lit up SP8's interior, and then wondered why Debian still hadn't activated hers.

"We've landed in the docking bay," Debian observed. "This is the passage that leads to the control cabin."

"Come on!" Valina said sharply as her anxiety increased. "And for moon's sake, switch on your light!"

Debian did what Valina told her, but instead of progressing calmly and carefully, Debian's attempts to walk were more like heavy stumbles across the pod's floor. She landed sprawling on her face or back at the end of each second or third step.

Valina heard Debian groan as she watched her hoist herself upright. "My muscles always attune to the force of gravity on New Dawn. Now, for the first time, I can't seem to cope with more gravitational pull and lower air pressure. It's good news the gravity is still online in here.

Valina agreed but only nodded. If gravity were offline, they'd have no hope of repairing the SP8.

With such slow progress, Valina wondered if she would have been better off alone. She gritted her teeth and made a dismissive gesture. "Can't you key some data into the PSPE controls to adjust your gravity requirements?" she said more sharply than intended.

With head bent, Debian keyed in a search on the sleeve controls of her protective suit. "There's no program installed. It's obvious someone has not developed the time travel suits to solve this kind of problem," she mumbled.

In silence, they watched for anything unusual as things ahead became visible in the darkness. Valina thought it strange that there were no signs of much upheaval. The equipment did not spark, and there was no smell of burning or leaking gas. It troubled her, for the silence here seemed ominous and unsettling.

Enough power remained for the door from the outer chamber to slide open, and Valina and Debian entered the central area. It was here that the calamity was evident. A faint intermittent bleeping came from the oxygen indicator that revealed just how low the oxygen level was. Their head beams lit up bits of broken components and showed small tools scattered across the floor. It looked chaotic like a miniature bomb had exploded and left a trail of debris.

In places, Valina could see that many pieces of equipment had stopped functioning, leaving one or two control keys flashing dimly and fading. On and off. On and off. Like a constant ticking that counted down the seconds. It caused disturbing thoughts that tormented Valina as she moved along the dysfunctional pod. *Please don't say we're too late. Please, don't say we're too late!*

Valina turned her head this way and that so the beam from her helmet scanned around the room. "There doesn't seem to be much damage to the main control panels; they're still intact. But most of the systems are completely down."

With an effort, Debian moved nearer. "You're right. These bits on the floor have come from something else."

Valina crouched down to inspect the small parts of debris. With her intelligence in System Engineering, she knew the cause of the problem at once. "I'm sure this means someone has damaged or disconnected the Central Power Core."

Debian tapped Valina's shoulder and pointed, "Look, Val, over there!"

Valina turned to where Debian was pointing, and her light beam shone on something that looked like a long pair of human legs sticking out from underneath one of the control panels. The head, shoulders, and upper torso were not visible.

In a quiet voice, Debian asked, "Cara?"

For a second, Valina hesitated., but who else could it be? "Let's look, shall we?" In one swift move, Valina sped towards the limp body, partly lying face down on the floor. She crouched next to the legs and waited for Debian to reach her.

"*Ow!*" Debian cried as she dropped heavily to her knees on the other side of the body.

They both peered under the control panel. Of course, it was Cara. At first glance, and to her horror, Valina could not see any sign of Cara's breathing. "Oh, no!" she cried. "I think we're too late!"

Chapter 15
An Urgent Response

Valina adjusted her light to grow brighter, revealing the tight-fitting black pirate suit Cara had been wearing when she left. "I'll turn her over gently," Valina said as she lifted Cara's shoulders slightly off the ground and rolled her onto her back. Cara remained motionless, her face ashen and her lips blue from the lack of oxygen. Valina frowned and noted, "Her eyes are closed, but she's trembling slightly! Do you think we can bring her around?"

"There's no air left in the oxygen app!" Debian said as she tugged at a side pocket of her PSPE and produced a small breathing apparatus. When Valina gently removed the empty oxygen device from Cara's face, Debian quickly inserted the small pipe into one of Cara's nostrils.

Nothing happened, and Cara didn't move. Valina put her hand on Cara's head and gently brushed her hair from the side of her face, "Putting oxygen through her nose isn't working, is it?" She bent over Cara's face. "She's not responding."

Debian unfastened Cara's jacket, "Loosen her belt!" she told Valina. It was Debian's turn to be bossy. After a glance, she shouted, "Come on, I need to get oxygen into her lungs!"

Valina felt numb, afraid, and helpless but did as Debian asked. Then she sat back on her heels, watching as Debian placed the palms of her hands upon Cara's chest and pressed. Debian lifted Cara's eyelids and looked into her eyes. Next, she put an ear to her chest and listened for a minute or two. Her expression was grim. "She has a faint heartbeat, but if we don't get her breathing right now, her heartbeat will stop altogether."

Valina blinked but said nothing. Even without putting her ear to Cara's chest to listen, her highly sensitive Listroc hearing told her just how faint the beat of Cara's heart was.

"Valina, we need to act quickly!" Debian said, putting her hand back onto Cara's chest and placing her other hand on top. "While I keep up the pressing rhythm, you need to open the valve more on the breathing app. Cara needs to get as much oxygen as possible," Debian urged.

Valina's mouth twisted in frustration. "Other than giving her oxygen, I don't know if we can do much more to help her." But she did as Debian asked and opened the valve.

Debian turned her head, "Leave this to me, Valina. Believe me. Cara will survive, but you must do as *I* say now."

Valina watched Debian work and swallowed back her anguish. *As First Officer, I should have taken responsibility from the start and threatened Cara with consequences when she didn't obey orders.* It was hard for her to see Cara in this state, and she placed the blame squarely on herself.

Debian stopped the compressions momentarily and rested two fingers on Cara's brow. She closed her eyes and lowered her head close to Cara's face. Seconds passed, but nothing happened. Then, to Valina's utter shock, Debian removed *her* protective helmet. A soft yellow glow engulfed Cara's sleeping face as Debian let her healing powers enter the unconscious girl.

Valina leaned in, face tight with concern. "What are you doing, Debian? What's all the light business? How can that help her breathe? She needs oxygen!… *You* need oxygen!'

"Hush! Have patience!" Debian replied in a whisper. Still, with her eyes closed, Debian put her two fingers on Cara's blue lips, and once more, a yellow glow appeared around them. Then, calmly, she said, "Cara, can you hear me? Open your eyes!"

Debian's hand gently touched Cara's face, and although Valina saw her eyes flutter, she was not sure the girl was entirely aware of their dark figures crouched next to her. As her eyes slowly opened, it didn't seem to Valina that Cara saw anything. She appeared utterly unresponsive. But Valina was more hopeful when she saw the young cadet's beautiful brown eyes with life in them.

Debian placed her face close to Cara's. "Get more oxygen into her! The dose of revival breath I've given her won't last long," she said.

Valina connected a breathing tube from her PSPE to the oxygen device and attempted to place it on Cara's face. Cara blinked a few times and seemed to come awake. She pushed the oxygen away and peered around through the dimness. She clutched Valina's arm in another second and struggled to sit up. Valina rushed to push her gently back down. "You mustn't do that, Cara. Just lie still until we've established your injuries. You need this oxygen."

But before placing it on her face, Cara gasped in shallow breaths, "The SP8. I've crashed it, haven't I? Won't lie down. Tell me what's going on. Why are you – *how* are you here?"

Debian and Valina shared a glance. "Tell me," Cara whispered.

Valina regarded her with a long, solid expression. "You've had an accident with SP8. Nothing that we can't put right." Valina's tone wasn't convincing, even to herself, because she didn't know if they could put it right.

Cara looked around, and with sadness, the First Officer saw a tear running down the girl's cheek as she gasped. "Is there much damage? Oh, Valina. Debian! I failed. Didn't get power transmitters. Made a dreadful fool of myself. Gorn's not a . . . thief. He *is* a diplomat. Serves Commander Predaton. Guess who's – *with* – Gorn? *Predaton*!"

Carefully and gently, Valina scooped an arm under Cara's shoulders and placed the oxygen device over the gasping cadet's nose and mouth. For a moment, she held her close to calm her. "Listen, Cara. We can't stay here with you. You want to know how we got here?"

Cara nodded.

"Well, Valina continued, "the only way we could get to you quickly was by using the new Time Travel Capsule. " Cara's eyes grew wide with surprise.

"But", Debian interrupted, "we haven't time to explain all that to you now. We must get back before the TTC goes without us."

Valina checked, saw a satisfactory oxygen level, and held Cara's hand affectionately. "At least we don't need to worry about those Power Transmitters anymore," she assured her crew mate.

Even as the words left her lips, Valina felt a shiver of fear and an ominous sensation that she was wrong.

CHAPTER 16

Count Down

Still huddled with Cara and Debian on the floor of the SP8, Valina blew out her cheeks and slowly shook her head to clear her thoughts. She mentally dismissed the feelings of foreboding, blaming them on nerves, nothing more. Their situation was not great, but they'd made it here, hadn't they? Cara was alive and already looked brighter and more alert.

Acutely aware of the time, Valina glanced at her sleeve controls. Then, she told Cara, "Before we leave you, we're going to fix all the damage and get Barnie communicating with you again." She gently pressed Cara's hand in hers and continued. "I'll set SP8 on an auto-course to bring you safely back to New Dawn and—"

Valina didn't get to finish what she was saying. Instead, Cara pulled down the oxygen mask, gripped Valina's hand and shook her head, "No, no! You don't understand. I can't come back to New Dawn."

Looking weak and unwell, Debian said irritably, "Cara, don't start all that nonsense again, please! We've no time to mess around. That TTC is in its early stages of development and has limitations on how it functions. Valina and I need to get away as soon as possible."

Cara sat up again and, in a miserable tone, said, "I can't return to New Dawn yet because I'm under vehicle arrest." Cara looked with watery eyes from one to the other. Then, with a rapid intake of breath, she went on, "Commander Predaton was extremely angry about how I'd tried to trick them into giving me the Power Transmitters. So, he ordered SP8 to shadow Gorn's spacecraft and follow it to the Galactic Conference on planet LB11."

Valina heard Debian sigh as she put a weary hand on her head. She guessed Debian was exhausted and losing sympathy. "In that case," Valina said, "we must locate Gorn's ship and return you there." Valina peered through her visor. "Why were you ordered to go to the conference, anyway? What will you do there?"

Cara sniffed. "The commander is handing me over to Captain Lydian, who will deal with me and my . . . mistake. Oh, if only I hadn't been such an idiot, Valina."

To Valina's relief, Debian's calm voice had returned and offered a hopeful smile. "Cara, try to relax. You don't appear to have severe injuries, but you must rest. So, I'm going to put you into a deep sleep. This sleep will slow down your anxiety and keep you out of trouble, " she said, attempting to replace Cara's oxygen mask.

Valina added, "We'll do everything possible to get SP8 shipshape and restore communication with Barnie, who will take over the rest. I'm sure Captain Lydian will understand that you acted in our best interests when going after Gorn."

Valina's tone became serious again, "For now, though, Cara, I think it best that you don't get in touch with Captain Lydian. We don't want her knowing that Debian and I risked using the TTC to come and rescue you from this crisis."

"Otherwise, we'll be in serious trouble, too!" warned Debian.

Cara looked at the pair in a trembling voice and mumbled, "No, of course. I won't tell Captain Lydian that you came. I'm so grateful to you both for getting me out of this awful muddle."

Debian leaned forwards and placed her fingers lightly on Cara's temples, "We'll get you back to Gorn's spaceship, but now you need to sleep. Then, the next time you wake, you'll feel stronger and more able to cope with things."

Cara smiled at Debian before looking startled. "What's happening, Deb? Your face is – is *glowing*!" A soft yellow light embraced Cara's face, and she immediately fell into a deep sleep.

Valina had known nothing of the light and energy Quistics possessed, which utterly mystified and intrigued her. She watched Debian replace her helmet and resume the oxygen flow to herself. Though she realised now that Quistics could reserve a substantial amount of oxygen in the lungs, she suspected it wouldn't keep Debian going much longer.

Valina sighed, then turned an admiring smile on Debian. "You used much of your light and energy to restore Cara's bodily functions, and there are still many tasks to complete. Do you think you'll be strong enough to carry on?"

Debian smiled back and nodded her consent, but Valina could see the worry in Debian's expression. Valina consulted the timer on her sleeve controls again, "I'm afraid the countdown for the departure of the TTC is rapidly running out. I'll carry Cara to her bunk so you can stabilise her while I get SP8 functioning to its total capacity before we leave," she said.

Debian's brow creased. "How much time do we have left?" she asked.

"About seventy–five minutes, but we need to work quickly," Valina said. After all that had happened, she hoped they would make it back safely to New Dawn Space Station.

*

Valina had been right about the damage she and Debian had found on entering SP8, so she first needed to restore the space pod's Central Power Core. The PSPE that Guylo had produced for them had a belt and pouches that held various essential equipment, such as micro tools and spare nano chips. Amongst the micro-devices was a small laser instrument Valina used to fuse the two red clips vital in the repair job that Cara had failed to complete.

With her Listroc knowledge and skill, Valina completed each task swiftly and precisely. She restored life systems, communications, control panel instruments, lighting, and, ultimately, the Central Core. As a result, SP8 had a stabilised oxygen output and was, once more, fully functioning.

As she keyed in the final codes and data, Valina imagined how desperate and frightened Cara must have felt when faced with such a daunting repair job. Not knowing what would happen to her once she realised she couldn't mend, it must have filled her with terror.

"Activate voice recognition!… Barnie, do you have voice recognition?" Valina finally said to Space Pod 8.

She waited a few seconds until she heard, "Voice recognition complete. Welcome aboard, First Officer Valina Skarn," Barnie responded.

Valina blew out a sigh of relief inside her helmet. With this voice recognition test, she knew Barnie was back in control of the pod. "Good. Now listen. You are in complete control of SP8 again. When we leave, you will have no other functional pilot onboard. Do you understand?"

"Yes, Valina. I understand." Barnie responded.

Valina nodded when the AI answered and proceeded with her instructions. "Although Cara is here, she cannot take control of the pod. So, I have reprogrammed you to locate the Zeg-Mar5 and encounter Mr Gorn. You must continue following his spaceship and immediately communicate with him when you reach him. Is that clear?"

"Yes, that is clear."

"Do you have questions, Barnie?"

The AI paused, then drawled, "Is Cara alive?"

Wide-eyed, Valina smiled. "Oh yes! Very much alive. I will connect you to her stabilising equipment, and you must keep her condition steady until she regains consciousness."

Finally, Valina touched the control screen to close the repair program and said, "When Cara regains consciousness, she may remember nothing that's happened to her. She'll probably be confused, so you inform her we were here to rescue her."

"Understood," he said.

As Valina made a few more adjustments to the control panel, with no other warning, she heard it. The humming sounds. The TTC was humming! Shooting around, she looked up and found Debian stumbling out of Cara's sleeping cubical. She'd heard it, too.

"Come on!" Valina yelled as she grabbed Debian's arm. "Can you hear it? The TTC is humming already." Valina felt her breathing quicken. "We need to get out of here. It looks as though something is wrong with that machine's time mechanism. According to the time gauge, it should not have hummed for another twenty minutes." She took another breath and asked, "Have you settled, Cara?"

"Yes, just about. Cara is sleeping peacefully, but it was a struggle with this gravitational-pull problem, and it took me quite a while." Debian gasped, listing to one side and propping herself up on the sliding door of Cara's sleeping cubical.

"I've attended to her minor injuries and stabilised her breathing. I also got her out of that crazy pirate costume and back into her cleaned-up and repaired officer cadet uniform." Debian said in a gush.

"Ok, let's go!" Valina shouted. She readjusted her helmet, ready for the journey, hoping luck was on their side. "It's up to you now, Barnie! You have complete control of everything!" she yelled. "Do you copy?"

"Copy," Barnie responded.

Valina set off with the staggering Debian to cover the distance to the docking bay. Then, after a struggle to get inside the TTC, they both lay side by side and in position with the safety clips trussing their arms and legs. The shield slid over them, and the humming increased.

When the bands of light encircled them inside the sealed capsule, Valina knew something was amiss. *Red? Why are they all red?* The light bands were not blue this time. Valina tensed, feeling that ominous sensation again as everything faded to black.

Chapter 17

Fire Storm

The buzzing vibrations deep in Valina's chest were so intense they caused her to feel sick. Although she found herself slumped headfirst over the side of the TTC, she had no notion of her whereabouts. "What's going on?" she murmured. "Debian?" She raised herself and turned to look for her crew mate. There was no sign of her.

Valina raised her eyes and squinted at an enormous crack in the visor of her helmet. She felt shaky, and her heart raced at the thought of what might have happened to her crew mate. *Where? Or* when *might Debian be?* The thought terrified Valina and robbed her of her usual self-control.

"So much for the wonderful PSPE keeping us so safe, *eh*, Guylo?!" Valina ranted in a bitter tone that quickly turned to shouting and mocking the AI. 'You must wear the PSPE at all times. Never remove it!' *Ha!* Not so *protective* against a crash landing, is it? Is it, Guylo?!" Shouting made her feel better, more awake.

I'm not dead, she thought, trying to calm her shuddering breath. *So, at least the TTC crashed us on a planet with an atmosphere and oxygen.* Valina felt no symptoms of oxygen deprivation.

She dragged herself out of the TTC and looked around. Low clouds of smoke drifted around her head. The place was far from inviting. Everywhere she looked, she saw the black rock. It was all she could see in every direction, rising into high, jagged peaks. Here and there, steam rose from some sort of liquid. And the smell that permeated even through her PPSE suit was noxious.

It was boiling inside the suit. Valina walked away from the hovering smoke cloud and released the clasp on her helmet. She pushed back her visor with tentative fingers and took a slow, deep breath. As she did, the stink of something burning mixed with the hot, dry air. She cleared her throat and coughed.

Debian, she thought. *Stay on task. Find Debian.*

But Valina didn't know where to search. The terrifying thought crossed her mind again. *Is Debian in another age and time while I'm stranded here?* It seemed highly probable.

Finally, she returned to the crash site and peered into the wildly smashed-up time travel capsule to determine whether Debian was under the wreckage. She bent and cautiously picked up the larger pieces amongst the smashed and cracked remains of the TTC. Valina found no sign of her crew mate. She was partly relieved but felt a fresh stab of fear when she wondered where or when her friend might be.

Noting how hot it was getting, Valina wiped the sweat from her brow. However, it wasn't only the heat making her sweat but the overwhelming sense of being lost and alone in this dreadful situation. "I've got to stop thinking that way. It's not helping!" Valina closed her eyes and concentrated on getting herself under control.

When she eventually turned to examine her surroundings, something caught her eye. A low cloud of yellow gas, a haze only a short distance away, drifted towards her. An unrecognisable shape floating in the cloud emerged as it came closer, and Valina inhaled sharply. Not until the figure was almost upon her did she release her breath.

"Oh boy! Debian! Am I glad to see you! You're safe!" Valina said as, at last, she recognised the familiar outline of her friend. "Are you hurt?" she asked, holding Debian at arms-length and peering intently into her crew mate's visor.

"I see your PPSE didn't hold up so well, either. At least we can breathe without it, but it's so hot here!" Debian gasped.

Valina nodded in dismissal and waved a hand towards the wreckage. "I'm not impressed with this time travel machine, either. Just look at the state of it! A complete wreck. I doubt whether anything inside will function properly."

Debian shook her head and huffed, "No, but there wasn't much inside of it right from the start, and as for it ever functioning correctly, that's another matter entirely. Luckily for us," Debian continued, "you still have your com-municator, *right?* Unfortunately, mine's broken along with the suit. I hope we're still in our own time."

"*Ha!*" Valina scoffed. "I was hoping your's still worked. Mine's as useless as the suit. I doubt we're in a different time, though. I don't think any part of this machine can function well at all. I know it's a prototype, but if dumping itself and us here is the best it can manage, it's hardly capable of travelling through hundreds of years in time, is it?"

"In which case, how do you reckon we'll ever escape? Is there an automatic distress beacon or anything?" Debian asked glumly. Valina couldn't, at that moment, give Debian an answer to her questions. So instead, she removed her gloves, wiped her brow and looked up. "Have you noticed a reddish glow up there?" she asked.

*

They had crashed in a dip with a prominent ridge of craggy black boulders on either side. Where the sky should be, there was a pinkish glimmer. The bewildered pair seemed small and helpless as they looked at their surroundings, and a sense of impending disaster seized Valina once more. They were silent for a while, observing the red glow above the rocks.

As Valina was first in command, she knew it was time for her to act. Turning to Debian, she said, "I'm pleased you've regained your levitation power. It must have been the time- travelling that caused it to stop. *"In which case,"* she said, pointing upwards, "Can you elevate to the top of that steep ridge and find out what's above those rocks? After that, we must find a way out of here as soon as possible."

Debian squinted up at the height of the black rocks. Then, in a slow, faltering tone, she said, "Ok, but I must levitate in stages. I can't tell from down here how high the top is."

"Right. Well then, be careful!" Valina said, patting Debian's back.

Valina watched Debian levitate to a small rock ledge, and after glancing over her shoulder, she began her ascent. After some zigzagging from one rock shelf to another, Valina watched as Debian soon reached the top. Then, Valina saw her give one wild look around and immediately drop back to the ground with great speed.

When she re-joined her, Debian's face was ashen, and her voice shook. "It's a dreadful fire,' Debian gasped. "It stretches across some rocky hills in an unbroken line. Surprisingly, there was little smoke up there because there was nothing to burn. It's all hot glowing cinders and flames."

Debian cleared her dry throat, "But it's also coming up from other directions at an alarming rate! A wind blows it our way and brings fumes across the lower ground. What shall we do, Valina?"

Through clenched jaws, Valina answered, "If this wretched TTC hadn't thrown us around and off our course, we might have made it back to New Dawn before the time ran out."

Debian flicked a switch on her sleeve, and a drinking tube appeared beside her mouth. She took a massive gulp of water, then gasped, "I don't relish the thought of burning to death in this fiery place. Look at how that gas is coming across now," she said, glancing above them.

Valina nodded. "We've got to get out of here, fast! But how and which way?" She looked in the direction from where Debian had come, then turned to face her and pointed over her shoulder with her thumb. "What's back there?"

Debian looked off in the same direction. "There's a narrow stream of a liquid substance where the TTC threw me out. Steam is rising off it, but it's not bubbling. I don't think the liquid's boiling, and I don't think it's water. I'm not sure what it is."

Valina turned instantly and said, "We'll follow that then, shall we? It might lead us away from the fire."

Debian grabbed Valina's arm, stopping her in her tracks, "No, wait, you can't! There are no banks to walk along and nothing but sheer jagged rocks reaching down to the flowing liquid. I found you easily because there was no other way to walk."

They both remarked on more smoke approaching from the opposite direction, and Valina concerned the fire might trap them, concentrated on their situation. She stared hard at the ground for some time, then looking up, she spotted Debian's fingers fidgeting nervously. "Ok, Debian, this is what we'll do!"

"What?" Debian asked, stilling her hands.

From the corner of her eye, Valina had again caught sight of the wrecked TTC lying nearby. It was black and scorched in places, with bits of smouldering wire sticking out of the top. The transparent panel had melted like jelly and left sticky blue lumps running down the sides of the machine. She was amazed they'd survived.

Valina walked around it and further inspected the defunct travel machine. Then she dropped down inside and examined the sides and bottom of the interior. "There's no damage done to the bottom of the TTC. No holes, no cracks," she said, popping her head out of the capsule. "The bottom is still intact, too."

Still appearing anxious, Debian hovered nervously, "But Valina, how will we get the machine working again? There's no way we can use that wreck to escape from here."

Valina's excited voice rose as she clambered out of it, "No, not as a time travel machine, we can't, but as a boat, we might. Come on, Debian, help me drag it into that stream of liquid!" she said enthusiastically.

Thankfully, the substance of the machine was exceptionally light. Still, since it was large enough to carry two people lying side by side, it was extremely cumbersome and awkward to manoeuvre. After much huffing and puffing, the pair hauled it to a low edge near the liquid stream.

"Can we stop now, please?" Debian said, sinking to the ground and wiping the sweat off her face. "This heat is making me feel ill," she said. Valina rolled her eyes and stood with her hands on her hips. But even she was panting now.

Valina watched Debian put the drinking tube to her lips and close her eyes. "Stay here, Deb. I'm going to walk back to the spot where we crashed. I've seen something in the debris that might be useful. I'll be right back," she said. Valina sped back to the crash site to sift through more bits of wreckage. Debian hadn't moved when she returned, and Valina dropped a piece of the wreck she'd brought back at the Quistic's feet. Startled, Debian opened her eyes with a jolt.

"Right, let's get this machine lowered into the liquid, shall we?" Valina said, and Debian levitated listlessly with a groan onto the bank. Then, with Debian's help and holding her breath in anticipation, Valina lowered the TTC into the stream. Would this thing float or sink? If it went under, then what would they do?

She need not have worried, and Valina was relieved that it buoyed up perfectly as they let go of the machine. Still, she knew they had to get in quickly before it drifted away. "You hold it steady while I get in, then hover in after me," Valina ordered.

"Isn't there one problem we've overlooked?" Debian pointed out. "There's no energy available to power it. So how is it going to move along?"

"Simple. We'll use our body's energy and the flow of the liquid to get it moving. And two of these," Valina said, picking up and waving the wreckage she'd brought back from the crash site. There wasn't time to explain that she knew about canoeing because it was an ancient aquatic activity she'd participated in after moving to Earth as a child.

"Now, hold the TTC still while I get in," she said, dropping the wreckage to free up her hands. As Valina lowered herself into the floating time travel machine, she sensed its tilt but brought it level again by transferring her weight to the opposite side. Next, she took a small instrument from her PPSE backpack and, from the side of the bed seat, quickly removed a long pole with a flat square piece fixed to the top. The flat part had been a head shield in the former time travel capsule.

She held up the removed piece and said, "We'll use these as paddles. Pass me the object that looks like this off the bank behind you. Then get in."

"What's a *paddle*?" Debian asked. Valina put a finger to each of her temples, closed her eyes and went Listroc. In a trance-like voice, she intoned, "The goal of the paddle is to guide the push against the water so that the boat goes forward."

Debian started to ask something else, but Valina cut in and said sharply, "For moon's sake, Debian! I've explained what a paddle is; now do you want to escape the rapidly spreading flames or not?"

Debian held the piece of wreckage in both hands and, with a jutted lip, levitated into the TTC. There was no wobbling when she sat behind Valina, and the machine remained balanced.

"Ok, we're off," Valina shouted as she pushed away from the rock bank with her paddle. In no time, they were moving swiftly downstream and – she hoped – away from the fire.

Chapter 18
Into the Fire

As their Time Travel Canoe moved away from the bank, Valina and Debian – sitting on each side of the boat – set off down the fast-moving stream of liquid. Debian, uncertain what a paddle was at first, soon found the action quite easy. "Oh! This was a great idea, Valina!" she exclaimed after they'd gone a short way. After that, Debian paddled like a pro.

This relieved Valina of one worry, at least. "Good job, Deb," she exclaimed over the noise of the rushing liquid.

Before long, the stream was a river, and their makeshift boat picked up speed. Valina half-turned and shouted to Debian, "Use the paddle to keep us from bumping into the banks! This flimsy TTC might crack up."

As she turned, Valina saw flames coming up behind them, dancing along the rocks that cracked loudly in the heat. "Can you hear me, Debian?" she said. She saw Debian almost drop her paddle.

"Yes, Valina, I can hear you," Debian answered in a quavering voice. "Those flames are getting close!"

"When the TTC crashed, and you got thrown out, could you see what this liquid is like further upstream?" Valina asked as they tried to keep up with their paddling.

"I could see that it flows swiftly. Then, through a gap in the smoke, I could see that it opens into a wider river of the same liquid," Debian answered in quick breaths. "It looks as if it runs right through large rocks. I hope it's not too turbulent."

"Don't worry! We can shoot the rapids if it is," replied Valina and dipped her makeshift paddle into the liquid. The action sent the TTC rapidly toward a bend in the river where more giant smouldering rocks towered above.

"Shoot the rapids?" Debian repeated, screwing up her face. "What does that mean?"

Valina rolled her eyes. "Yes, well. If we have to do it, you'll know," her retort was more terse than she'd intended.

A black cloud of vapour swept overhead, and some burning embers, wind-driven, dropped with a sizzle into the flowing liquid. Flares were coming over the top of the ridge. As the TTC raced through the liquid, brown foam curled in a wave at the front, and they forced them to put every bit of strength into their paddles' strokes. The whole place seemed to explode and burn around them, and the heat was overwhelming.

"Come on, Debian, paddle faster! We need to get ahead of these flames and burning rocks. If the fire overtakes us, we won't get through," Valina urged.

Already the fire was getting stronger. Great flames flared up on one side of the liquid river, burning and waving like giant torches high above the rocky crags. Rocks cracked with the heat, and acrid vapours stung their throats. It was like being trapped inside the deepest part of a volcano. Valina worried that she'd taken them in the worse possible direction. *What choice did I have?* She thought woefully.

"Look over there!" croaked Valina and pointed ahead. "At last, we've reached the opening to a channel!" she cried as the TTC darted into the arched shadow of more black boulders. The current was very swift here, and the channel took them through a long rocky avenue of low overhanging slabs. So low-hanging they could hardly pass underneath.

"Keep your head down!" Valina turned her head and called to Debian, who, she saw, was so exhausted that she could scarcely paddle.

Suddenly, roaring flames caught the rocks on the top of the overhang as they sheltered beneath them. In less than a minute, the stones were blazing ferociously above them. Valina and Debian, stifled with heat, bathed in blinding gas and glare, bore steadily on. Debian scooped up some liquid with her paddle and soaked both of them.

"Stop it! That won't cool us down, and we don't know what this liquid is. It might be caustic. Our suits will only protect us for a while," Valina shouted.

They gasped in terror as more flames swept across their way and made a scorching archway of fire.

"Well, perhaps you're right," Valina yelled, reconsidering. "The liquid is not eroding the TTC. So, it might help protect us." Debian didn't reply but splashed more liquid onto herself and Valina.

The river of strange liquid reflected the lurid glow from the flames until it appeared to Valina as a vast stream of human blood. Both girls gasped for breath in terror, and Valina realised they might have lost the chance of ever getting through. Their chances of survival seemed to run away with the gushing liquid.

"We better get ready to plunge into this liquid or take our chance of surviving the flames," Valina shouted to Debian. Just then, as she was preparing herself to jump, the TTC shot out into the red, glassy swell of the river. For the moment, they were safe, and both of them glanced back at the screen of fire they'd just come through. Valina wondered how they'd made it through unharmed.

Once she'd recovered from her fright, she looked around and saw that they hadn't come through completely unscathed. "Debian, stow your paddle and put out those live embers in the bottom of the TTC. I'll keep paddling. "

It startled Valina as her crew mate smacked her on the arm smartly. "Your right sleeve was smouldering," she said flatly.

She could hear Debian grunting as she smashed burning spots with her boots and flung the liquid over the cinders. "It's out," she said. Then moaned in despair. "Oh Valina, I so desperately want to leave this horrible place!"

As Officer Cadets, they'd never trained to steer a tiny makeshift boat through a rapidly flowing river strewn with many jutting and sharp rocks. So, Valina and Debian learned to "shoot the rapids" as they went. Already the long, loping flow of the fluid had caught them in its steaming current, and it whirled the TTC onwards. Suddenly, the vessel did a weird dance on the edge of a small bubbling whirlpool that once threatened to engulf them. Valina tried to remember everything she had ever learned about canoeing and guiding an out-of-control spacecraft. But a whirlpool was something entirely beyond her experience.

She fixed her anxious mind on the treacherous slope above the worst stretch of swirling liquid. Then, all at once, she spoke anxiously, "Debian! Dig your paddle deeply into the liquid. We must try to steady the craft and guide it close to the bank!"

But the TTC refused to obey and swerved closer and closer into the deadly foam that swirled madly in mid-stream around jagged boulders.

"Watch out!" shrieked Debian.

Valina ignored Debian's warning and yelled, "When we crash, get ready to jump!" They both dropped their paddles and waited, ready to spring clear. But once again, the TTC swept through another narrow passage between toothed rocks, so tight that the sides of the machine scraped the stone, slowing them almost to a complete stop.

Debian's frantic tone rose again, "We're not going to make it!"

Valina wanted to scream, *Shut up, Debian!* But she restrained herself. Just then, the scraping stopped, and the capsule broke free, once again joining the rushing current. The burden of stress from so much danger all around interfered with her transcendent genetic intelligence. She could feel it deteriorating, and she couldn't stop it. She struggled to push her mind into the upper levels of the Listroc mindset, trying to work out where they were.

There has to be a way out of this fire. Unless the entire planet is burning up. Unhelpful facts began peppering her thoughts. *A burning planet or star could mean one of several distinct possibilities – likely outcomes include –* She felt briefly trapped in her thoughts as they swirled in circles.

What worked when we escaped the whirling liquid? With that thought and much effort, Valina focused only on the problem to be solved – *our boat, the currents, relative speed, the rocks, the flames.* Valina began calculating the TTC's motion and weight ratios as she concentrated. Every so often, she adjusted the angle of the paddle according to the flow.

"Debian!" she shouted finally. "When I tell you to, I want you to take your paddle out of the river and lean all your weight to the left. Understand?"

"Ye-es!" came a strangled, frightened reply from Debian.

Valina focused and waited for the calculated moment. The moment when the TTC would be at the exact right point in the river of liquid as they approached the turbulence of the rapids. "NOW!" she yelled, yanking out the paddle as they pitched all their weight to the left.

The TTC swerved sharply and then shot out with a dancing glide onto the smooth liquid below the rapid. Valina grabbed her paddle and guided the TTC smoothly into a small backwater of liquid beneath a sloping ridge away from the intense flames.

*

"For one dreadful moment, I thought this machine would cause the death of us!" Debian said. Valina thought 'one dreadful moment' was an understatement but didn't say so. "Me too!" she agreed as they climbed onto the bank.

With shaking legs, gasping for breath, and a *bit* of help from Debian, they heaved the TTC up and out of the strange river. After dragging it a short way, they placed it high and dry among some much cooler rocks. Valina stared at it for a moment, shaking her head. "Look at the state of it now. What a wreck! But at least it stayed watertight and kept us safe."

Debian folded her arms and frowned at Valina, "Well, I didn't feel one bit safe through any of it!" she scowled.

Valina screwed up her face but didn't snap back. *Probably insensitive of me,* she thought with a pang of guilt *when she's so frightened.* She knew enough about Debian's peaceful life to know that her friend hadn't been this close to losing her life since the Chortons invaded her planet three hundred years ago.

Valina watched Debian open her visor to take a deep gulp of air. Then, in a quivering voice, she asked, "Now what?"

Chapter 19
Looking for Shelter

Valina opened her visor and wiped the sweat off her forehead. How much more of this intense heat could they take? She looked away from Debian, who was still staring, waiting for Valina's next plan.

"I don't know," she replied finally to Debian's question., breathing in and out in quick gasps. "At least we're away from those terrible flames," she said, hoping the firestorm wouldn't catch up with them soon. Then, exhausted, she took off her helmet, wiped the sticky sweat from her scalp, and sat beside Debian, who had perched on the edge of an enormous black boulder.

They sat in silence for a while until Debian said, "I can't stand much more of this hideous place. And the heat! My water supply is getting low, too. What about yours?" She blew a strand of bright orange hair out of her face.

"Same. I guess the Nanochips are finally out of power. There's nowhere to charge anything, so I'm just taking enough water to moisten my lips and throat. Then we'll share what's left of it," Valina said. "Can you put out a distress signal? Nothing on my suit is working. Except for the water."

Debian pointed at the small, red, flashing light on her sleeve. "I already have, right before we started down that river."

Valina frowned. "Surely someone's picked up the signal by now. We had no trouble picking up Cara's distress beacon."

Debian wiped the sweat off her face and took another tiny sip of her water. "Who knows where or in what period of history we are, though," she said. "Maybe we'll have to wait until scientists invent space travel." She took her helmet off and dropped it at her feet.

Valina stood up, put her hand on her hip and rubbed her forehead with the fingertips of her other hand. She paced off a little way before retracing her steps to look at Debian. She silently agreed, but the idea of being lost in time filled Valina with such terror that she wanted to reject even the thought. No matter whether it might be true.

"Do you really think that's why no one's received our distress beacon yet, Debian?" she asked. She attempted to challenge the idea, but her fear was apparent, and she felt embarrassed.

"It's one possibility," Debian said in a more soothing tone. "But don't worry. The signal will repeat, even if nothing else in the suit works. There must be someone out there in this galaxy or time period capable of picking it up,"

When they'd rested a bit more, they set off again. After walking a short way, Debian said. "Maybe this place is inhabited. Except where it's on fire, I mean. Should we look for inhabitants?"

"Well, if you're right, we must find a way out of the fire first. There is oxygen, so we might determine whether the place is inhabited." Valina didn't want to consider what type of inhabitants they might find or whether they'd be friendly.

"Unless, of course, they are some sort of fire creatures. Valina, what if they actually are? What if they live in the fire or feed off of it? Maybe that's why the whole place is burning," Debian worried.

Valina blew out her cheeks and shook her head at Debian's remark, and when she spoke, there was a bitterness to her tone. "There's quite enough doom and gloom in this place without you adding to it, Debian," she said, walking off to follow a ridge of cinder path.

Valina followed the same cinder path on the side of a smouldering black hill for over an hour, with Debian following. They walked along silently; the constant crunching of grit under their boots and the heat made it hard to go. Finally, Valina stopped, sat on some charred grey rocks, and unclipped her helmet. "That's it. I've had enough. I'll risk taking this PSPE suit off and go along in my uniform. It's just too unbearable in this heat," she said.

Though the firestorm had scorched and blackened their protective suits, the girls remained relatively unharmed. Debian's panicked voice rose again. "But we need the equipment. What about the distress beacon? And what's left of the water supply? It's all attached to our suits!"

Valina didn't reply but started stripping off the protective suit. And it wasn't long before she stood beside the pile of PSPEs in her uniform. "Look, Debian, the oxygen and air pressure on this planet – wherever we are – seems to meet our needs! We only need the bare essentials."

"Mm, like food and water, do you mean? I can't remember the last time we ate proper food." Debian said.

Valina shook her head and resisted thinking about food. "No, we'll have to take our nutrient pills for now, though I doubt there is anything edible in this place, anyway."

"Toast, maybe?" Debian said sarcastically, taking off her helmet. As she removed the rest of her PSPE, a small, blue light on her sleeve controls flashed. "A response! Look, Valina, someone is sending a response signal." Debian called out.

Valina got up and shot over to Debian's side. "Can you get any details about where it's coming from?"

Debian tried but got nothing. She sighed, and her shoulders slunk. "No. Of course, none of that's working. It could be coming from millions of miles away. But if they're responding to our distress signal, it means at least someone's received it."

Valina nodded in agreement. "Hopefully, they're able to track our position." They watched the blue light for a while, but to their dismay, it soon faded.

"Oh no! It's dying," said Debian. "Well, that's the end of that, then. They must have given up responding."

"Maybe they're searching different zones. Come on, cheer up and get out of that stifling suit!" Valina said as encouragingly as she could manage. She tried not to let Debian see, but Valina felt increasingly disheartened and panicky. *Don't give up,* she urged herself, *think what to do next.*

Valina began to rummage through her PSPE and detach equipment from the sleeve controls. Forever practical, she meticulously laid the small pieces of technology on the black grit and said without looking up, "Start unclipping the equipment from your suit. But watch you don't spill the last precious drops of water. We can use the clips to attach these essential pieces to our uniforms. Take the sleeve control off the PSPE and attach it to your—" Valina glanced at her crew mate and interrupted herself. "Debian? Are you alright?"

Debian pulled her long, orange plait forward over her shoulder and held it tightly in her fists. "I can't go on! Valina, I really can't," she cried. "You'll have to go on without me. I'm too exhausted." She slowly lowered to the ground and covered her face with both hands.

Valina hurried over to her, "Oh, Debian, don't cry!" she said, dropping beside the weeping girl. Valina suddenly remembered that Quistics – although they can live for hundreds of years – need much more sleep than most other beings. So, while others enjoy weekends or holidays, a Quistic usually hibernates, sleeping for days at a time.

"Don't cry!" Valina pleaded again. "I'm sorry! I should have realised you would need much more rest than me." Debian's tears ran down her cheeks, leaving pale green incandescent streaks on her sooty face. Valina gently patted her friend's shoulder. "Come on, Deb. There's no way I'm going on without you. I'll sort your gear, and then we'll find a place to rest. I think I've spotted somewhere suitable."

Valina, who always observed and memorised her surroundings, had noticed something in the distance that looked like giant holes in the sides of the rocks. She hoped they were caves; fortunately, there were no visible flames in that direction, either. As she removed and sorted the equipment from her crew mate's suit, she noticed that Debian seemed more composed and calmer, although her eyes were still full of helplessness.

"What about the distress beacon? It's still sending the signal, but how will we know if anyone is tracking it? It's not detachable from the PSPE, and I don't have the energy to drag that whole suit along with me! What's more, I can feel my floating powers diminishing again. I need to sleep, but not out here in the open," Debian pleaded.

Valina shrugged and flapped a hand. "Leave the suit there! That distress signal will go on almost forever. And eventually, someone will track it and come for us. Hopefully." Valina knew the equipment she took from the protective suits was essential, and she didn't mind carrying it all. But, unfortunately, leaving Debian's suit behind meant anyone who might track them using the distress beacon would find empty suits. *Will they keep looking, or assume the worse? Should I carry Debian's empty suit with us, too?*

When Valina noticed Debian was nearly asleep again, her thoughts were interrupted. *I've got to keep her moving, or I'll end up carrying her, too!* Valina spotted more large craters on the sides of the prominent ridge, and she pointed to them.

"Look up there, Debian! I think those are small caves. If I strap most of this equipment to myself, do you think you could make it to them?" She helped her friend stand up. "It's not far." Debian sniffed and nodded her head.

"At least that area's not on fire. And we'll have some shelter from the hot winds and smoke if they blow this way," Valina said as she clipped the technology to herself. "You can sleep while I keep a lookout." She took hold of Debian's arm as they set off towards the caves.

Debian dried her eyes on the sleeve of her uniform jacket. "But you must rest too. We'll take turns," she said.

It took longer than they expected to reach the caves. It wasn't an easy climb, especially for Debian, who seemed to weaken with every step she took.

Her lack of levitation energy kept causing her to stumble and drop to the ground. Valina, too, felt herself sway in the heat. She reached out to grab a large rock for support as they began the climb. Flames burned in the distance behind them, and the smell of choking smoke seemed to smother any hope of escaping.

Chapter 20

Scuttling

After resting briefly, Valina and Debian continued to climb. When they reached a flatter ridge, Valina looked up to see how far they still were from the cave. It would be hard going now, much steeper, but many flat banks were visible on the way up.

Almost looks like stairs for some giant, she thought, making mental pictures to study later. *Regrettably, we're at least another hour's walk away from it. Poor Debian.*

"We're almost there," she fibbed encouragingly. Valina could see the dark entrance she hoped was a cave at the top of the ridge more clearly now. *So, not a complete lie,* she thought.

As they trudged along, Debian leaned heavily on Valina's arm. Each time they had to climb the grade to the next ridge, Valina pulled her crewmate up and over. They walked slowly across each flat shelf, and every step they climbed was steeper and more challenging.

Something about the place felt more foreboding than the rest of their surroundings. Tired as she was, Valina noticed the area approaching the cave was smoother, a lot less loose rock and cinder, for one thing. *Could it be inhabited? Who or what else might take shelter here?*

Worse, Valina thought, *what if something is lurking in the darkness, ready to defend its lair? What could we possibly do?* She knew they had no hope of survival if they couldn't take refuge in this cave or another one nearby. As the ground got steeper and steeper, and Debian kept wanting to stop and rest, Valina continued to urge her onwards.

"Come on, Deb! We're almost there. If we stop now, neither of us will want to start again."

At last, they reached the top and drew nearer to the ominous black craters on the side of the ridge. Valina chose the nearest opening so they didn't have to travel farther up. She chewed her bottom lip as she peered into the dark nothingness and led Debian into the cave.

The place seemed to close in on them as they entered, tightening the strange darkness around them. Yet, even in there, they could smell the burning rocks, and at that distance, Valina could hear them cracking in the heat.

"It's slightly cooler here, but where can we rest with all these black rocks and grit covering the floor?" Debian whispered through quick breaths.

Hundreds of black cindery rocks of all sizes covered the cave floor, but Valina couldn't see them until she switched on her arm beam and adjusted the diode to give a brighter light. Then, as they made their way over and through them, they could feel sharp shards digging into their boots.

"Once we find somewhere suitable for us to sit down, you can rest," Valina responded, also in a whisper, afraid that speaking too loudly would cause an echo around the cavern. The last thing they needed was someone or something to know they were there. When they were farther into the cave, Valina could see that the rocks on the floor were not so close together, and at last, they found ample enough space to sit.

"It almost looks as though…" but Valina stopped herself from saying it.

". . . as though someone has come in here and cleared the rocks away?" Debian said, finishing Valina's statement for her. Neither wanted to continue that conversation, so they sat down on the grit.

"Here, use this as a pillow. I won't need it in this heat," Valina said, taking off her jacket, screwing it into a ball and handing it to Debian.

It didn't take long before Debian fell into one of her deep coma-like periods of sleep that all Quistics drift. So, with no proper weapon to defend Debian and herself, Valina was utterly alone and highly vulnerable.

All officer cadets carried a small Taser stun gun, but it was no match for some of the advanced weapons many beings and aliens used. Yet Valina couldn't help smiling to herself as she thought, *At least perhaps it's a little more protection than Cara's 3D model laser gun. But not much more.*

She missed Cara and her heroic optimism. *If Cara were here*, Valina thought, *she'd have carried Debian up to the cave with little trouble. Then she'd have tossed rocks into the cavern to check for inhabitants.* Valina laughed a little at the thought of Cara rousting some creature with only the model laser to defend herself. It sounded just like her.

She hoped Cara was still in her restful induced coma and that Barnie continued steering the SP8 nearer to Gorn's Zeg-Mar5. Now that she knew of Gorn's legal position, she was sure he would send out some tracking system once the space pod got within a reasonable distance. What would happen to Cara after that? *There's no way of knowing,* Valina thought.

Soon, a great weariness crept over her. After the terrible ordeal – the crash landing, shooting the rapids in a time travel canoe to escape from the fire, and finally climbing up to this cave – Valina was exhausted. She took a small glug of water, ensured Debian was ok, and then got to her feet. She needed to move before she dozed off. She clipped her light around her head and took a few steps.

It was then that she heard something behind her, a scuttling sound. Fear froze her and stopped her breathing for a few seconds. Her heart raced, and she felt a powerful urge to run. Then, as she got herself under control and took careful, even breaths, Valina slowly turned around to face whatever was behind her. Nothing moved or made a sound.

The beam of light exposed more of the cave, though, and she saw it wasn't as small as they'd first thought. *Something could hide anywhere in here.* Turning slowly, Valina directed her four hearing canals from one side of the cave to the other. She could still hear Debian's two beating hearts, the gentle rhythms of her quiet breathing, and the raging fire in the distance. But no more scuttling for the moment.

When her eyes became accustomed to the surrounding darkness, it amazed her that the cave ended in a dark opening. But not an opening that had formed naturally. It looked like a giant hole or a rough opening into a mine. *Someone's made a doorway.*

Something scuttled again into that dark maw, to her left this time. She felt her heart jump and spun to look in the direction the sound came from. Despite that, Valina saw nothing unusual until, following the beam of light to the opening, she saw that stone steps led downwards.

Steps? Valina hesitated, startled at the discovery. *Should I investigate?* It was another sign of life on this planet. But she was unarmed, bone-tired, and had no backup. Who knew who or what was down there? *Or how many of them?* She thought. *And I hadn't ought to leave Debian alone, either.*

Weary and overwhelmed, she retraced her steps and lay beside her crew mate, listening intently for the scuttling sound to return. She heard nothing for a while except Debian's regular breathing. Soon the soft sound became hypnotic, and Valina drifted off into a sound, exhausted sleep.

CHAPTER 21

Captured

Valina's sound and peaceful sleep inside the cave ended abruptly when her keen hearing picked up the sound of voices. As she listened, she reckoned the mix of unfamiliar accents was about two minutes from the cavern entrance.

We must hide! She thought.

Two minutes wasn't much time to hide both herself and Debian, who was still in a deep slumber. She looked around desperately for a place nearby. The sound of voices drew nearer, and she preferred to see who it was before showing herself. She gathered up the equipment and stashed it behind some rocks. Debian was not heavy, and Valina quickly picked her up in both arms.

But where to hide?

The cacophony of voices was near now, so she resolved to lay Debian well concealed behind a massive boulder at the side of the cave. But unfortunately, there was only room for Debian. *So close! I can hear them breathing,* she thought, close to panic. She crouched low and dashed to another nearby boulder.

Before she shifted farther back into the blackness of the cave, to her terror, she heard the scuttling sound again, moving up behind her. She struggled not to let her imagination riot, but whatever caused that noise sounded like some awful creature. The voices she heard came from the cave entrance, which trapped Valina between them and the scuttling thing. She drew out her taser and turned her light beam onto a dim level, just enough to see directly ahead.

She saw it then, the scuttling thing.

A giant scorpion rested in the glow of her light, squatting on a flat ledge of rock. The light beam was enough to reveal the yellow creature with its pincers outstretched and its venomous sting quivering at the end of its tail, bracing to strike out. It was enormous. Slightly larger than an over-fed house cat.

Valina froze as its many eyes glared straight at her. Her pulse raced as she pointed the taser gun at two of the eyes on top of its grotesque skull. She inhaled rapidly, and every muscle in her body tensed. The time seemed to Valina to have stopped as her mind grappled with choosing whether to fight it or turn and flee in the other direction. Neither option was safe. *But which is worse!?* She had no time to think or judge. She'd threatened the gross scorpion. And the gross scorpion had reflex actions.

Without warning, the hideous creature leapt at her. In a split second, before it landed in her face, Valina pressed the taser button, and two things happened. First, a sickening high-pitched scream almost took out her acute listening powers, followed by a disgustingly messy explosion. Some scorpion bits had spattered over her shirt and left thick greasy stains of yellow gunge here and there. But right now, that wasn't her prime worry. Instead, she noticed she could no longer hear the weird voices behind her.

When Valina turned around and peered ahead, the voices' owners stood motionless before her. She could do nothing but scan the row of grim beings staring at her.

They were as strange in appearance as their voices had been. Some more normal looking wore all-black outfits. Built like a pile of boulders, one stood almost eight feet tall. Dense with muscle, the creature had a broad, lumpy face jammed low on a neck as thick as a stone pillar. He lifted one arm, rippled with muscle, and signalled to the rest of the group in a circular motion. At once, the other group members spread out to encircle Valina. Then, with the loudest, most resounding voice, he hollered, "Grab that creature!"

Before Valina had time to move, two of the group dashed across and grabbed each of her arms. One of them was so skinny he was almost skeletal. "I've got it!" he screeched as his bony fingers with long yellowish fingernails dug into Valina's soft skin and made deep scratches where he gripped her arms.

Valina screamed and tried to kick him, "Get off me! Get off of me!" she cried. But to her horror, he pulled her close, and she could smell his tattered, filthy clothes that hung stiffly for want of a good washing. Then, as he bent his head towards her, she saw that his strange helmet held back wispy, black greasy hair strands. His round, red eyes peered at her. "Now then, now then! Stop ya' strugglin'! You won't escape from us!"

The several armbands of bones and teeth chattered as he yanked on Valina's arm. A vile fishy stench came from his breath, and yellowing fangs, and Valina fought back the urge to gag to stop herself from throwing up. Instead, she tried again to kick out, this time behind her, to catch his legs. "Get off me!" she shrieked again.

Another Radican, a Garlap, grabbed her other arm. A short, squat, bulky ogre-like creature dressed in an outfit of patches of brown animal skin roughly sewn together. It hung from his broad shoulders down to his knees. His laugh was thick and menacing. "Oh! So, what we caught 'ere, then?" His short legs were like stumps with boots at their ends, so his body resembled a cube. Valina heard the others in this criminal group joining in with grunts and whoops as she struggled to free herself.

"Where you come from?" the Garlap said, leaning into Valina. His dark grey face, significant with wrinkles and lines, reached his slit eyes. He had no nose, only wart-covered nostrils, and his down-turned mouth made Valina think he, too, was about to throw up. She didn't answer and attempted to wrench her arm from the creature's horrible, fat fingers. He was not tall but was at least three times as wide as Valina and held her in a painful, vice-like grip.

The skinny one's bulging red eyes had the menacing stare of an insect, and Valina found him more frightening than the Garlap creature. "Get off me! Let go of me!" she screamed in panic, trying desperately to fight against them.

But Valina was no match against their strength and numbers. *No wonder they're hooting and laughing at me.* She was smaller than most of the creatures. She was alone and completely unarmed. Valina had hidden what remained of her survival equipment behind some rock. Her crew mate was a sound sleeper, and the remains of her taser and uniform were a slimy mess of foul-smelling scorpion guts. When she fought against them, she only injured herself. So what choice did she have but to surrender?

CHAPTER 22

Another Creature

Bug-eye and the Garlap dragged Valina backwards, still gripping her tightly although she was no longer struggling. As they pulled her along, the heels of her boots dragged across the gritty floor.

"I'll walk if you let me get on my feet," she shouted. They ignored her. Valina realised they were dragging her toward the stairs she'd discovered earlier. "*Hey*! Where are you taking me?" she said, still not resisting but twisting her head to look around for any possible way to escape. As she did, she noticed someone new approaching.

This creature was not smelly, hideous, or vile like the others. Instead, this person was a young, human girl around the same age as Valina and Cara. Very slim, pretty, and dangerous looking.

"Wait!" the girl shouted to the Garlap and Bug-eye. She wore all-black clothing that stood out compared to the others, dressed chiefly in filthy rags. However, her bodice, edged with finely twisted leather strips, and her equally black skirt, which hung nearly to the floor, seemed out of place to Valina.

The mob stopped. The woman approached, quickly leaning in to face Valina. "*Hmm*!" she murmured in a silky tone. "I believe, gentlemen, that we have caught a Listroc." She narrowed her eyes and stared as if she'd never seen a Listroc before.

This close, Valina saw that the feathery ends of the woman's long, jet-black hair touched the top of her bodice and fluttered with her every move. Her green eyes, lined with black, were beautiful yet menacing from beneath feathery bangs. "Now, we shall need to *do* something with our captive to make sure she doesn't escape," she said.

In a desperate gasp, Valina said, "What do you want with me? I've done nothing to harm you. I got lost, that's all." She let them believe she was alone, for now. After all, Debian might be the only one to save her *if she wakes up in time.*

The girl turned and walked away, her black skirt swishing from side to side as she walked. Beneath the dress, Valina saw black leggings tucked into high boots. To her horror, Valina also saw long metal weapons glinting from the top of each boot.

Turning back to face Valina, the girl ignored her questions. "I am Shansa," she announced amiably. "But if we're to get to know each other, I need to know what to call you, don't I?"

At Valina's silence, in an entirely different tone, Shansa snapped, "What's your name, Listroc?"

Valina didn't answer. She was determined not to give anything away, not even her name.

Shansa smiled with one side of her mouth, "Oh well, never mind. We can make you feel a little more like talking later. You'll be much more sociable when we, *er*," she paused. Valina was sure Shansa's eyes grew greener as she stared at her, "Well, shall we say when we've got to know each other a little better?" she continued.

She was so close that Valina noticed a scorpion tattooed down Shansa's left cheek, partly hidden by the girl's hair. Then, with one quick action, she attached a small round device to Valina's neck.

Shansa leaned in closer until her face was within inches of Valina's, with a look that made goosebumps race up Valina's neck. "We don't want you to run off and hide somewhere, do we?" Shansa said in a low, eerie voice that matched the menace in her eyes.

Shansa paused, straightened, flapped her hand, and shouted, "Take her to the cage and lock her in!" As the creatures dragged Valina, the device on her neck pulsated, and she cringed at the vibration and the high-pitched, whining sound. It quickly became such a distracting and hypnotic vibration that Valina could not think clearly. Though she was still aware of her surroundings, she became increasingly confused about what was happening to her.

The mesmerising effect of this strange girl's eyes or the device on her neck made Valina feel faint. She wasn't sure, but she knew it was fear, not smoke, choking her breathing this time. With great effort, she shut her eyes tightly, gathered her strength, drew a deep breath, and screamed as loud as she could, "DEBIAN! *HELP ME!*"

Valina hoped the terror in her scream was loud enough to wake Debian from her deep Quistic sleep as the group began chortling and hooting all around her again, dragging her down the steps and farther into the cavern's depths.

Chapter 23

A Malicious Gang

When Debian came awake with a start, she looked around, wondering what woke her. At first, she couldn't see anything and the sensation of not seeing brought a wave of panic that woke her completely. In the pitch blackness, she groped around and found the ragged lump of rock that had hidden her. When at last fully awake, her superior eyesight kicked in, and she remembered Valina and herself entering the cave.

She could now see the small area where someone had jammed her behind the low rock wall. She wondered how she got there but quickly realised that Valina must have hidden her as she slept. *But where could Valina have gone?* That was the terrifying thought.

"Valina!" she called in a low voice. "Valina, are you here?"

She listened, but her crewmate didn't respond. Instead, Debian heard distant, muffled voices too far away to hear what they were saying. *Voices!* The small cadet floated a little way off the gritty black floor of the cave and looked around. This time, when she called out, she spoke with quiet urgency.

"Valina!"

Cautiously, Debian headed towards the back of the cave, where the fierce voices were loudest. It sounded like they were questioning someone, but she couldn't hear anyone answering them. Did they have Valina? *Of course, they do!* She scolded herself. Debian hovered in place, eyes closed, struggling against a strong survival instinct that compelled her to flee.

"I'll try to save you, Valina, " she called softly but loud enough for Listroc's ears to pick up. She then floated forward, following the sound of the voices, and soon discovered the top of the steps. For her crew mate, she risked gliding down them. As she descended, an orange glow of light was ahead, bright enough to see more clearly.

The stairs curved sharply to the left as she approached the bottom, so Debian remained concealed behind the curve, slowly floating upward until she had a better view. This lower cave was cavernous. She could see this thanks to the pale orange lights that were everywhere. Dimly lit passageways led off in all directions.

What is this place?

Most alarming was what she saw just up ahead. The source of the sounds she'd followed was a group of fierce creatures gathered around in the middle of the chamber. She recognised a few species, but no two looked the same. Every one of them radiated with malice, viciousness and danger. They chanted a weird, tuneless melody as they focused on something. Then, when the group lurched from side to side in an awkward sort of dance, she could see who was in the centre.

At the sight of her friend, Debian gasped, "Valina," then clamped her hand over her mouth to stop herself from shouting.

She kept her mouth covered as she stared. They'd secured Valina's hands behind her back, and the horrible group's taunts seemed to have cowed her somehow. Her head hung down, and she seemed to care for nothing except the ground at her feet. *What have they done to you?* Debian thought. Something foul looking and green glistened from Valina's hair and clothing. Was it poison?

Debian watched the group cavort, noting a Garlap grab her friend's arm and yank her up when she seemed about to fall to the floor. It was then she knew who they were. The Garlap's ragged uniform told her all she needed to know.

She had sometimes encountered these nefarious creatures throughout her long life but had always kept a safe distance. Now they were right there in front of her – a vicious gang of Radican Pirates.

While the pirates were still chanting and distracted, Debian hovered, hid in the shadows and took out her taser weapon. She looked down at the group of menacing pirates and realised her chances were not good. Her small weapon would feel like an annoying tickle to some of them. Her only advantage was her ability to levitate.

Unfortunately, there was no one else here. *So it's all up to me,* Debian thought.

CHAPTER 24

Shocked into Action

As Debian stared in horror at the scene before her, another voice shouted, "That's enough now! Stop!" The Radicans stopped chanting, and a foreboding silence prevailed. Then, a young woman, whom Debian thought was probably human, emerged from a nearby corridor. Her manner and appearance suggested that she was a highly-ranked Radican. That and the way the other pirates obeyed her commands with no argument or hesitation.

"You had your fun. Now take the Listroc away and lock her in the cage." She turned to Valina and snarled into her face, "Don't fret; we'll talk soon!" Then she shoved her hard.

Valina offered no resistance and would have fallen had the skeletal Radican not caught her by one arm. Instead, the Garlap grabbed her other arm, and the pair dragged Valina toward the corridor, following the female pirate.

At last, the shock and surprise of seeing what was happening to Valina urged Debian into action, and she aimed and fired the taser gun at the group of Radicans.

Her first shot hit the bug-eyed skeleton, who went down like a rag doll. The shock immediately prompted the Radicans to draw their weapons and run about, searching for the shooter.

Debian tried to hide herself, but she was too slow. The Garlap spotted her and pointed. "Quistic!" he yelled. "Another intruder! Shansa! Up there, on that rock crevice!"

They all looked up to where he was pointing, and one of them aimed an enormous weapon straight at Debian. Thankfully, his aim was clumsy, and the great flash from the weapon missed her, hit the chamber's roof, and sent a large segment of rock tumbling down into the chamber. Debian tried to hide and headed for the stairway as rocks and dust showered down.

Through the cloud of dust, Debian saw the woman in black run over to the gunman and furiously kick the massive gun from his hands. "*Fool!* Do you want the whole cavern to come down on our heads? Go get the Orb!" she screeched.

In all the confusion, Debian took a chance and changed her position. She floated silently up to a place closer to the exit. One creature cried, "Quistic! Over there!" Something blew an intense current of air in her direction, clearing the dust and exposing her more. Before they could do anything, she took another potshot. This time, she hit one of them on the head, and he dropped to the floor, stunned.

Debian knew she should try to make it up the stairs and escape from this underground pirate's den. She glanced over and saw Valina standing where the startled Radicans had left her, making no attempt to fight or flee. "Run! *Run*, Valina! Valina, over here!" Debian yelled, hoping her friend would snap out of it and run toward the stairs.

Valina glanced up with a vague look of recognition at the sight of Debian, then ran awkwardly into the corridor toward the cage. Someone hollered, "The prisoner!" And two Radicans hurried over, grabbed Valina roughly and dragged her away. Debian saw again how painfully disoriented, uncoordinated, and unusually slow to react Valina was. *It's almost,* Debian thought *as if she was half asleep.*

She glanced towards the other side of the chamber and, in horror, saw two other Radicans wheeling out an even larger weapon that they mounted on a stand. As she levitated with speed toward the stairway, Debian desperately hoped she could move fast enough to dodge whatever they were setting up.

With vague thoughts of escaping, returning to stay with her abandoned PSPE suit until somebody answered the distress beacon, Debian flew down to enter the stairway.

A powerful blast of air hit her, and Debian instinctively covered her head with her arms and curled herself into a ball as she crashed into the stone-carved stairs. Then, quicker than her attackers expected, Debian forced her body upwards, turning over and over in mid-air and continuing flying up.

As the wind current they'd created helped her speed away, Debian barely had time to think; *I'm going to make it!* – when something else hit her in the side hard. She saw the ground coming up fast to meet her, protected herself again and closed her eyes as she almost hit the ground. But she didn't hit this time. Instead, she stopped at the last second, suspended just a few inches from the bottom step.

Debian barely moved. Pirates moved in quickly, but Shansa's tight control over the Radicans kept them from grabbing their new captive.

"Gently, now. Gently! We've caught this precious creature, and I want to keep it as a *pet…*" she mocked, throwing back her head with a manic laugh. "Even your rescue attempt was adorable! With your little taser gun. Are Quistics trainable, I wonder?" She asked the group, smiling quizzically around at them. "Let's find out."

"Get up!" She said in a firm tone. "Get up, Quistic!" Shansa yelled. "UP!"

Debian staggered to her feet, wasting no time trying to float away. Her entire body ached, and she realised now that they'd used a magnetically charged Orb shield to trap her and bring her down. There was no escape from the power of this type of weapon.

"Turn it off," Shansa commanded. The second they deactivated the magnetic power, Shansa leapt forward, grabbed Debian's long braid and viciously yanked her sideways so the taser fell from her hand. The rest of the Radicans clamoured around to prevent any further chance of escape.

"You can join your pal Valina in our cage," Shansa snapped, thrusting one of those humming devices towards Debian's neck. "And thank you, by the way, for telling us her name; she wouldn't."

Shansa laughed again, and all the pirates joined in. No one noticed that the device did not stick to Debian's skin, and it slid away, rolling off somewhere into the grit. Debian realised then that this device must be the reason for Valina behaving as though she were half asleep. *I have to get that thing off Valina's neck,* she thought.

"I'm sure your friend will enjoy some company. Then we'll decide what to do with the pair of you after you've answered a few questions. And make no mistake; you *will* answer my questions!" Shansa snarled. Another pirate grabbed her arm, and they headed for the cage with Shansa still grasping Debian's braid.

They moved along a dimly lit passage that sloped downward, deeper into the ground, until it opened into a large area with a cage-like cell built in the centre. As they approached the cage, Debian saw Valina behind bars, sitting on the floor in a corner, clutching her knees. She squinted across at them as one pirate deactivated the door and another shoved Debian inside.

Shansa's eyes flashing with menace, pointed into the dark shadows beyond the cage bars. "I don't recommend trying to escape. You'll have the guard set upon you, and then you'll be dead," she warned. Shansa touched one bar on the door, and it slid shut. Putting her face close to the bars on the other side, she smiled, but her green eyes remained cold. "Well, I'll leave you two to settle in while I inform the Grand Master Radican that we have two intruders in our midst."

She was a little way down the passage when, as if it was an afterthought, she turned back and called, "You'd better have some answers ready. He hates it when uninvited guests intrude on his plans. He'll want to know how you got here and why you came. And you *don't* want to make him angry." Her maniacal laughter faded as she walked up the passage.

When Shansa had gone, Valina slowly stood, stumbled over to Debian, and took one of her hands in both of hers. She was shaking all over. "Oh, Debian, are you – ok? I'm so – so sorry. I got us into this. My fault. Using the TTC." Valina paused and held her head in her hands before continuing. "To rescue Cara. I should never have – never have. Brought you with me, she said, struggling to speak.

Debian looked at Valina's troubled face and said calmly, "Well, we had to rescue Cara somehow. And I wouldn't have let you go alone. It's not your fault we accidentally landed here instead of returning to New Dawn."

In her head, Debian questioned whether Cara was to blame that they had ended up in this terrifying situation. And in her present state of mind, she concluded – *yes, darn it!- It's all Cara's fault for being so hot-headed and chasing after Golbat Gorn and the Power Transmitters. But unfortunately, it was all for nothing, and now we have to deal with the consequences.*

But she snapped out of her anger when she looked up at Valina. "I can tell you're not well, Valina. What have they done to you?" she asked.

At once, Valina's hand went to the side of her neck. "It's this device. It – somehow affects me. I – I can't think clearly. That Radican, Shansa, put it on. I tried, but – too painful. Can't remove it," Valina winced.

Debian peered at the small, round metal device protruding from Valina's neck and said, "I think she tried to attach one to me, but it didn't stick, thank goodness. It may be something to do with my healing powers that made me immune to it." She gently touched the device on Valina's neck, which made Valina draw in a sharp breath and hunch her shoulders. Debian snatched her hand back and said, "Oh! I'm sorry. Is it so painful?"

Valina's mouth opened, but no sound came out as she sank to the cage floor, holding her neck. Debian squatted next to her, and then, looking at the bars around the cage, after a moment, she whispered, "Perhaps I can find a way for us to escape."

"No! Look," Valina said in a low, weak voice. "It's guarding us! See?"

She followed Valina's gaze to the darker area outside the cage. As her vision quickly adjusted to the low light, Debian saw. She gasped and covered her mouth with both hands.

Squatting, perched on a higher ledge of rock, eyes shining, giant pincers stretched, sat a colossal and hideous Kaligiabeast. With a head like a gigantic lynx, it opened its mouth and bared hundreds of long, vicious fangs. It rattled its curved scorpion tail, and the massive stinger quivered, ready to strike.

When it let out a terrifying hiss, Debian dropped next to Valina, and they clung to each other, hiding their faces away from its black, bone-chilling eyes.

PART THREE

CHAPTER 25

Cara Awakes

"Come on, Cara! Bring the picnic rug and see what's for lunch. Ham sandwiches, crisp cucumber salad, and lots of lemonade!" Granny called. Cara smiled at the sweet, familiar voice. A warm breeze smelled vaguely of the lake, and the sun felt hot on her skin. It was blissful.

"Okay, what about here?" Cara said, dumping herself onto the first patch of grass they saw. Yikes, it's skagin' hot on Earth today. Maybe I'll take a swim in the lake first." Her grandmother raised her eyebrows and tutted. "Sorry!" Cara said, realising that she'd sworn.

Cara reached out to seize a glass of ice-cold lemonade and clutched nothing but the air. She hesitated, then let her hand drop because her ears immediately picked up the smooth purr of the space pod. Trying desperately to hang on to the vision of her grandmother's smiling face, she whispered, "It's been lovely seeing you, Granny. You've cheered me up no end. Thank you."

Wakefulness didn't cause unhappiness or fear. *I feel so relaxed; I really don't want to open my eyes.* It was the most restful sleep she'd had in a long time, and the mind journey from Granny came just at the right moment. She sighed, not wanting to let go of her visions. Grudgingly, Cara sat up and opened first one eye and then the other. A loud, dull voice spiked her peace of mind.

"Have you finished your mind journey, Cara? Are you awake?"

"Well, if I wasn't before, I am now!" she huffed.

The AI's tone brought Cara back to reality and into the present time. She sat up to discover she was on the bunk in the sleeping section of SP8. At once, she noticed she wore her now clean blue Officer Cadet uniform and the rip in her sleeve mended with almost invisible stitches.

"Focus, please, Cara!' Barnie said, "You need to disconnect yourself from me."

"What? What do you mean, 'disconnect from you?" she asked. Then she felt something snagging at her neck and, touching it with her hand, realised it was a tube attached to her skin.

"I've been keeping you alive, Cara, but you can gently remove the life-stabiliser tube from your body now," Barnie said.

"Oh, I see. Thank you, Barnie," Cara winced as she pulled the tube from her neck. "And how did this get in my neck, exactly?"

"You were very sick. You almost died of oxygen deprivation, among other serious problems. Valina and Debian used some time travel capsule to come and save you. You probably have no memory of it," Barnie said.

Cara swung her long legs around, sat on the edge of the bunk and stretched them as thoughts came vaguely back from the recent past. She noticed the Radican suit crumpled in a heap on the floor. Before doing anything else, Cara got up and gathered up the costume. "Wretched thing," she muttered, slamming the whole bundle, helmet and all, out of sight in a spare overhead locker.

"As I was saying," Barnie continued, "You need to focus! Focus, Cara! There are things you must do."

The last of the mind journey's calming effects were dissolving quickly, partly because Cara found her AI's nagging very irritating. "Barnie, stop telling me to focus! Your remarks are not helpful." She paused and sighed, coming fully awake and realising that the SP8 and Barnie were working again, also thanks to her crew mates from New Dawn. "Although, I must admit I'm glad to have you functioning again after all that's happened to us, Barnie."

She glanced around the pod. "So, where are Valina and Debian now?"

Barnie answered, "They've gone. The officer cadets left in the time travel capsule. Cara, would you like something to eat and drink? You've been asleep for precisely three days, two hours, six minutes, twenty-five seconds, and one arcsecond – and three milliseconds, two nanoseconds, ten femtoseconds – and three attoseconds and six zeptoseconds…"

Cara frowned, "What! Do you mean I've been asleep that long? Surely not!"

But Barnie was insistent. "Cara, you've been asleep for precisely three days, two hours, six minutes, twenty-five seconds, and one arcsecond – and three milliseconds, two nanoseconds, ten femtoseconds – and three attoseconds and six zeptoseconds…."

Cara rubbed her eyes in disbelief and screeched, "Yes, yes! Okay, Barnie, so you said. You don't need to keep repeating it! But it seems I've had only one good night's quality sleep," she yawned but stopped herself just in time from stretching.

Feeling lightheaded, Cara moved towards the pilot seat and slumped into it. She smiled as she saw the steaming beaker of coffee and a couple of doughnuts sitting on the armrest of her chair.

"*Yummy*! Thanks, Barnie. I didn't realise SP8 had such delightful goodies onboard," she grinned as she sipped the steaming coffee from the beaker. It tasted good after the long, heavy sleep, and it soon revived her enough to bring back thoughts again – thoughts of her two crew mates on New Dawn Space Station. She took a bite from a doughnut, and between bites, she asked Barnie, "Where are Valina and Debian? I mean, where did they go when they left here?"

"I have no information to answer that, but I can calculate a simple probability," droned the AI.

Cara drank her coffee. "Well, I hope they travelled back in the TTC to New Dawn."

Had they got clearance from Captain Lydian to use the TTC to save her? The very idea shocked Cara. If so, how had they managed it?

"Yes, after they had saved you and put everything back in order, that was their intention. However, it may not have been immediately. The time could have varied as much as seven minutes, four seconds – " the AI went on.

Cara ignored him while she finished her coffee. After that, she put down her empty beaker and stood. "Well, I hope you're right, Barnie, because when Captain Lydian first showed us the machine, she warned us not to meddle with it. She told us it's still in an early stage of development."

"I am sorry, Cara; I have weak data on time travel machines," he said. Then he started rattling off how long it might take him to research the topic.

"What's the matter with you, Barnie? Perform a diagnostic on yourself." Cara sighed and looked at the screen in front of her. The caffeine and sugar were working; she alertly noticed two arrow-shaped images on either side of SP8. "Why are those crafts shadowing us?"

"They are trackers from Gorn's ship. He sent them out to escort us, and now they've locked us into their magnetic fields. Please note, Cara: There is no way of escaping now!" Barnie informed her. Rather sternly, she thought.

Cara groaned. "How long will it take us to reach Gorn's ship? We should try to contact my crew mates. *Ugh!* I need to take a shower and freshen up," she cringed. " I've never gone so many days without a shower. It feels horrible!"

"You say you have never gone three days, two hours, six minutes, twenty-five seconds, and one arcsecond – and three milliseconds – two nanoseconds, ten— ”

Cara closed her eyes, pinched the bridge of her nose, and said flatly, "Barnie, shut up!"

Barnie went entirely silent. She waited. The seconds passed.

"I *said*. How long is it before we reach Gorn's ship? I need a shower to freshen up," Cara repeated. There was no answer from the AI. Cara waited impatiently and said in a lofty tone, "Well?"

She feared she'd somehow crashed his systems again and yelled in a short-tempered, nervous shout. "*Barnie?* Why aren't you responding!?"

After another long pause, Barnie's function light finally flashed on the control panel. "Your command was confusing, Cara. I am sorry. I interpreted '*shut up*' as '*shut down!* I have stored that bit of *misunderstanding*. However, for safety reasons, it may not be wise for you to use such terminology in the future," the AI said.

Cara's eyes widened. Was that Barnie's way of telling her off for being disrespectful? She frowned and opened her mouth to say something, but Barnie interrupted.

"Calculating distance and time of how long it will take to reach Mr Gorn's spacecraft," Barnie continued in his matter-of-fact voice. "We are not too far away and will catch up with the Zeg-Mar5 in one hour and *approximately* four minutes. But our destination, the Golden Dome Conference Centre, is still nearly ten hours distant."

Cara smiled, thinking perhaps she'd fixed Barnie's detailed time description issue by accidentally shutting him down. She shook her head and grabbed the remains of her doughnut. "Brilliant, I'm off to the shower cubical. And then maybe a nap. By then, I'll be hungry," she mused. She popped the last morsel into her mouth and had unfastened her jacket when Barnie stopped her.

"Wait, Cara! Captain Lydian has scheduled an AV meeting, and she has ordered you to attend."

Cara froze and gulped down the food, almost choking. "What!' she sputtered, "A meeting with Captain Lydian? Why am I just now hearing about this?"

An icy feeling of dread engulfed her. Advanced Virtual meetings were rare, especially with a senior officer. Instead, crew members usually met with officers via audio microwave or holograph. But an AV meeting meant Captain Lydian would teleport straight onto SP8.

"Barnie, did the Captain say what the meeting was about?" she asked, though deep down she knew.

"No," the AI replied.

Cara felt uncomfortable as she recalled Captain Lydian's departure for the Golden Dome Conference Centre. The Captain had inspected the crew and formally announced, for the record, that Valina was in charge. She'd offered words of encouragement to both Valina and Debian. But, like so many times before, the Captain hadn't had one kind word for Cara.

Cara cringed at the memory of how she'd overslept that day and dressed in a hurry, not noticing she'd accidentally put on her dirty, torn jacket. The Captain, who never missed a trick, had surveyed her with half-closed eyes.

"You're a wreck, Cara Davis. There is a split in your sleeve. *Again.* And is that tomato sauce on your jacket? It seems to me you are out of uniform, Cadet. Guylo, make a note of that."

She'd given Cara a very hard look. "Get yourself in order, girl!" she had scolded.

Cara, of course, had tried a feeble apology, but that only further angered the Captain. "You talk too much, Cadet Davis when you should focus on your duty! All you need to do is to be quiet and get on with your work!"

It was clear to Cara that Captain Lydian disapproved of her. Knowing this made her nervous whenever the Captain was around, and her jangled nerves led to mistakes, which led to more disapproval.

Cara wrapped one arm around herself and bit her knuckles. After everything she'd done, she was terrified of what the Captain would say now. Calling an Advanced Virtual meeting was the last thing she'd expected Captain Lydian to do, and she felt sick with dread.

Advanced Virtual meetings produced a sensation of absolute reality. It felt like you were standing beside the person you were talking with. She had attended a few at the Academy when lecturers were too far away on other planets to speak in person. There, the people appeared to you as solid matter. However, Cara had never touched someone during an AV encounter, so she didn't know whether it was possible to feel them as solid matter. There was no way she'd find out in this meeting.

Unless Captain Lydian slaps me! she thought.

Cara's heart picked up a beat, and her breath quickened. "Barnie, do I have time to clean myself up, at least a little?"

"You have two minutes. "

"Where is the Captain holding the meeting?"

"Right here in the control cabin. It would be best if you faced the door, Cara. The Captain will teleport through it."

"At least she won't be coming through the wall," Cara said, feeling goosebumps run over her as she sat down and swivelled the pilot seat to face the door. "That would be very scary!" Her mood was jittery as she sat staring at the door, awaiting her fate.

CHAPTER 26
A Call to Account

Cara stepped up and stiffened to attention as the inner door of SP8 slid open. Although she directly faced the door, she could not see the face of the tall, slim figure who bent somewhat so as not to catch her head when entering. At once, Cara inhaled a delicate, expensive perfume that filled the air inside the pod.

"Welcome aboard, Captain!" Barnie announced.

Cara didn't risk making eye contact with the Captain and instead looked straight ahead as she saluted. In response, Captain Lydian glared at the young cadet standing before her and huffed. "Well, let's start with you presenting yourself smartly in the presence of a senior officer, shall we?"

Cara realised her jacket was half undone and, with flustered fingers, fastened it up. Her lips quivered. "I'm sorry, Captain, I— " she murmured in a small voice but thought it best not to finish the statement. All she ever seemed to do was infuriate this woman.

The Captain raised her eyebrows, tutted as she strode past Cara, and seated herself gracefully in the pilot seat. "Turn around and face me!" she ordered.

Cara obeyed, gradually turned around and glanced at the intelligent, blonde woman dressed in her immaculate, perfectly fitted uniform. Barnie was right. With her high cheekbones and perfect complexion, Captain Sarah Lydian inherited her Earthling mother's beauty. She exuded authority as she scrutinised Cara, her expression unyielding.

"First, may I ask," she inquired icily, "was it through you alone that this present situation has occurred?"

Cara was sure the Captain noticed at once the terror in her eyes. She swallowed hard. Her lips and throat were so dry no words came out when she opened her mouth and tried to speak.

The cultured, velvet voice continued. "I hope you realise that while you were playing pranks, wasting resources, and amusing yourself, the rest of the

New Dawn Space Station crew had to fulfil your duties."

It seemed to Cara, who stood rigidly that neither Mr Gorn nor Commander Predaton had reported everything that had happened. Only the parts that made her look bad.

With angry eyes, the Captain leaned forward and snapped, "So, is it just yourself I will need to investigate, or have you involved the other crew members in your stupid little game?"

Cara was desperate. How was she going to answer this? Neither Valina nor Debian had prevented her from going after Golbat Gorn. And in the end, Valina allowed her to carry on. So maybe her actions *had* involved them all. The Captain tapped her foot and continued to stare, waiting for her response. "Well? Have you nothing to contribute to this conversation, Davis? You're usually so eager to speak!"

Cara certainly knew her reckless actions had brought nothing good, but she hadn't been playing any prank! How could she make Captain Lydian understand how much they'd feared the strange alien and the loss of the power transmitters? Although Cara always tried to be honest (mostly), the last thing she wanted to do was get her crew mates into serious trouble. So she'd take the blame.

She licked her dry lips and took a deep breath. "It was me, Captain. I thought up the idea of going after Mr Gorn. Valina and Debian didn't help me." Cara said in a small voice.

Again, the Captain looked her up and down with a keen, disconcerting gaze. Eventually, she leaned forward and continued in a low voice. "And what are you doing in this space pod now, on your own? According to your service record, you're not even fully qualified to pilot a space pod."

Before answering, Cara cleared her throat. She thought it best to ignore the Captain's last comment and get to the point of the mission. It was time to mention the power transmitters.

"We . . . Came to believe that a clever rogue had stolen precious cargo from New Dawn's secure storage. I thought that after using the pirate ruse to re-capture the Kwaidum crystals and Imperium domes for the power transmitters, I could safely return to New Dawn and return them to their rightful place." She finished and looked with apprehension at the Captain.

Captain Lydian clenched her left gloved hand into a fist. "Oh, did you?"

Cara didn't feel threatened by this gesture. It seemed to be a habit of the Captain, who often did it with her left hand, perhaps to relieve some pain she suffered. She never wore a glove on her right hand, just her left.

"Well," continued Captain Lydian tightly, "because of your impulsive behaviour, it now involves your crew members and me in an exceedingly embarrassing situation."

Cara, usually daring and excitable, stood frozen with anxiety as Captain Lydian rose from her seat, "I shall have to decide what I'm going to do with you, won't I?"

Though Cara stood to attention with her head held high and too proud to let her fears show, she quaked inwardly. She guessed what awaited her. "What I ought to do after the conference is to take you straight back to HQ and haul you in front of the Galactic Court for a full investigation and hearing," the Captain stressed firmly.

Cara didn't know what would happen after that, but she was sure it would be terrible beyond words. Commander Predaton would undoubtedly be involved if it went to the Galactic Court. The Commander was a powerful man she didn't altogether trust. She saw something sinister behind his steel-grey eyes and hoped never to see him again, just as he'd ordered.

With Captain Lydian's last threat, Cara's shoulders slunk, and she could barely suppress her shaking. She hoped it wasn't visible, but when she glanced up, she noticed something now preoccupied Captain Lydian with her thoughts. She looked troubled, almost. Cara suspected that failing to keep her crew in order might weaken the Captain's authority on New Dawn. After being confronted by the tyrant, the picture of Commander Predaton's control over the Captain and her crew was unpleasant.

Captain Lydian glared at her again, and Cara wondered whether she would escape this trouble. "It would have been bad enough if Golbat Gorn *was* a Radican Pirate who had stolen the power transmitters!" Cara braced as the Captain continued to criticise her. "All the time, you would have been risking your own life and possibly the lives of others by your rash behaviour." Finally, she moved in closer to Cara and, with a cutting stare, said, "You are disobedient and irresponsible. Consequences be damned!"

But Cara was not entirely without spirit, even at such a difficult moment. That last remark from the Captain had stirred something like anger within her, and this time she met the senior officer's eyes full-on. "That I am not, Captain!" she shouted, instantly forgetting her fear.

Cara spoke quickly and confidently, hoping to finish before the Captain cut her off. "I took the actions I did because I felt partly responsible for allowing some stranger to enter New Dawn and steal the most valuable possessions we've ever had on board. It was I who accidentally told him where he would find them. It was no prank! And, as you reminded us before you left, Captain, we three handled the safety of New Dawn, including those domes and crystals. I assure you, I – that is, *we all* – took our responsibilities seriously."

Cara took a breath and carried on. "Gorn's appearance shocked Valina and especially Debian. We were all shocked! He frightened us with his abrupt actions. We had no prior communication or warning of his arrival."

Captain Lydian glared, but Cara hadn't finished. She took another quick breath. "If you knew anything about me, you'd realise I'm a loyal Officer Cadet. I would rather have *died* than let a thief make off with such powerful objects! I took an oath to protect the galaxy!"

The Captain looked Cara up and down again. "Indeed," she said in a stiff voice. "Are you finished?"

Cara wasn't. "Just one more thing," she said, a little quieter now. "I am extremely loyal and protective towards my fellow crew members. They're both very dear to me."

Captain Lydian dropped her gaze and looked down at the floor. For a moment, Cara had silenced her. But the Captain's lips thinned as she looked back at Cara and said dryly, "Well. Thank you. I know all now, don't I? And I suppose *you* know what will happen next."

With a flushed face and dry throat, Cara blinked and nodded. Her spurt of anger had abruptly dried up, and she couldn't utter another word for her life. So, with a clenched jaw and lowered eyes, Cara faced her sentence with stoic patience and the bit of pride she had left.

Captain Lydian paced deliberately around. "Do you realise, Cadet Davis, that as your commanding officer, I can discipline you and hand out many punishments?"

As she nodded, unwelcome tears pricked Cara's eyes. She knew what was at stake. She might lose everything, at least her desire to show everyone what an ordinary human can achieve.

The Captain, standing directly behind her, leaned in, her voice low and menacing as she rattled off the punishments and continued to call the shots. "... Or I could confine you to your cabin for days and reduce your food rations. I could give you extra duties and downgrade your position so you would never be part of the New Dawn squad again!"

Cara's throat and heart ached at the thought of the terrible consequences. Her bright new career would be over before it had even begun. What would she do then? Valina and Debian would want nothing more to do with her. Where would she go? Too ashamed, Cara would never have the courage to return to Earth and look her family in the eye. She'd let everyone down, including herself.

Crushed and with her ego beaten, a large tear rolled down Cara's cheek as far as her chin. She hadn't realised how hard-set Captain Lydian was. But then she wondered, *do I deserve such harshness?* She let out a troubled breath, which felt more like a sob to Cara, who rarely cried.

Once more, the Captain loomed over her and said unexpectedly, "I can do *all* of those things and worse. But – I'm not going to."

Cara looked up, startled.

Captain Lydian strolled away toward the door. "I've got my reasons, which you are too inexperienced to understand. But I shall neither punish nor report you to the Martial Court." She returned a pace nearer and bent her face towards her bewildered cadet.

"Only on certain conditions," she said.

Chapter 27

A Door Closes

The lights in the control cabin of SP8 shone directly down on Captain Lydian, who resumed her full height and stared down at Cara with a steady, unwavering eye. There was a long silence as Cara braced herself, expecting the commanding officer to resume her reprimand. Nothing like that happened.

Instead, Captain Lydian changed her gaze and surveyed the control panel. "The autopilot is flying this pod now?" she asked.

Cara considered the question most unnecessary but opened her mouth to assure Captain Lydian that SP8 was now on autopilot. But, before she could speak, Barnie cut in with a sudden and surprising interruption.

"Yes, Captain, I am in full control now. All systems are reporting normal," the AI announced. "We are now shadowing the Zeg-Mar as ordered."

Cara was both surprised and worried. She hoped Barnie would not blab on about how she'd nearly died because of her own incompetence. Or talk about Valina and Debian using the experimental TTC to save her. *How can I shut him up?* She thought, frantic, her eyes searching for an idea. Her discarded coffee cup caught her eye. *I'll ask him to beam us a coffee, something like that.*

"Barnie, I want you to—" Cara began, but this time Captain Lydian interrupted.

"And tell me, Barnie, what communications have you received from the New Dawn Space Station crew?" she inquired.

Cara closed her eyes and wished for Barnie to shut up and stop interfering; she was anxious about what he might say next. She'd worried that the Captain might ask her this precise question. It was worse that she'd asked Barnie instead!

In her nervousness, Cara forgot to stand at attention for a moment. She fidgeted with her jacket sleeve. A frown returned to the Captain's brow as she gazed back at Cara. Cara's mouth twitched, and she returned to attention, eyes forward, head up.

Barnie said: "I can confirm that First Officer Skarn appeared briefly as a holograph before we lost communication," he continued. "After that, unfortunately, I have no record of further contact since –" The AI began rattling off the number of hours since that contact. Barnie made it to thirty-seven nanoseconds before Captain Lydian silenced the litany. "That'll do!"

Cara's struggled to stay at attention but couldn't help her eyes opening wide at the AI's words. Had Barnie *lied* to the Captain? No! That couldn't be. He'd be incapable. *An AI would only lie if someone or something carefully programmed it to.*

Then Cara thought of Valina, who'd likely broken many rules to use the forbidden TTC without permission. If Valina did something like that, she had probably been careful to delete any record Barnie might have made of either herself or Debian visiting (or talking to) Cara on the SP8. Was it because of Valina that Barnie kept counting down time in excruciating detail? Was that a programmed *distraction?*

He didn't do it unless asked about something concerning Valina and Debian! She realised, surprised. Cara had never imagined Valina being so devious. She didn't know what to think.

Captain Lydian stood and scanned the rest of the pod's interior. Then, she focused on Cara once more. "You probably consider yourself gallant, protective, and intelligent. You may be all that, Cara, but you must find better ways of showing it," she said in a gentler tone.

Captain Lydian continued to stare at her. She put a finger under Cara's chin and lifted her face so they both looked directly at each other. Cara had the impression the Captain could see right into her mind and somehow knew things about Cara that even Cara herself didn't know yet.

"You remind me of myself. When I see you, Cadet Davis, it brings back memories of what I was like at a similar age."

Cara watched Captain Lydian turn away and gaze into the distance. "I'd just completed my training as a warrior and graduated with outstanding results," the Captain recalled. "Unfortunately, my first squad leader drove his troops without mercy. On one particular mission—"

The Captain didn't finish. Instead, she turned with a grimace, removed her glove and held up a bionic hand in front of Cara's face.

Cara blinked several times, asking, "What happened to your hand, Captain?"

Captain Lydian gently placed her hands on each of Cara's shoulders.

"When I was your age, I, too, was hot-headed and proud, and I decided I knew better than my commanding officer. So I didn't stop to evaluate things. Maybe I was afraid, but I still went ahead. I acted out of fear instead of logic and reasoning," she shrugged and paused.

For a moment, there was silence between the cadet and officer. Then the Captain resumed her official tone as she stepped away and put her glove back on before crossing her hands behind her back. Finally, she turned around again and said, "And in a moment, Officer Cadet Davis, I will tell you the conditions of your not being punished. I scheduled this meeting to end in a few minutes, so I must be brief."

Cara waited in suspense for the Captain to go on. "I dare say you are already loyal, protective, and intelligent. But to be gallant, you must always stop momentarily and judge whatever situation you find yourself in, even when you're scared or unsure of what to do. Fear is a tough emotion, and sometimes you can't avoid it – but I'm convinced that facing it will strengthen you."

She cocked her head gently and looked into Cara's eyes. "We would all try to avoid being afraid or uncertain if we could, but sometimes we can't. As an Officer in the Galaxy Patrol Force, you will meet many challenges, and reasoning carefully is your path forward through those challenges."

With a quiet breath, Cara blinked and listened as the Captain continued in a sombre but gentle tone. "Trust me, Cara, self-control, logic, and a kind heart are some of a person's most superior characteristics. These are the things that make you become a good leader. But first, you must love yourself and remember that people love you. From that, you will find strength and success."

Captain Lydian's voice became strained for a moment, and her brow creased. "You can't go on like this, Cara! I don't want you to keep getting into trouble because it might be fatal one day!"

Their eyes locked, and Captain Lydian moved closer to Cara. "Always try to stop and make your thoughts clear before you act. Clear thinking will be the most potent weapon you will ever have. So, I want you to promise to do that now."

Then, just a few inches from Cara's face and with such a steadfast look, she said, "Do you promise, Officer Cadet Davis?"

Cara sniffed and let out a great sigh of relief. "Yes, Captain Lydian. I promise," she replied sincerely.

The Captain's brow creased. "Alright, Cara, carry out your orders and continue to follow the Zeg-Mar. I'll be in contact with Gorn. You'll need to replenish the pod's atomic thrust for the long journey back to our space station, so I'll order a refuelling squad to attend to you as soon as you arrive at the conference centre. After Gorn releases you and you've refuelled, program the autopilot to take you back to New Dawn. At a safe and proper speed."

Cara nodded. "Yes, Captain."

"And for moon's sake, Officer, keep out of trouble! You must never forget: think critically, assess risk, and make safe decisions."

"Permission to interrupt, Captain?" Barnie's voice pierced the air, and Cara thought that was strange because the AI hadn't bothered to ask permission whenever he'd interrupted earlier.

"Go ahead," the Captain said.

"This meeting is due to end in two minutes, ma'am. Therefore, it would be best to enter the docking bay as soon as possible and prepare for return teleportation," Barnie said.

The control room door slid open then, and Captain Lydian turned and made her way towards it. Then, pausing and looking back at Cara again, she resumed her official tone.

"Oh! By the way," she said. "I'm delighted you've finally mended the rip in your jacket sleeve!"

With raised eyebrows and a flicker of a smile, she ducked her head and departed from their Advanced Virtual meeting. Cara, however, remained rooted to the spot, staring for a long while at the closing door. *I don't know who mended my jacket, but it wasn't me!* She left the words unspoken.

Then, as she came to her senses, she said quietly, "Wow! Guess what, Barnie? I found out you *can* feel the touch of someone in an Advanced Virtual Meeting!"

Feeling mentally exhausted from the interview with Captain Lydian, Cara slid back into the pilot seat and asked aloud, "So what now, I wonder?"

Part Four

Chapter 28
Time to Act

After the SP8 caught up to Gorn's ship, Barnie received a brief communication with official orders for Cara. With her usual impatience, Cara partly listened as he recited the Captain's orders. He wouldn't stop his recitation no matter how many times Cara said, "I *know*, you idiot. She just told me! Be quiet!" (Not daring to say *shut up* again).

Since her captain ordered her to do nothing and go nowhere for the next ten days, Cara decided extended Rec/rel time was her best option. So for the next three days, she enjoyed long showers and made Barnie clean every bit of the space pod, including her clothing. She ate like a king, drank, rested, and occasionally ran and climbed for hours with the SP8's holographic exercise equipment. And, of course, she napped a lot.

She was napping comfortably three days into the dull journey when Barnie woke her with an alert.

"Cara, there is an interference with communications," he announced suddenly.

His interruption annoyed Cara, who grumbled, "Oh, do shu – *er, uh* – shovel off, Barnie! I'm sick of listening to the droning voice of artificial intelligence. So, give it a rest for skag's sake, will you?"

But the AI continued, "No contact signals are coming from Zeg-Mar-5. Neither long- nor short-range. Everything has gone silent, and they do not respond when hailed."

"What?" now suddenly awake, Cara shot across the cabin to the controls and switched the exterior surveillance camera back on. To her horror, she saw something she'd hoped never to see again.

A strange green and glowing object hovered above Gorn's spaceship.

"What the….?" She tapped various keys, focused on the camera, and zoomed in."*Ugh*! That looks like one of those huge arachnids that roam the outer planets." She shivered and remembered facing dozens of those horrible creatures during her training. As an exercise, the academy regularly sent cadet squads out to capture the disgusting giant spiders. She shuddered again at the memory as she stared at the creature's image and focused on the surveillance screen showing Gorn's spacecraft. It looked, or someone had made it look, very much like those hideous beasts.

"Barnie, project a probe wave onto that object hovering over Gorn's space-craft because I need to determine whether it's a living creature."

At once, a blue wave shot out from SP8 and hit the object that hung over the Zeg-Mar5. "Do we have a reading yet, Barnie?" she asked.

"The reading is coming in now," the AI informed her.

As impatient as ever, Cara pinched the bridge of her nose, forcing herself to count to ten before asking, "Well, what are the results?"

"It is not a living creature. Its surface is metallic. It has pulsating energy, and therefore it is a type of spacecraft," Barnie replied.

This information worried Cara. Who would make a spacecraft that looked like a hideous spider?

"What's going on?" she wondered aloud. She returned to the pilot's seat and watched the strange craft. "Barnie, open all communication channels," Cara ordered.

"They are open," Barnie replied, "but all our signals and sound waves are bouncing back at us. Some invisible shield or barrier is blocking them. You cannot contact anyone on Gorn's spacecraft or the craft hovering over it. SP8 is not even visible to them," Barnie droned.

Still staring at the screen, Cara stood up. "I can't just sit here passively and merely watch. Something strange is going on. Perhaps it's some kind of inva-sion. It has to be. Are we still on autopilot?"

"I can confirm; we are still on autopilot," said the AI.

"So, take us in closer. If something strange is happening on there, I need to find out," Cara demanded, throwing on her jacket and fastening it up.

"I cannot do that, Cara. Captain Lydian has programmed me to follow Gorn's spacecraft from a certain distance. We have a pre-set trajectory," Bar-nie answered flatly.

Cara put her hand on her hip, looked up and spoke into the surrounding space, "And I, Barnie, can end that certain pre-set program and devise one of my own. Now take us in closer to Gorn's spaceship!"

Nothing happened. "Barnie, I said to take us closer to Gorn's spaceship – now!" she repeated. Again, nothing happened, and SP8 remained in the same place. Finally, after at least twenty seconds, with still nothing happening, Cara had enough. Her brow creased. "Barnie, can you hear me? Take us nearer to the Zeg-Mar spaceship. That is an order!"

"That is not a wise decision, Cara."

Cara's voice cooled a few degrees. "And why not, may I ask?"

"For safety reasons. At present, we are at a safe distance. We have plenty of time to escape if the spider craft moves to attack us."

All this 'safety stuff" was getting on her nerves. So eventually, Cara snapped, "It's always the same with artificial intelligence, isn't it, Barnie? Fear is your weapon to persuade living beings to do what *you* want them to do." She clenched her hands into fists, "Making us fear stuff gives you the power you crave, doesn't it?"

Cara paced restlessly, "Well, don't delude yourself! Artificial intelligence will never have control over living beings. Trust me, Barnie, that's never going to happen!" *Well, not this time,* she thought.

Cara grunted in frustration and continued to pace the floor. "Don't you understand? Gorn and his crew may be in danger and need help." She paused for a moment and tried to calm down. Cara recalled how Captain Lydian had spoken to her about making the right decision. But, concerning the present state of affairs, her immediate decision was excruciatingly hard to make.

Should I get involved with Gorn's spacecraft or not?

Yet she had that gut feeling that always urged her to continue. It was that gut feeling that always motivated her. "I'm certain something strange is happening on the Zeg-Mar," Cara snapped, losing her temper and patience. She bit her lip and frowned. It was apparent to her that Barnie could not comply if Captain Lydian had programmed his orders because the AIs could not override a senior officer's program.

But Cara did. And now she not only knew how to shut the AI off, but she also knew how to get Barnie back if needed. In her present situation, she felt she had no other choice.

"If I can make this right and help Gorn and his crew, everyone, including the Commander, will see I'm not a screwup. I *can* do things right. I'll make Captain Lydian and my grandparents proud of me," she whispered.

She moved cautiously towards the master function key, and her hesitant hand hovered over it. Barnie spoke. "Cara, I do not advise you to…."

"Here we go again! Sorry Barnie," Cara said and turned off the AI, putting him out of action.

Still, the SP8 remained at the same distance from Gorn's ship. Cara was alone and in charge, but she needed a plan if she were to investigate the spider-craft. True, she hadn't fully qualified to pilot a space pod, but she knew enough to approach the two crafts without being seen. With Barnie out of action, she could not use the Stealth system. Nevertheless, she knew the time had come for her to carry out this mission.

Cara's stomach churned as she sat down in the pilot seat. She didn't know what she feared most – facing the evil-looking spider-craft alone or Captain Lydian finding out that she'd disabled the autopilot and approached the spider-craft without permission.

She pushed those thoughts away and focused on piloting SP8. She would need every bit of concentration she could muster. As she surveyed all the controls, something else caught her eye. The tip of an object stuck out from under one of the control panels, and it looked at first like a gaming control; it was about the same size. Cara got up and squinted, then sliding her finger under the panel ledge, she flicked it out. "Ah! My faithful 3D model laser gun," she joked. "Pity I never got to find out if this baby works!"

At once, she looked around the pod for a potential target. She spotted the bed in the sleeping cabin and aimed. She was about to squeeze the butt when an unsettling thought came. She didn't know how powerful it was; therefore, if the weapon did work, she also didn't know how much damage it might do. *What if it sets the bed on fire?*

She looked at the nozzle of the gun. *Nah! It's only tiny.* And with no more consideration of the consequences, she aimed at the bed and, this time squeezed the butt. Cara screamed and froze in disbelief as a needle-sharp blue laser beam hit the bed. Then, with amazement and in a low voice, she yelled, "It skagin' works!"

She dashed to the bed to inspect the results and found a black mark where the beam had struck the bed's fabric. With further inspection, Cara saw it had pierced the bed, too and left a tiny, clear pinhole. Though relieved that the weapon had done less harm than expected, she immediately remembered with a jolt and a gasp. *Yikes! I pointed this thing at Valina and Debian to make them think I was a threatening Radican.* Cara peered closely at the model weapon again and exhaled a long breath. *Oh, boy. It's a relief I didn't fire it then. I could have injured one of them severely!* She shuddered at the thought.

So, accepting it might be better than having no weapon at all, Cara shrugged, tucked it into her belt, and returned her attention to the task at hand. She buckled into the pilot seat again. "Now, let's investigate, shall we?" she said aloud.

CHAPTER 29

Flying Alone

In the pilot's seat, Cara reached with her left hand and located the tilt key in the centre console. *But first, I must look carefully at all the controls and realign the space pod.* Her eyes flicked to the grid display screen straight in front when she'd done that.

Now I must get control of the navigating function. Cara hesitantly tapped a key to scan lower down until her gaze locked on the position of Gorn's spacecraft. Then, through mindful use of the control, she could pick out the top of the Zeg-Mar, showing the alien spider-like craft that hung above it.

Ok. So now I'll check *every instrument on the control panel.* Cara reminded herself of what input she needed as she touched various screen pads and keys. *Let's see! Yes. Power, distance, and speed calculation!* Cara thought everything looked stable and routine, remembering how it had all looked in the virtual flights she'd perfected.

She smiled. "Cool, I'm doing a great job here. *Ha!* Unlike that time, I worked as a vendor stacker, and everybody who ordered coffee got fish soup. No wonder Granny doubted me when I told her I wanted to join the Galaxy Patrol Force." She giggled.

Whoops! No giggling. Keep it together, Cara! Get back to the controls. She took a deep breath. "Yes. Here I am, absolutely focussed and solo-piloting SP8."

Cara calculated the distance at minimal thrust. "We'll be in position in about five minutes. You couldn't have done it better yourself, Barnie." She enjoyed talking to the AI when he couldn't answer back.

Even without the AI in control, the pod progressed well. One look at the audio control panel told her there was still no communication between the two crafts. But soon, if her plan worked, she might get close enough to board the Zeg-Mar5.

The controls filled the width of the pod in front of the pilot seat, and the equipment made constant, repetitive, familiar sounds that gave Cara a little more confidence in what she was doing. Some pieces occasionally bleeped to draw attention, but others were silent against the gentle humming. Satisfied that SP8 had the correct position, Cara began the final approach to Zeg-Mar-5.

A loud, crackling sound spiked straight through her ears and into her head, shocking her and somewhat overloading her eardrums. Cara jolted slightly in response, and her right hand instinctively moved towards her ear. Her throat tightened, and her lower jaw went rigid.

What the skag was that? Her hands surged forward to the controls with a sensation of numb clumsiness. *What's happening to me?*

The sudden, sharp sound had done something strange to her hands, and worse, it somehow induced instant anxiety deeper than she'd ever felt. *What am I afraid of?* She tried to ask herself, but almost immediately realised she couldn't speak. *Help! I need help!* She screamed inside.

She heard the Captain's voice, telling her to stop and take time to think clearly before making choices as she struggled to calm herself. *Fear is a very tough emotion, and sometimes you can't avoid it – but I'm convinced that facing it will strengthen you.*

As she focused, Cara began to see that she had chosen to go it alone, but if she needed help, she could decide to turn the AI back on, and Barnie would take back control, per orders.

Whoever said choices are free probably didn't have to worry too much about life and death consequences, Cara thought.

That awful sound felt like an attack, and it shook her earlier confidence. Now she found it an effort to breathe evenly. But instinct and training urged her to continue her investigation of the menacing spider-craft hovering above the Zeg-Mar5.

Cara located the volume level on the internal audio control and slid it down to shut out the scraping sound. Whatever it was. She wiggled her jaw, stretched her neck a little, and consoled herself. "Probably just space noise," aloud. Her hands felt almost normal again as she flexed them stiffly. She knew that weird noises often got picked up on sensitive equipment when you travelled this deep into space. Even so, her back felt sticky-wet against the seat, although the air temp in the pod was normal.

Cara turned to face the Primary Flight Display and peered out of the thick glass that formed the pod's front shield. Her jaw tensed as she increased the thrust of power.

"Do I have control?"

Cara didn't know why she'd asked that. There was no one to argue, confirm, or answer the question. She scanned the flight display while trying desperately to counter the balance of the pod. Unfortunately, her hands were still too clumsy, and SP8 suddenly dropped like a bomb at hundreds of miles per hour.

Cara screamed and cursed her "clumsy skaggin' hands" as the space pod plummeted. She looked at the nose cone target at the bottom of the display and was relieved to see that although SP8 had taken a considerable drop, they were still on the assigned gradient she'd keyed in. However, the display screen showed a slight curvature, and the pod was not relatively straight. She swallowed hard.

Her unfocused gaze swept across the multicoloured screens and blue-grey panels that covered a back-lit keypad. She closed her eyes, held her breath, and then blinked, willing her vision to focus. When she could see clearly, Cara's eyes darted to two screens up and to her left. This display showed system failure and other catastrophic warnings. She checked for the MASTER SYSTEMS WARNING and MASTER OPERATIONS CAUTION lights.

Thank goodness those haven't lit up! Cara released the breath she'd been holding and opened a small compartment on her right side where she found and pulled out the 'Emergency Quick Reference Handbook.' palm computer.

Cara placed her finger at the top of the screen and dragged it down past item after item until ELEVATION CONTROL was at the tip of her finger. She selected it then, still scrolling through the manual, she found the heading, *'Maintain Flight Elevation Level Without Autopilot.'* Following the instructions, Cara checked that the atomic thrust was still correctly engaged, and verified everything, just as the manual directed.

To her great relief, SP8 now slid upwards on the right trajectory. They would shortly be in position above Gorn's ship. Cara breathed a sigh of relief. Minutes later, the SP8 arrived just as she'd programmed it to, right above the Zeg-Mar5 but still a safe distance from the alien craft. Then, with two deft taps of the correct keys, Cara engaged the manual elevation control. The ship stayed put.

Yes! I've done it. I've done it! Cara celebrated silently – with no punching in any direction.

Chapter 30

The Emblem

The SP8 was swift but had nothing in the way of firepower. Space pods are meant for fast travel – not for combat. In contrast, somebody built this spider craft which bristled with weapons for battle. A blast from just one of those direct energy weapons would obliterate the SP8, Cara knew, leaving nothing except a small cloud of micro-nano particles and dust.

So, Cara didn't want to make it obvious someone was paying a visit. *I need to find out what I can, and then maybe I'll find a way to board the Zeg-Mar. I might save the day if I can catch them off guard.*

She manipulated the visuals on the screen, studying the two ships and their connection. Then, spotting an insignia on the spider-craft, Cara zoomed in on it. She gasped at what she saw.

There, emblazoned on the craft's underbelly, was the colossal image of a Kaligiabeast. The emblem of The Radican Pirates! She recognised it from her research on Radicans. One training video she remembered, in particular, echoed in her thoughts now. "The pirates chose the most vicious and deadly beast in the galaxy as their symbol and mascot. These Radicans are a ruthless group – and 'ruthless' is a compliment in the pirate world. No one knows who the supreme leader of these space criminals is, but we've learned enough to know that if any of them questions their supreme commander, they pay with their lives."

Seeing the horrible emblem caused Cara's urge to rush to the rescue, waiver and dip.

Radicans! She realised with a jolt that real Radicans had taken Gorn's ship this time! Everything she'd speed-read about the fearsome pirate gangs returned in a rush. *They won't obliterate us with their weapons. Instead, they'll steal the SP8 and let me choose to either work for them or die slowly in a cage. They'll harvest my organs to sell while I'm still alive!*

Since no one was here to see, Cara covered her face in her hands and shuddered. "No, no! *No*, stop it! " she whispered. She breathed steadily into her hands, banishing those thoughts.

When she had calmed herself enough, she began steering the ship back the way she'd come. "Just carefully, *carefully*," she whispered in shaky, soothing tones. "Back away, get clear. Get clear of the ships, then re-activate the AI. But first, get clear."

Even after such hurried research into the Radicans, Cara knew better than to attempt this rescue alone. She had to find help, somehow.

She felt slightly more confident once the SP8 was again a safe distance from the Radican spider-craft. Still, her hands shook a bit as she moved to reactivate Barnie.

I'll need the volume back on to hear his test voice, Cara reminded herself. To her surprise, Golbat Gorn's voice called out her name as soon as she slid the volume level back up.

"Officer Cadet Davis. Come in! Officer Cadet Davis, are you there?"

Chapter 31

Another Chance?

It took her a few beats to manage a response. Cara tapped the comms screen and then sat there, mute and staring.

"Officer Cadet Davis!" Gorn rasped again.

"Copy!" She stammered, "*Err*, copy that. Cadet Davis here. Sir, I thought. – err, that is, I saw. I mean, *see* an alien spacecraft hovering over – And my AI informed me that your comms were down, sir?"

"Davis, we have dealt with the situation. I will discuss this further after I board the SP8 momentarily, along with two others. Please direct your AI to prepare for my boarding party." The communication ended there.

Although she tried to be quick about bringing Barnie back online, Cara took too long, causing Lieutenant CyJay to contact her again, demanding to know why they could not yet board. Ultimately, using the 'Quick Reference Handbook' to let them board was faster than restarting the AI.

After the brief delay, Gorn, Lt. CyJay, and a maintenance crewman boarded the SP8. Cara rose, saluted, and stood at attention as if frozen. All she could think was, *Please don't check on Barnie or the autopilot.* But it seemed inevitable that Gorn would. Then they'd know she'd gone against the Captain's direct orders.

"Davis," Gorn said, seeming in a hurry, "here's the situation. A rogue Radican attempted to breach our security to steal the Power Transmitters. As you know, Davis, they blocked all communications during the attempt. As it turned out, by some coincidence, this second Radican invader again turned out to be alone and probably nothing more than a pirate imposter."

Cara's breath caught. Were they accusing her of being part of another fake pirate attack? She resisted the urge to speak up and defend herself by holding her tongue between her teeth.

"Although," Lt. CyJay added in a snide tone, "*this* fake pirate stole his ship and uniform from actual Radicans and claimed to be—"

A sharp look from Gorn cut CyJay off mid-sentence. "Lieutenant, there's much to do, and our time is short. Please direct the modifications to the SP8 while I escort Officer Cadet Davis to the Zeg-Mar." He turned back to Cara. "I will explain along the way."

Cara remained quiet as they boarded a small shuttle and travelled to Gorn's ship. He quickly explained what was happening as he piloted the shuttle himself.

"As you know, we cannot take the prisoner on Zeg-Mar5 because of the strict calibration of thrust power. This nuisance 'invasion' has delayed us far too long. We cannot wait for another ship to take control of the prisoner. My engineers will modify your space pod to allow for secure prisoner transport. First, we must officially remand him to your custody on board my ship, where you will receive further instructions."

"What modifications will you make to the SP8, Sir?"

Hopefully, nothing involving Barnie, she thought, wishing she'd been able to reactivate the AI before her guests arrived. She struggled to think of a plausible reason to offer for Barnie and the autopilot being off. *Should she pretend to be surprised that she found something had deactivated the AI and Autopilot? What? How did* that *happen? I was talking to Barnie right before you hailed me!*

"Since we are putting you in charge of this prisoner, you will require a way to secure him. Therefore, we will install a force field and keep the prisoner in a secure area. A crewman will also bring onboard the SP8 other necessary equipment," Gorn answered while guiding the shuttlecraft back to his ship.

As they approached the Zeg-Mar's docking bay, the hideous spider-craft loomed above them. "So," Cara said, staring at it, "that's a *real* Radican ship?"

With a sigh and a disgusted shake of his head, Gorn said, "As far as we know right now, it's either a failed prototype or a ship they stole some time ago and couldn't properly use. It has no actual weapons other than the comms blocking equipment. Radicans probably use it to frighten their less advanced victims. As soon as our instruments determined the spider-craft's weapons arrays weren't real and had no living or robocrew aboard, our security team moved on the attacker and easily disarmed him."

"And he was . . . Dressed as a Radican?" Cara longed to ask if the prisoner's Radican suit was as good as hers had been — after all, that one even had the vocal modulator to make her sound like an angry pirate — but it didn't seem appropriate to bring that up.

"Oh, I suggest you watch the video record of his so-called attack. You'll have to try and gather information from him on your journey anyway, and watching and listening to that will probably fill you with questions."

"*Er* – yes, sir. Very good, sir, but – " she faltered, full of doubt. "Has the Commander approved of me taking this responsibility?"

Gorn raised a scaly hand and said, "Yes, he has agreed, and under the circumstances, you would do well to show the Commander your best abilities as an Officer Cadet. Due to highly unusual circumstances, Davis, you are being given a chance to redeem yourself."

Almost as soon as they were back on Gorn's ship, he handed Cara over to one of his crew. "Take Officer Cadet Davis to security and deliver her to the Chief." He leaned in and lowered his voice to say, "Keep her in your sight until you arrive there. Do not under any circumstance allow the Commander to so much as lay eyes on Davis."

The crewman nodded. "Yes, sir. I understand."

"Davis," Gorn said, "I'll contact Captain Lydian to apprise her of the situation and your new orders. I'm sure you'll hear from her soon." Then, to Cara's surprise, he wished her good luck before turning abruptly to address the crewman. "I've got to find the Commander. Wixon, alert me as soon as Davis is with Chief of Security."

Cara watched as Gorn hurried away. "This way," Wixon said. He headed up the opposite corridor from Gorn, and Cara followed. As she wondered again what to do if confronted about disabling the autopilot, the crewman turned left down another sizable gallery. He turned and said, "It's just at the end of the—"

He was interrupted by the Commander's shrill, almost hysterical shout. "I asked you a question, and I WANT AN ANSWER!"

At the sound, Wixon jolted to a stop and looked at Cara with wide, frightened eyes. He glanced around, looking for a quick escape or hiding place. Cara herself felt like running back the way they'd come.

"He must be in with the prisoner!" Wixon whispered. He took a few steps forward, tapping the wall. A door to the right slid open. "In here, quick."

Cara hurried into the small office, followed by Wixon. "Stay out of sight of the door just in case," he said, " I'm contacting Mr Gorn."

To be out of sight, Cara went to the back right corner of the small room. From what she could see, she guessed this was the Chief of security's office. She could still hear the very loud commander screaming at the prisoner. While Wixon spoke quietly to Gorn, Cara leaned close to the wall and listened.

"Who were you working with? ***TELL ME, OR I'LL HAVE YOU TORTURED!***"

Tortured? Cara thought, surprised. Radicans were known to torture and kill their victims, but the GPF had strict rules forbidding such methods. Then she heard what sounded like someone being slapped.

"Radicans!" another voice shouted. "I was workin' with Radicans."

"Tell me who. I want names!"

"Nobody you'd know." This person, the prisoner, had an accent Cara didn't recognise.

"I. Want. *Names.*" The Commander sounded menacing now. Cara could picture the snarl on his red, angry face.

The prisoner's voice changed, too. He sounded worried now, even frightened. "Hey there, mister Commander Predator, sir? Didn't nobody ever tell you it ain't safe to fire one of those on board a spaceship?"

Cara backed away from the wall. Was Predaton going to shoot the prisoner?

Just then, she heard Gorn's voice. "Commander! Here you are. The boarding party on the Radican spider-craft have informed me it is safe for us to join them now. I know you were eager to see – "

"Yes. Good. I simply needed a few moments with the prisoner," the Commander spoke quietly as if he hadn't just been yelling and waving his weapon around.

"Yes, of course, Commander. Shall we go, or – ?" Cara couldn't make out what Gorn was asking Predaton.

Wixon came up beside her then. "Alright, Mr Gorn is clearing the way for us. We're to wait here for the Chief."

They waited. Wixon sat next to the Chief's desk, but Cara had to stand in the back corner, away from sight of the door. When she objected, saying Gorn and the Commander were no doubt on their way to the Radican ship by now, Wixon noted, "Mr Gorn's orders." She wondered again at her strange assignment.

Gorn said the Commander knew. No, he said 'he agreed' to me taking charge of a Radican prisoner. A high-up person like Gorn wouldn't dare lie about something like that. What might've happened if Predaton saw me in the corridor?

The Chief, suddenly arriving, interrupted her thoughts, and the next few minutes were full of new orders and instructions. There was a full itinerary and detailed lists of what she agreed to be responsible for. It turned out that being responsible for a prisoner was like being imprisoned herself. By the end of the ordeal, Cara fully understood her new situation better. So, *this is actually my punishment,* she thought as she followed the Chief to the shuttle bay to "take custody" of the prisoner.

The Chief must have noticed Cara's discomfort because as they arrived, she stopped and whispered close to Cara's ear. "Listen, none of us believes this guy is an actual Radican. I doubt he'd survive as one. But they can be devious, so be on your guard."

Before she could ask anything at all, the door to the shuttle bay slid open. When she saw the prisoner, Cara understood the Chief's whispering.

Chapter 32
From Prisoner to Guard

At first, Cara thought it was Valina, but she knew that was impossible. It couldn't be her, even though she recognised the same hairless, pale blue head and delicate features. And again, the same refined contoured jawline, the beautifully shaped lilac eyes, and high cheekbones Cara had always envied. It was not until she noted his height and broad shoulders that Cara realised it was a male version of Valina from the same Listroc race. At a second glance, she wondered how she could have thought him female. He was clearly a man, looking handsome and dangerous, clothed in the foreboding black rags of a Radican pirate.

The young Listroc did not resist when the Chief took his hand and scanned the restraint on his arm. Then she scanned Cara's ID chip.

"There it is," she said, "the prisoner calling himself 'Zedok' is now officially in your custody, Davis."

Zedok laughed. "What's this now? Her? You, people, are whack—"

Cara knew she needed to show this Zedok she was in charge right away, or she'd have nothing but trouble with him. She thought *I'm likely to be stuck with him for a while.* She stood straighter, rising to her full height and gave him a sharp look. "Quiet!" She demanded. "Get into the shuttle. Now."

The Chief nodded her approval. "Yes, that's the way, Davis. But, *uh*, the pilot has to get in first in these tiny shuttles."

Zedok kept laughing and chuckling to himself as they settled into the shuttle. Cara gave him a threatening scowl.

CyJay and the crewman he'd been supervising were returning to the Zeg-Mar5 in the shuttle, so the Chief nodded a quick goodbye to Cara and stayed put.

CyJay took command when Cara and the prisoner stepped foot on the SP8. "Over here!" He snapped at the Listroc, "Sit down!" he ordered, and as soon as he sat, CyJay activated a transparent security screen around him.

Although Zedok remained visible, the unseen barrier prevented any escape attempt. Furthermore, they'd created the cell around one side of the sleeping area, effectively giving the most comfortable bed to the prisoner. Cara frowned, confident that CyJay, who for some reason hated her, had done this on purpose.

The crewman looked at Cara. "This is for you, ma'am," he said, offering the security screen activator. "And you may need this as well," he said, taking a taser from his belt. "For when you have to let him out."

"What? Oh, yes, thank you," Cara said in a small voice when she realised the crew member had addressed her. *Let him out?* She thought. *Why would I do that? Oh, yeah. The bathroom's over there. Shouldn't I have something more potent than a Taser? Should I ask for that? Or demand it, maybe.*

Distracted, Cara was slow to notice that the crewman was standing there, waiting. Then, just as she recognised the palm of his right hand was on his left shoulder in salute, Lt. CyJay said, "He's waiting for you to return the salute, *Officer Cadet* Davis," putting a snide emphasis on her lowly rank. Cara didn't have to look up to see the sneer on the lieutenant's face; she could hear it in his voice. She returned the salute quickly before turning to give CyJay a stern look. "Have you informed my AI of our itinerary?" She was going with the story; *I had no idea Barnie was shut off-*

"No," he said over his shoulder as he and the crewman headed for the shuttle. "We had to disable it during construction. No time to restart it. You'll have to do it. As for your orders and itinerary, we've sent it all. Your AI will receive it when you activate it. The additional supplies you'll need are stacked in the storage locker."

He paused, turned and said much louder, "Have fun with your pirate buddy, Cadet Cara! It was NOT nice knowing either of you. Goodbye."

Cara stood, fists clenched, staring as the door slid shut behind CyJay. She wished she'd thought of a terrible, witty insult to hurl at him before he left. "I hate you more every time I'm forced to lay eyes on you," she muttered, still staring at the door. But of course, Zedok, with his Listroc hearing, heard.

"I agree with that, Cara. A genuine piece o' work, that one. What do they teach at those posh Galaxy Patrol Academies? Certainly, not manners, judging by that twisted little git! He seems more like a Radican than I do!" Zedok guffawed.

Cara clenched her jaw, turned and glared at him. She chose not to bite back at his comment, even though she wanted to. Instead, she swallowed hard to calm herself.

"So," he said, looking around, rubbing his hands together, "what now? I suggest we eat. I'm about starved."

"I have to reactivate the AI. Not that I need to inform you about everything I do."

As she worked, Cara kept glancing over at her prisoner. Zedok's appearance and colour were much like Valina's though his features were more rugged. He looked about Cara's age, a little older, perhaps. Like Valina, the same metal spiral hung from his left earlobe. An adornment that would make him stand out from the rest of the Radicans. His lilac eyes were lively and questioning, and he regarded Cara with genuine curiosity. There was a certain spark behind them. Even before she spoke to Zedok, Cara sensed he was not like other Radican Pirates with their terrible ways. He was barely more than a boy. Surely, he wasn't capable of carrying out such daring, high-profile crimes and atrocities.

When Cara reactivated her AI, she was pleased to see Barnie's visual screen appear with additional data that showed the recalculation of the pod's calibre to include an extra living being on board. "Welcome aboard, Cara! Do you wish me to activate further safety restrictions on the passenger?" Barnie's monotone was back, and strangely, Cara found that comforting.

"That won't be necessary, Barnie; the prisoner is secure. You have our detailed orders?" she said with a perceptible sigh.

"Yes, I have them. Are you hungry, Cara? Would you like something to eat and drink? It will do you good and lower your stress levels. Perhaps those dumplings you like so well?" Barnie droned.

Cara sat down in the pilot's seat and put a hand to her brow with a cringe. *Great. He sounds like my grandma!*

Zedok chuckled. "Hey! Your AI sounds like a mom. Hah! Nice to meet you, Mother Barnie. You may call me *Zedok*. Just so happens I'm starving. Some dumplings would hit the spot to start!"

"You'll have to wait!" Cara snapped over her shoulder. "Our first stop is for refuelling, Barnie. Please set the dumplings, er, I mean, the coordinates and engage autopilot." Barnie acknowledged her command, and the SP8's familiar hum assured Cara everything was well.

As she fastened herself into the pilot seat and brought up the control panel, she turned to the prisoner. "I'm releasing the power cuffs from your wrists so you can buckle up and prepare for take-off. We'll be departing at once, per orders."

"Very good, Cara," Barnie said. "Ready to depart."

Cara watched as they travelled away from the Zeg-Mar5. It was a great relief to leave Gorn and his ship behind finally. But, once it was entirely out of sight, Cara's mind returned to the dumplings Barnie had mentioned.

When did I last eat? She couldn't remember, but it was definitely before the spider-craft appeared and interrupted her nap.

"Barnie," Cara called, "Dumplings sound good. And that root vegetable thing." She listed a few other favourites, watching Zedok as she did. He'd closed his eyes and seemed to imagine something pleasant. Food, she supposed. She let him think she would eat it all in front of him for a minute before adding, "And Barnie, make up two plates, please."

A few minutes into the journey, Barnie announced the meals were ready. Cara picked up one of the two trays and put the security screen control on the tray. She carried the tray in one hand and the taser in the other as she walked to the makeshift cell.

Zedok lay on the bunk behind the security screen, either sleeping with his eyes open or mulling over something. It was hard to tell with Listrocs. Finally, she said, "*Ahem!*" He startled, sat up, and stared at her with interest. He was alert and watchful, but not in a sinister way. He wasn't menacing or angry the way Cara imagined pirates to be. But she remembered the Chief's advice. *No matter how mild-mannered he seems, I won't let my guard down.*

She cleared her throat. It was apparent why Cara was in front of the screen because she held a tray with delicious aromas rising from the hot food. She waited, hoping he would speak first, perhaps even to ask about the meal. But he continued to stare at her. *Watchful and cautious,* she thought. So, she said, "Food's ready."

"Well, Cara," he began.

She cut him off. "That's Officer Cadet Davis to you," she said. Then she put the tray down and picked up the security screen controller, aiming the taser directly at Zedok. Cara deactivated the force field. As the screen melted away, Zedok leaned forward as if to stand, and for one awful second, Cara thought he might attack her. She was ready to fling the entire tray of food at him and simultaneously fire the taser, but he'd only been moving to sit on the edge of the bed, closer to the side table.

She took a breath, calmly entered the cell, placed his food on the side table, snatched the controller off the tray, backed away, and then reactivated the security screen, keeping the taser trained on him throughout.

"Much appreciate it, *Officer Cadet Davis.*" Zedok turned his full attention to the tray and ate hungrily after sniffing the food a little.

Again, Cara noted how familiar his voice and mannerisms were. He sounded so much like Valina, though his voice was full-toned in pitch, and he had that accent she couldn't place. Because of the bold and sarcastic way Zedok had spoken to Commander Predaton, she'd expected him to mock and try to intimidate her. But he didn't growl or hurl abuses, no grunts of temper, no threats of violence. Instead, just small moans and groans as he thoroughly enjoyed the food.

When he briefly glanced up at her, she glimpsed amusement in those lilac eyes, which surprised her yet caused a stab of annoyance. *He probably thinks a young female cadet on her own is no threat to him.*

Cara took her tray to the pilot's seat, eating slowly and watching the view as SP8 sped through space. Before too long, they arrived at the refuelling ship. Barnie, programmed with his orders, handled everything.

"Cara, there will be a brief wait, and refuelling will begin. However, we can depart for our next destination in approximately one and a half hours."

"Alright, Barnie. Take the tray from the prisoner's table now and mine." She saw that Zedok had stretched out on his bed and eaten every bit of his food. She was supposed to question the prisoner and gather as much information as possible. But she also felt a little tired and wanted a nap. Yet it would be embarrassing if someone on the refuelling ship tried to contact her and found her sleeping. She sighed.

Gorn, she remembered, suggested she ought to watch the video of Zedok's invasion and attempted robbery. *He thought that might help me know what to ask the prisoner,* she thought. So, she told Barnie to find and load it for her. She typed the command. The prisoner didn't need to know every little thing she was doing.

Chapter 33

Reviewing Zedok's Invasion

When the security recording began, Cara recognised the interior of the Zeg-Mar5. But it was hard to see details on the small screen. So, she paused the playback and selected the 3D hologram view, but even as a hologram on top of the screen, it was too small to see everything accurately.

"Barnie," she typed, "project this recording as a full-sized 3DH on the deck." After a short delay, the official recording of Zedok's invasion appeared near Cara, nearly life-sized.

"Good," she said, pleased. She swivelled her chair, and it felt like she was right there, on the Zeg-Mar5's control deck. She restarted at the point where the huge Radican wearing some sort of armoured suit first entered. He entered casually as if he was just a regular crew member. Cara reversed and played his entrance in slow motion.

How did he walk through the ship dressed like that without anyone noticing? And why didn't the Zeg-Mar5 start failing? You would have upset its calibration, surely?" She asked aloud.

"I had help," Zedok said with a yawn. "A Radican operative on the ship,"

Cara paused the holographic recording again. "Barnie, record this conversation and mark it as Prisoner Interview One."

Zedok laughed. "Don't you mean 'interrogation,' Cara – er, I mean Officer Cadet Davis?" He was sitting on the edge of the bed now, also looking at the hologram of his daring invasion.

Ignoring his question, she asked: "You say you were working with someone on Gorn's ship? So that's how you could board and get to the control deck unnoticed?"

With a deep sigh, he said, "Yes. It was all planned by somebody big – probably the Supreme Radican himself or that witch Shansa. Of course, nobody tells me that kind of thing. I'm just a slave. If I follow orders, I don't get tortured to death. Simple, right?"

"Who was it helped you onto the ship? If you don't know their name, say what you do know. What'd they look like? Male or female? You at least know that." But, she thought, *Gorn was right; I've barely watched the beginning of the recording, and it is helping me with the questioning.* Her thoughts raced ahead with other things to ask about.

"I never saw or spoke to them. But I do know one thing. You're in trouble, too," Zedok said with a mischievous grin. "For doing something similar to what *I* tried."

Zedok's comment offended Cara, so she ignored him and pressed *Play*. The invasion hologram played again, but Zedok talked over it.

"Or at least you were in trouble until they foisted me onto you."

"This is not about me," Cara said. She paused the holograph again and started it again when he stayed quiet. The Radican in the giant suit was still only entering the control deck, thanks to having paused so many times.

As soon as Cara tapped *Play*, Zedok started talking again, forcing her once again to tap *the Pause*.

"Bein' a Listroc, I overhear *so* much, you know. And that Zeg-Mar ship is practically ancient – thin walls and all that. I been wonderin' this one thing since I picked the big guy up with that power arm. What is an important high-ranking officer like Commander Predicate fellow doing on a creaky old ship like that Zeg-Mar5, anyway?"

"It's Commander Predaton, not *Predicate.*" He distracted Cara by saying he picked up the Commander with a power arm. "Are you saying you picked *up* the Commander? Sorry. I don't believe that. He's pretty, uh, large, compared to you."

"It's the suit. Let's watch the rest of the security recording. Seein's believin', right?"

Cara tapped *Play* again. The recording continued as the giant Radican entered the deck quietly. Nobody seemed to take notice. He took a few steps, then suddenly darted forward. The suit was colossal and heavily armed, yet the pirate crossed the deck with impressive speed and agility. Before anybody could react, he grabbed Commander Predaton by the front of his uniform. Cara gasped at the speed and strength as the Radican picked the large man up and shook him like a toy.

The invader's deep unnatural voice, slow of speech, echoed around the Zeg-Mar's control room while everyone there froze. "Get down, everybody – or the Commander here dies! Everyone down! Now!"

The colossal figure clad in black stood, holding Commander Predaton up, leaving his legs to dangle in mid-air. In the other gloved hand, the creature held an enormous blaster weapon, which he brandished with precision around the crew members in a threatening display of terror. Everyone, including Gorn, dropped to the deck.

Cara paused the scene again and stood to get an even better look at Predaton hanging there.

"What'd I tell ya?" Zedok said. He folded his arms and looked proud. Cara stood with one hand over her mouth, trying to hide her laughter at seeing the angry Commander so helpless. Finally, she turned her back to Zedok and allowed herself a silent burst of laughter, starting the playback again as she did.

"Now somebody," the monstrous voice boomed, "bring me those precious power transmitters you lot have on board. Don't take too long, and don't try any tricks." He gave the Commander another shake. "Because he could get badly hurt, you know? And if I kill one of you, I gotta kill *all* of you. Don't I?"

The huge Radican pointed his blaster at Gorn. "You. You get them. NOW!" As Cara and Zedok watched, Gorn scrambled to his feet and hurried out of the control deck area.

"This," Zedok sighed, "is where everything goes wrong."

In the holograph, Gorn came back almost at once. *Too quickly to have got the power transmitters,* Cara thought. Instead, he placed a box with a handle on the deck near the Radican.

Cara tapped *Pause*. "Were you suspicious at how quickly he came back? He wasn't even gone a minute."

"That's why I threw the hostage. I knew something was wrong and had to make a quick getaway."

Cara gaped across the deck through the frozen holographic images. "You *threw* him?" Then, without waiting for Zedok's response, Cara tapped *Play*, and the action commenced.

"*Eeeaaahhhhhaaa!*" the Commander screamed as the giant Radican tossed Predaton without ceremony directly at the armed security force who'd rushed in behind Gorn.

Cara said, "Barnie, stop recording the interview." As soon as Barnie confirmed, Cara rewound and then watched the Commander fly across the deck again, laughing out loud as he did.

She watched it again and then again in slow motion, laughing along with Zedok. After playing it forwards and backwards in both fast and slow motion,

Cara finally wore herself out from all the laughing. She carefully froze the holograph with Predaton flying upside down, mid-scream.

"I guess that's when they captured you," she said, stifling a laugh.

"Well, sort of. There's a bit more to it. But I didn't get to make my big exit, and I didn't even get to deliver the little farewell speech I'd planned. 'Well, ladies and gentlemen,' I was goin' to say. 'I shall be on my way. If anything is missing from this canister, or you're stupid enough to stop me, we will attack and turn you all to dust. I hope I make myself clear!'"

Cara laughed again. "It's just as well you didn't. Let's watch the rest, I guess." She tapped *Play*.

The enormous black figure backed out of the area, heading back to where he'd entered, keeping his blaster trained on everyone. Unfortunately, more armed security immediately encircled Zedok when the door slid open. Before the invader could shoot someone, he took a hit from behind and another from the front.

A terrible eerie moan erupted from the Radican suit, and the pirate veered to one side before toppling over. He fell stiffly, like a tree crashing onto the deck.

Cara said, "Wow." Then, looking across at Zedok, she saw him cover his face with one hand.

"I can't watch," he said.

The holographic image kept playing, but no one on the Zeg-Mar's deck moved. Not even the Radican. He lay where he'd fallen, unmoving and silent.

A medic hurried in behind security and rushed to the Commander's side. Just then, Cara noticed someone else arrive. Lieutenant CyJay. "It seems odd that CyJay wasn't on the control deck during the attack," she mumbled.

In the hologram, Golbat Gorn walked over and picked up the decoy transport case. He exclaimed. "Security reports the ship that's been holding us is unmanned and unarmed,"

The Commander struggled to his feet, breathing heavily. "Another imposter, posing as a Radican! She's come back for a second attempt!" Predaton shouted.

Gorn was about to respond when something unexpected happened. The huge Radican, lying motionless on the ground, moved. At once, all the security crew aimed their weapons at him, ready to fire.

Mesmerised, Cara stared at the colossal figure clad in black as he struggled and finally grasped his helmet. When he sluggishly pulled to remove it, there was a collective gasp from the surrounding onlookers. For beneath the helmet, there was nothing. No head, no face. Nothing.

"Didn't see that coming, did you?" Zedok said, laughing again.

Cara again paused the playback. "This is you getting captured. I'm surprised you find it funny."

Zedok waved a hand, shaking his head. "It's the look on everybody's faces, I guess. Including yours! I couldn't see any of this when that git shot me and broke the suit. I nearly suffocated." He laughed again as if at the memory of his near death.

Cara shook her head and started the security recording again.

In the nearly life-sized hologram, everyone on the Zeg-Mar5's control deck stared down at the colossal figure of the headless Radican Pirate. Cara heard a tapping noise from the middle of the Radican's chest, and at the sound, Gorn's security crew raised their weapons again. As everyone watched, a panel in the Radican's chest slowly slid open, and Zedok's blue head appeared.

Two crew members grabbed an arm each, lugging him out. "Get him to his feet! Bring him to me," the Commander shouted.

Zedok, who Cara noticed was struggling to catch his breath, moved his feet slightly apart and straightened up. His lilac eyes were alert and watchful, and he continued to stare in silence. The Commander glared at him. "Who are you? I've never heard of a Listroc being Radican. Who are you working with? How did Davis convince you to try this?"

Cara thought, *Davis! He really thinks I had something to do with all this!*

Still, the boy said nothing, so the Commander, whom Cara saw was growing red with rage, continued with a growl, "Did you two honestly think you'd get away with this?"

The Listroc stood straight, and his expression remained unchanged like a statue. For a moment, Cara figured he would never speak, but he looked up at Predaton. "I would have got away with it if someone hadn't knocked out my oxygen."

The group's attention turned back to the Commander as he growled in a low tone at the boy, "I'll ask you again, and this time, I want an answer. Who are you, and who were you working with!?"

"I'm a Radican, of course," he replied evenly, returning his attention to Predaton. Cara guessed he was probably trying to sound braver than he felt.

The Commander took a threatening step nearer to him. "Stop wasting my time and tell me your name – or else there'll be trouble!" he warned.

The Listroc shrugged. "Zedok. My name is Zedok."

He drawled it as though he enjoyed saying it. Cara wondered if that was his proper name or just a pirate's name he'd made up. It sounded cool whether it was or not, and she liked it.

Predaton grunted, turned his back, and paced away from the young Radican. "Well now, Mr Zedok!" he continued as he turned back to face the boy, "I'm arresting you for the forced entry of a Galaxy Patrol craft, attempted robbery, physical abuse, and carrying a dangerous weapon." He glowered at the young Listroc, "From now on, you are my prisoner, and we'll deal with you accordingly when we return to HQ. You *and* Davis."

Golbat Gorn, slinking in the background, made a rasping sound in his throat, "Commander, sir, may I remind you, we cannot take on board any more passengers because the calibration of the set program of travel is—"

"I'm tired of hearing the limitations of your ship and crew! How do you propose we deal with this second prisoner!? Leaving that devious cadet on her own has led to this!" Predaton's voice boomed into a hysterical screech that stopped Gorn and made Cara visibly flinch.

"Commander, I apologise for these limitations. I've had security checking all details of this attack. Davis has not communicated with anyone other than our ship since Captain Lydian dealt with her. There is no evidence suggesting that she was involved here, and the ship that locked out our comms is identifiable as Radican. I should also point out that this pirate's costume was fitted with real weapons and armour, whereas Cadet Davis's was—"

"All right! All right! Just get this creature locked away and out of my sight, Gorn before I do something I will likely regret!"

"Take him to security and lock him up," Gorn ordered, sounding almost as weary as he looked.

Cara tapped *Pause* again. "Well," she said to Zedok, "I guess that's about—"

"There's a little more before they drag me out," he said cryptically. He waved his hand toward the Commander's holographic image. "Watch it to the end."

With a sigh, she tapped *Play*.

Two security crewmen dragged Zedok away while the others collected and dragged the Radican suit off the control deck. To Cara's surprise, she saw CyJay move towards the Commander and whisper something close to his ear. Predaton narrowed his eyes and scowled but nodded. He said something she couldn't hear to CyJay before calling Gorn over. It looked like Predaton told CyJay to tell Gorn whatever he'd said. Again, CyJay kept his voice very low, probably whispering.

Gorn responded by shooting Zedok a grave and ominous glance. "Very well, Commander. It does solve both our problems," Gorn said. "You're certain you want to trust—"

The Commander snapped something at him in a hiss.

"Very well. I'll arrange it. But, if anything goes wrong, I cannot take responsibility for—"

Predaton became loud again. "JUST HANDLE IT! CyJay will help you with the details. I don't want to be bothered with this again, do you understand? I don't want to lay eyes on either of them again. Have I made myself clear? Nobody will hold me responsible for what happens if I see either of them again. Especially Davis."

Predaton flapped his hand and snapped, "Cyjay, go with Gorn! I'm going to my cabin, and I do not wish to be disturbed!" Then, he stormed off, the medic following.

Cara wondered whether the Commander had always been as aggressive as this. The more she saw of him, the more she wanted to tell Golbat Gorn how sorry she was for mistaking him for a villain. She realised now that appearances did not always indicate personality.

The security recording ended then, and Cara stared across at Zedok. He looked very calm and unthreatening. Not at all like a vicious pirate. *But,* Cara reminded herself, *appearances can be deceiving.* Was Zedok a true Radican pirate, or just their slave, as he claimed?

Chapter 34

Conversation with Zedok

"Refuelling is complete, Cara," Barnie announced minutes later. "I'm setting a course to the nearest HQ station. ETA 13.4 hours."

"Barnie," she said aloud because she wanted the prisoner to hear this time, "let's go to silent notifications and interior lights down. I'm going to get some sleep now."

"I'm for that," Zedok said.

Cara ignored him, focusing on getting ready to sleep. Being alone all this time on the SP8, she hadn't bothered with the privacy shield when sleeping, so it required some help from Barnie to activate it. After that, it took her no time to fall into a deep sleep.

She awoke nearly five hours later, only to be shocked when she got up to see that the prisoner was not in his bunk! But it turned out he'd set his own privacy shield. How had he known how? *Why would they let a prisoner have a privacy shield?* She wondered. *It's probably the rule about fair treatment.* Cara never remembered so many details like that.

I'm used to leaving the details to Valina or Debian, she thought now, feeling homesick for her friends. She made a mental note to have Barnie check on their whereabouts. They should be back on New Dawn by now.

After breakfast, Cara began Zedok's interrogation again. But she struggled to get much information from him. He wasn't particularly forthcoming, and she wondered whether she would complete his statement.

"Who are you?" Cara asked for the third or fourth time. She cocked her head to one side and looked stern. He repeated only his name. "Why did you attempt to steal the Power Transmitters from the Zeg-Mar5?"

Zedok surprised her by answering. "I'm an apprentice Storm-Pirate. I storm quickly onto spaceships and loot stuff. Sometimes, they order me to take certain special items—"

"Like Kwaidum Crystals and Imperium Domes for power transmitters, you mean?" she interrupted.

Zedok only nodded and waved his hand vaguely. "Yeah, all sort of nonsense like that." He closed his eyes and went quiet again.

Finally, Cara glared at him through the electronic barrier and said, "Perhaps you could start again by first telling me how you became a Radican Pirate!" she exclaimed and paced up and down in front of him.

"Why do you care? I'm a nobody. They orphaned me at birth. If you got no family, you get taken to the Gasamba colony on Planet PH14," he declared.

When he said the word *orphaned*, it struck a familiar chord in Cara's chest. *I'm an orphan, too. But I was lucky to have my family.* "I've never heard of the place or the planet," she said, more to herself than to Zedok.

"It's true, I tell ya! But I don't expect you to believe anything I say," he shrugged.

"I don't have to believe you; I'm just taking your statement. Law enforcement will determine whether you're speaking the truth or not."

"I tell ya, Gasamba is a horrible place. The authorities set up an enormous camp for orphans, asylum seekers, travellers, quacks, misfits, deserters, aliens," he said flatly, counting them off on his long fingers. "You name 'em; they're all there. Every one of them dragged off and removed from their home worlds."

When Cara glanced at him again, she saw the lilac in his eyes had dulled. "What did you do there?" Cara asked, studying him closely.

"Nothing!"

"Well, that doesn't tell me anything," she snapped. Cara could think of better things to do than record a criminal who wouldn't cooperate. She preferred to return to New Dawn, for she missed Valina and Debian's company and wondered if they were alright. She stood and walked away.

Zedok blurted out, "I did do something there. I escaped!"

Cara turned her head and studied Zedok over her shoulder for a moment. "Do you want to tell me about it, or shall we continue this pointless game where I have to guess the next part of your story?" She replied icily.

Zedok leaned forward behind the barrier and peered straight at her face. "I'd like to talk to you, Cara, Cadet Davis, but can we chat properly? I ain't good at answering legal questions. It makes me feel kind of – you know – edgy."

Cara sighed but admitted to herself that she felt much the same. She stayed silent but turned round to face him. Zedok's statement needed completing. She was also keen to find out who on the Zeg-Mar5 was a Radican operative.

With his Listroc ears, what might he have overheard?

Earlier, he'd hinted that he knew why the Commander had decided she should transport and question him on the SP8. At that moment, she felt utterly confused about that specific command decision and wanted to know more.

"All right," she exhaled in consent, "we'll do it as a more relaxed discussion, but I still need my AI to record it."

Zedok nodded in agreement, and Cara gave directions to Barnie, "Make a note of the date and time, Barnie. File it under 'Conversation with Zedok.'"

"Yes Cara!" droned Barnie. Since she'd messaged him about not talking in front of the prisoner, Barnie was a lot less chatty.

Cara sat back down, facing Zedok. "What took place after you departed from the orphan camp?"

"*Escaped*, you mean. I met up with some other guys, and we trekked from one colony to another, taking whatever useful things we found."

Cara squinted at him and leaned forward in her seat. 'Stealing, were you?"

Zedok cleared his throat but didn't directly answer her question. "One time, I met this Garlap creature, and we became pals. The trouble was, I got to be his partner in crime. He told me, 'Don't waste more of ya time with this lot son, when there are bigger rewards to go after.'"

That surprised Cara, "You joined up with a Garlap? You mean one of those unintelligent, cube-shaped beings?"

"Oh, trust me, Garlaps are not as dumb as you'd imagined," Zedok said in a low voice. "One night, he must have put something in my drink that sent me to sleep because I found myself trapped inside some magnetic orb when I woke up. There were three other guys in there, too – all beings from various worlds. We couldn't talk to each other 'cause there was no translator system," he hesitated for a moment as if recalling the details.

"Go on!" Cara said, her tone rising. But then she lowered it and cleared her throat, afraid of sounding too eager to learn more of Zedok's story. "Who'd captured you?"

"The Radican Pirates," Zedok said evenly.

Cara's eyes widened. "You mean they forced you to enlist and that you didn't volunteer?"

Zedok stood up and folded his arms. "That's how they recruit. Kidnapping men, women, whatever. Usually young ones, but they're not overly picky."

Cara leaned towards the cell barrier, gaping a little in surprise. "I didn't know there were *female* Radicans." She gave a nervous little laugh, realising how unworldly she probably sounded.

Her expression of surprise amused Zedok. He smiled a crooked little smile, eyes twinkling again. "Oh yes, there are one or two of them. And hey, I tell ya what, Officer Cadet Davis. You'd pass as a convincing Radican Pirate yourself. Tall, athletic, attractive, and *brave*. No wonder they almost fell for it when you dressed up and played Radican." He winked.

Cara felt the colour rise in her cheeks and found she couldn't speak for a few seconds. "Yes, well, as I said before. This isn't about me. And for the record, I'll never dress up as a Radican Pirate again. Ever!" She glanced at the overhead locker, where she'd stuffed the Radican costume.

"Ah, yes! But, of course, sorry, I forgot," Zedok continued to watch her, puckering up his face and speaking in a false, swanky voice. "You're one of them goody-goody human girls from Earth, trying to become a big shot in the GPF!"

Cara fumed, "Life's not like that. You must earn respect, you know. I imagined my Captain hated me, but she doesn't."

"Oh Yeah! And how do you know?"

"Captain Lydian talked to me. She told me about herself. Respected me for some things I'd done but advised me on how I might stop to think first and other ways to improve my behaviour," Cara said in a steadier voice.

"Ha, HA!" he screeched, "I was right earlier, wasn't I? You *were* in trouble!"

Cara couldn't hide how uncomfortable she was at his jibe. And maybe Zedok noticed because he added, "Well, you're lucky, Cara. Nobody was ever interested in what I said, thought, or did. So, I've had nobody to tell me how to do better. No parents, no friends. Nobody."

Cara thought this conversation was veering too far off course. After a pause, she said, "So, back to your capture. That's when you decided to become a Radican?"

Zedok laughed harshly, and his eyes took on a hawk-like frown. "You've just got no idea, have you, Cadet Davis? They enslaved me. I didn't have a choice! I told you before, I'm an apprentice Storm-Pirate," he said bitterly. "One of the deadliest jobs a Radican can have."

Cara gave him a look from under her brow. "Who ordered you to storm onto the Zeg-Mar5 and get the power transmitters?"

Zedok took a deep breath and let it out as he considered how to explain. "All we pirates know is everything, every order, comes from the Grand Master Radican. No one knows who he is or what he looks like 'cause a huge helmet and visor always conceal his face and disguise his voice. The rest of him looks like an armoured suit, vicious spikes, power arm and all."

Cara felt a surge of excitement. "Do you mean like the one you wore to disguise yourself?" she asked.

"Yeah, exactly like that. The leaders ordered me to disguise myself as the Grand Master in one of those enormous suits I operated from inside," he said.

In awe, Cara listened to more of Zedok's statements. "The Grand Master Radican is shrewd and gains followers for his gang by cunning. He wants them loyal and is pleased they'll do anything for him. So, he insists everyone must pledge allegiance and swear an oath that they are prepared to die for him."

"Did you swear the oath, Zedok?"

Zedok returned Cara's gaze and said, "What do you think? 'Course I did! I had no choice, did I?"

When Zedok looked at Cara this time, his face was steely and alert, "You don't need to ask me any more questions. But, if you want to know so much, I'll tell you the truth about these terrible Radican Pirates."

Cara frowned and waited, seeing his eyes that darted from one thing to another. "Go on then, tell me!" she said finally.

Zedok's words came out in a rush, "First up, they're a bunch of mad, wicked deadheads and so sly, so cruel. I hate them. I wish I'd never trusted that Garlap. And now, because I failed my assignment and lost one of the Grand Master Radican's armoured suits, they'll hunt me down and punish me."

Cara grimaced. "And the punishment?"

Zedok looked away from her and said grimly, "They'll torture me. Make me wish I was dead, but they won't let me die for a long time. Then they'll shoot whatever's left of me out into deep space. That's if the Grand Master's in a good mood."

Cara looked at him with mixed emotions for a second, then said calmly, "Well, they won't catch you, will they? Not while you're my prisoner – er – I mean not while you're a prisoner of the Galaxy Patrol Force."

Zedok laughed bitterly, "*Ha!* Well, we might make it to your HQ without them catching us. There's a slim chance. But the Galaxy Patrol Force will charge me with my crimes and send me to prison on Planet Canton for the rest of my life – straight from one hell into another."

He blinked his eyes and became aloof again. "I don't want to be your prisoner, that's for sure. Nor do I wish to be a Radican. These pirates are growin' more and more forceful. And they get away with it too often, so they think they can do whatever they want. Can't you see how powerful they would be if they got those power transmitters? They could turn them into weapons and tramp through every world until they'd taken the galaxy. That's what the Grand Master and his loyalists want – to rule over everything. They want to enslave every living being."

Zedok looked Cara in the eyes, lowered his tone, and, in a conspiring voice, said, "Somebody should stop them. But to do that, they'd need to slay the Grand Master Radican. Not a simple thing to do."

Cara sat unmoving as Zedok continued. "Besides that, there's a others ready to take his place if anything happened to him. His second in command is a human from Earth who's just as ruthless as he is."

"And what do they call him?" she asked.

With a half-smile, Zedok leaned towards Cara and said in a low voice, "Oh, it's not *him*; it's *her*. A woman called Shansa!"

Cara opened her mouth to respond, but Barnie suddenly cut in. "Recording paused," he said, "Cara, we are receiving a signal from an emergency distress beacon within our range."

Chapter 35
Distress Beacon

Cara returned to the pilot's seat and checked the control panel. She tapped on the flashing red signal and tried to pinpoint its location. It was impossibly erratic. "Barnie, can you track the signal? I can't get a lock on it," she said as she watched the image. Her wristband vibrated with Barnie's confirmation. Once again, Cara considered how much she liked this quieter, security-mode AI.

She was unaware of Zedok standing right up against the cell barrier, his neck straining to better view the screen. "I'm sure I know where that distress signal is coming from," he said.

Cara turned and shot him a look. "How?" Then she thought better of asking the prisoner for his opinion and added, "No thanks. Barnie's working on it."

"If you switch the cell barrier off, I'll come over to the screen and show ya."

"You wish!" Cara said harshly, turning back to peer at the screen.

Barnie messaged her again via her wrist comm. "Cara, I cannot detect the location of the distress signal. Something unknown to my database is interfering with the signal."

A few seconds later, Barnie spoke aloud, and everything unravelled: "Cara, prepare to receive an urgent audio message from Captain Lydian!" Barnie called out.

For a split second, Cara held her breath. *In trouble again, am I? What is it this time?*

"Davis, this is Captain Lydian. Do you copy?"

Anxiously expecting to get another ticking off, Cara hesitated. "Cara Davis! This is your Captain. Can you hear me? Copy."

Cara answered shakily, "Yes, Captain, I'm receiving you. Copy."

The Captain's voice sounded tense. "Unfortunately, I have some bad news.

Copy."

Here we go. What is it this time? Cara gulped and squeezed her eyes tight. "Copy, Captain!" she said.

"Right, listen carefully!" Captain Lydian announced, "I'm instructing all personnel to report any incoming distress signals directly to me. So far, we can't locate the one we've received. Are you detecting anything at the moment? Copy!"

Cara relaxed. *Phew! Not in trouble.* "Yes, Captain, we are. But it's too erratic for me to pinpoint the location. Copy."

"That's what we've encountered, too, so far. Copy," the Captain said.

The next moment, a loud whisper came from the electronic cell behind her. "Cara! Tell her I know a way to locate it!" Zedok said.

Turning to look at him, Cara snapped, "Shut up! I'm trying to concentrate," much louder than she'd intended.

"I beg your pardon, Cadet? Explain yourself," the Captain said.

Cara cringed, "Oh no, Captain! Sorry! No, I'm not telling *you* to 'shut up'. I have a prisoner on board who keeps talking. *Um*, copy." *And all this skagin', copy this copy that business confuses me!*

"Yes. Mr Gorn contacted me about your – *er* new assignment. I knew you might be in range to receive the distress beacon, considering you are en route to HQ in that sector." Cara heard caution in her voice, but Captain Lydian returned to the business immediately.

"Now listen, we've got an emergency. Valina and Debian are missing. I know they came to help you by using the TTC – otherwise, you wouldn't be with us now, would you? Yes, I know about that. We'll talk about all of that later. Right now, we need to focus on finding them."

Cara went rigid, clenched her jaw, and didn't answer. Fortunately, Captain Lydian carried on speaking. "The problem is, we don't know what happened to them after they saved you; they've been lost since then."

Cara's throat tightened. She only vaguely remembered Valina and Debian coming to save her. Barnie told her they'd arrived in the TTC. Valina had repaired the SP8 while Debian tended to Cara. *She even sewed my ripped sleeve,* Cara thought, staring at the impossibly neat stitching.

It startled her when the Captain repeatedly said, "Cadet Davis, are you there? Come in, please. Copy?"

Cara's eyes widened, and she breathed sharply, "Oh yes, sorry. Sorry, Captain. Copy."

When Captain Lydian spoke again, Cara thought she seemed a bit rattled.

"You know full well you should have told me about this incident during our meeting on SP8."

All Cara could think to say was, "Yes, ma'am, I . . . I'm sorry, Captain." The Captain was right. "I felt responsible for what they did. It was all my fault. I didn't want them to get in trouble. I didn't know they were lost, but I felt responsible for what they did. If I'd known—"

The Captain's tone was softer now. "Yes, I thought so. And at that point, none of us knew."

Reverting to her command voice, she said, "Well, you can start putting things right by thinking clearly now. You need to be vigilant and keep working on pinpointing their location. As of now, we know almost nothing. Except that the SP8 is closer to where their beacon *might* be. Inform me at once if you can find out anything. Copy?"

Cara cleared her throat and said shakily, "Yes, ma'am. Copy."

"Very good. Stay alert, Davis."

"Yes, Captain. Copy," Cara said in a flat tone.

"Audio message ended!" Barnie informed everyone loudly and abruptly.

Cara sat with her head in her hands, confused and upset about the awful news. *They could be anywhere*, she thought, suppressing a sob that emerged as a sorrowful moan.

"Hey, I really can help if you'll trust me just a little and let me out." Zedok sounded so sympathetic and reasonable.

Cara straightened, got up and walked away from him, fighting to regain her self-control while all she could think was, *We have to find them. We have to save them. But I can't let him out!*

Chapter 36
Cara Takes A Chance

Cara tapped different codes into the device relentlessly but was getting nowhere. "I *cannot* pinpoint the location of this distress beacon," she said, gritting her teeth. "It's bouncing around like a ping-pong ball."

Zedok sat in the electronic cell, not stirring a muscle. Instead, with hands-on knees, he stared at Cara's frustration. Finally, fighting back the tears of rage, she swiped the screen to turn it all down. She stomped over and returned Zedok's glare. He ignored her and maintained his gaze on the darkened tracking screen.

Cara flicked a hand in front of him. "How in moon's name do you Listrocs sit as still as statues for such a long time?" He ignored her. "Zedok!' she shrieked, hoping to startle him. Still, he didn't budge. "That distress beacon could be from my two crew mates, and if I don't pinpoint their location, nobody can do anything to help them!"

Zedok turned his head in slow motion and fixed his gaze on her. He watched her but said nothing.

"Zedok," she repeated in a much calmer tone to not give way to tears, "your race is far more technologically advanced than ours. Instruct me, please, on how to re-program this tracking device! Tell me how to locate the signal!" She waited as he stared.

Finally, he answered, "Sorry, but I can't instruct you."

Cara's hands fisted at her sides. "Just now, you told me you could help me. Now you're saying you can't. Unless I let you *out*? If you're so trustworthy and it's not all a trick, help me first."

Zedok stood up casually and leaned on the invisible barrier. "I can help you because of all the time I spent around Radicans, see? Because I pay attention and because I'm a good listener, I'm pretty sure I know why you can't track it. I can't show you or tell you how. Nobody taught me; I just figured it out." He hesitated, thinking for a few seconds. "I learnt it in a Listroc way I have. I have to do it myself. Hands-on, see?"

Cara bit her lip and knitted her brow. "You're asking me to take an enormous risk. I don't even know whether or not you can find them. What am I supposed to think?"

Zedok straightened to his full height and folded his arms, looking stubborn. "I promise you I can do it. First, I'll help you, and then you'll help me. If you want my help, let me out. Now."

His lilac eyes were bright and intelligent, almost hypnotic. Cara looked away from his gaze. It distracted her, and she desperately needed to focus. If the distress beacon was from Valina and Debian, it was her duty at all costs to find where it was and act accordingly. She swallowed hard and stared back at him. "Ok," she said after a pause. "What are the conditions? You said you'd help me if I helped you. What is it you want?"

He inclined his head towards her. "Simple. I want to escape from the Radican gang."

If Cara hesitated much longer, she knew it might be too late to save her friends. Everything about this situation frightened her. She folded her arms, mimicking his stubborn stance. "I'm not sure I can trust you, Zedok," she said sternly. "And how can I possibly help you escape the Radicans?"

"You only have to let me go somewhere later without taking me to headquarters. Just leave me someplace where I'll have a chance to get away. That's all. And anyway, it's a risk you'll have to take, ain't it? I mean, you'll have to trust me if you want to save your friends," he said.

Cara glared at him, thinking.

"Listen," he added, "I'm not going to attack you or try to take the ship. And you don't have to trust me completely, right? Just hold a weapon on me the whole time I'm out. Then, if I make a move to steal your ship, you shoot me dead."

Cara considered for a few seconds. "That's not a bad idea, but I don't have any weapons. Just the taser that crewman left for me." She didn't bother to mention the little laser from her Radican costume.

"I heard the big fellow telling a crew guy to load extra supplies and weapons onto the SP8. The git mentioned it to you before he left in the shuttle. Said they'd stacked boxes in a locker or something."

Cara remembered. She hurried over and found the crates from the Zeg-Mar5. The first one held an assortment of miscellaneous supplies marked Culinary. Cara put it aside and opened the second crate. There she found an impressive and sleek blaster, fully armed.

"What'd I tell you?" Zedok said with a low whistle. "I'm going to have to ask you to be careful with that weapon when you're holding me at gunpoint, Cara. You could kill me by accident very easily. Also, if you're not careful, you might blow a hole in the SP8."

Cara cautiously set the blaster aside, pulled out some packing material and then stared, stunned, at the other thing in the second crate.

"There's no way — it can't be. It — It doesn't make sense." She reached forward to grab the handle but pulled her hand back, wary, muttering to herself. "This has to be a decoy. Something like that."

"What is it? An even bigger weapon? What did they think we'd be getting up to, anyway? Let's see it."

Cara tried to stuff the packing material back into the crate but wasn't quick enough. Zedok saw the canister.

"Is that!?" He pointed, nearly getting a shock from the barrier when his arm almost passed through it.

"No!" Cara shouted. "It's definitely NOT."

"Do you think they didn't show me what they'd look like? Do you think I didn't have to memorise every detail of those things before they sent me off in that rattle-trap spider-craft with that monstrous suit? I *know* what those are!"

Cara packed everything, including the blaster, back into the crate and stacked both boxes in the locker. Then she slammed it shut. "NO!" She said.

"Yes," Zedok said. "We both know what they are. It's the Kwaidem Crystals and Imperium Domes. The very same power transmitters the gang sent me to steal!"

Without responding, Cara stepped away and turned her back on him. For a while, she didn't speak. Then, without turning to face Zedok, she said, "All right, I'm letting you out. But remember, I shall have my taser ready if you try to trick me." She turned, strode over to the release control and picked it up. Then, as she stepped back to the electronic cell, she took the taser from her belt and pointed it at the prisoner. The barrier slipped away, and Zedok looked at her.

"Well, I can't say I'm disappointed you're not using that blaster."

Cara only pointed at the tracking equipment.

"Don't want to talk about the unexpected cargo, then?" He said.

Cara frowned and waved the taser. Zedok stepped toward her and said, "I get it. One crisis at a time. Let's take a look at the tracking screen, shall we?"

The light caught the rotating spiral dangling from his earlobe as he moved.

It made Cara blink, but she sensed no threat from him and lowered the Taser. Together they crossed over to the control panel, and Zedok activated a minor key at the side of the pilot's seat.

"Oh, I hadn't realised that was there!" Cara said as a second pilot seat emerged from the floor.

Zedok grinned and said, "Are you confident you can handle this space pod properly, Officer Cadet Davis?"

Cara's lips thinned. "Don't you start," she said, "I've had it with folk asking me that question. Thank you very much!"

When Zedok reactivated the screen, they sat and watched the pulsating red dot bouncing around. Cara waited for Zedok to key in the codes. But he didn't. The Listroc did nothing except stare at the screen. He didn't move. "Zedok, have you passed into statue mode?" Cara murmured impatiently.

For at least three minutes, he remained perfectly still. Not even his eyes shifted to follow the signal, and he barely breathed. Cara fidgeted, not knowing how to react, and when at last Zedok took a sharp intake of breath and yelled, "GOT IT!" she almost fell out of her seat. He keyed in hundreds of codes so rapidly that Cara's vision couldn't keep up. There was no warning before the red dot eventually froze in the centre of the screen and stopped pulsating.

"What did you do?" she asked.

He didn't take his eyes off it, "I've achieved what you asked me to do, of course. I've found where the distress signal is coming from. I had my suspicions all along that it was in that place."

There was a long pause until Cara said sharply, "Tell me then! Where *is* it?"

Zedok's face was intense. "You won't like what I'm about to say, Officer Davis."

Cara leaned in with slitted eyes. "Tell me, and let's see if you're right!"

"The signal is coming from—" he hesitated like it was some game show. Cara held her breath until he exclaimed, "It's coming from Carbonica!"

Cara huffed and flipped her hand irritably. "That doesn't mean a thing to me. What's Carbonica, and what am I not supposed to like?" she asked in a steely tone.

"Carbonica is a burning planet, probably a dying planet – eventually. But Radicans don't care. It's their main hideout. Nobody can find it, except usually by accident. They've got some kind of scrambling device that keeps the place hidden. That's why the distress beacon seems like it's moving around, too. What's more, who knows when a big enough eruption will break up the entire planet? When I was there, it felt like that could happen at any moment," Zedok warned.

Cara raised her eyebrows. "And it's one of the Radicans' secret bases?"

The colour of his eyes paled. Valina's eyes always did the same when she had certain unsettling emotions. But he said nothing. Instead, he tapped a few more keys that caused some curious white symbols to appear. Cara drew in a sharp gasp and instinctively grabbed Zedok's arm. "What do those symbols mean?" she asked.

He squinted at the screen and deciphered the symbols. "Let's see. The signal is from a small distress beacon attached to…" he faltered and squinted at them. "TTC-PERSONAL SOLAR PROTECTION EQUIPMENT?" Zedok read.

Cara stood and gnawed on her knuckles for a second. "Oh, Zedok! I think that has to belong to either Debian or Valina." She sat down beside him again and looked into his eyes. "While flying the SP8 alone, I had a bit of trouble with it. Well, more than just a bit," Cara admitted. She read the concern in Zedok's eyes while she related the entire story and told him what she remembered of Valina and Debian travelling in the TTC and saving her.

Zedok shot her a worried glimpse. "What do you think happened?" he asked.

Cara looked down at her hands and fiddled with them. "I think something terrible might have happened on their return journey to the New Dawn space station. And maybe they crash-landed on Carbonica."

Zedok didn't say anything. Instead, he keyed in another code with the same remarkable speed, and the symbols formed an image on the screen. There it was – a personal solar protective spacesuit. Cara gasped, and both hands shot to her cheeks. "Oh no!' she whined. "I'm sure that's the suit they wore when they showed up to save me!"

Zedok sat, still staring at the image of the PSPE suit on the screen, but Cara got up again and began pacing and wringing her hands. "I don't know what to do or where to start. How in moon's name can anyone rescue Valina and Debian from a whole nest of Radicans?" she exclaimed tearfully.

Chapter 37

A Change of Course

Cara stood with one arm clasped around herself and her other hand supporting her forehead. "I should inform Captain Lydian right away," she said as she moved away from the screen.

Zedok stood and walked over to her. "I've got an idea if you want more help."

Cara sighed, folded her arms, and sighed with resignation. "Go on!" she said.

"Well, we've got the power transmitters on board, ain't we? So why don't we make use of 'em?"

"We don't know that we have them. They're probably just fakes. A decoy or something." Cara couldn't think of any reason someone would have hidden the real ones on the SP8. And she said so to Zedok, explaining how little sense it would make. "In fact," she added as Zedok kept shaking his head in disagreement, "someone was probably supposed to explain that to me. Probably that jerk CyJay."

"Well, what I see is one intrepid young Officer Cadet on her own on an unarmed space pod. Besides that, she's got a potentially deadly prisoner to guard all the way to HQ. It's a long way across a pretty empty stretch of space, Officer Cadet Davis. So let's give you some really crucial cargo, too. Cargo, some pirates have got wind of and are plenty keen to have. I'm sure you can see what I'm saying?"

Cara frowned, "What's your point? Are you saying someone's setting me up?"

"Well, setting both of us up. We're sitting ducks here in this little pod. The only thing it's got going for it is comfort and speed."

"How would any pirates know we had the power transmitters? Unless you contacted them somehow?"

Zedok held his head briefly, then dropped his hands and sighed. "First, if they know, it is *not* because I told them. How could I, anyway? Somebody on that Zeg-Mar put those transmitters in that crate and dragged it onto this ship. On purpose! If it's Radicans who show up, I guess we'll know that someone on that ship told them where to look. But we know someone in the GPF is a crook. Somebody helped me get onto that ship. Maybe *they* want those crystals and domes for themselves to get rich and be powerful. So, they put them in a place where they'd be easy to find and easy to take. See?"

Cara began thinking about how the Commander and Cyjay had acted at the end of Zedok's failed robbery. Why had they so quickly put her in charge of the prisoner?

"Zedok," she asked, "what did CyJay say to the Commander right as they took you off the Zeg-Mar control deck? Remember? You told me I should definitely watch that part. And that's all it was – them talking, then telling Gorn their plan. But what did they say that nobody could hear? I'll bet you could hear them."

Zedok sighed. "I heard some of it, yeah. That rude git –"

"CyJay, the lieutenant?"

"Yeah. Him. The cyborg. He said something about 'it' solving all their problems. He said, 'This couldn't be better, sir. Think about it. It's perfect. Almost made to order.'"

Cara frowned and stared at the floor. It was all very suspicious. The power transmitters should not be on the SP8.

"Wait!" She exclaimed, hurrying over to the storage locker. "Maybe they are decoys. Before we – I mean, *I* – decide anything, we should at least see if they're the real thing or not."

Once she opened the case and saw the official seals, Cara's heart sank. "If they were fake, we could just jettison them," she moaned. "I don't want these things with us!" She looked up from where she was sitting on the floor next to the locker and saw Zedok holding the taser she'd left on the arm of her chair.

"What are you doing? Zedok!" She scrambled to get to her feet, but he pointed the Taser at her.

"Oh, nothing," he said with a frown. Cara heard an unexpected menace in his tone. "I've decided I'm going to shoot you into the great wilderness of deepest space, and then I'll escape in SP8 with the power transmitters and my new gramma, Barnie." His face looked ferocious.

Cara felt the colour drain from her face. Zedok's lilac eyes glinted as he held her at taser point, and she went rigid, hoping he would kill her before ejecting her from the pod. But just as suddenly, the menacing expression on his face dissolved, and he threw back his head and howled with laughter.

"Oh, Cara! I mean – Officer Cadet Davis – your face is a picture, ma'am!" Then, standing to attention and clasping his left shoulder, he gave her a mock salute. Suddenly he chuckled loudly and placed the taser back where he'd found it.

As she jutted out her chin and frowned, Cara's expression changed, too. "That's not funny!" she yelled, getting to her feet, grabbing the taser and pointing it at the laughing Listroc. "I'm putting you straight back behind the electronic barrier. *MOVE!*"

Zedok stopped laughing and looked at her with a hint of a smile at one corner of his mouth. "I can't help you if you do that," he said in a calmer, quiet voice.

Cara's heart was still pounding, and her breathing was shallow, "You frightened me! And now I'm not sure I can trust you at all. In fact, why should I even contemplate trusting a criminal to help me?"

Zedok put up his hands with palms turned outwards. "I was joking, but you're right, and I am sorry. I couldn't resist making fun when I saw your little gun lying there."

His expression became serious again. "It's true, though, what I told you. I don't want to be a Radican anymore. I don't want to be a criminal. And I'm desperate to escape from all of that." He looked at her and cocked his head to one side. "If you please forgive me, I promise to do nothin' stupid like that again."

Cara huffed, "Zedok, I've serious concerns right now, and I'm not in the mood for jokes and silly games. You offered to help, but then you scared the living daylight out of me!"

As he moved closer towards her, Cara saw his lips part to show Listroc's small pointed canine teeth like a wolf's. There was a flash of white in his warm, friendly smile. "Forgive me?" he said as he put out his hand to take hers. Cara ignored the gesture, and he let his hand drop to his side. "But I do have an idea about how we can help your friends escape Carbonica," he said.

More desperate by the minute for her crew mates, Cara gave him a stern look. "Go on then!" she said with reluctance.

Zedok returned to the screen with the image of the PSPE, "I'll tell ya, we can travel in this space pod and land right on Carbonica. I'll work out how to get there, travelling at warp speed."

For a moment, Cara paused. "I'm not sure," she sighed, turning away from him and shaking her head, "I'm not sure that would be wise."

"Listen. This is the truth. Even if your friends weren't in trouble, we'd need to get off this course and go – I d'know – anywhere else! To another HQ or somewhere else where nobody would expect us to be. Because *somebody* expects us to be right here, Officer Davis, in this nice little space pod with no proper way to defend ourselves from bigger, badder ships."

"But," Cara began.

"No time to discuss it much. Whoever's on Carbonica is not safe. We're not safe. And who besides us – with me knowing the way and knowing my way around that god-forsaken hideout, who else but us is in a better position to sneak onto that planet and rescue them?"

Cara saw his point. In fact, it seemed like a plan she might devise herself. Still, she'd made promises to the Captain. And she remembered the security Chief's warning about underestimating Zedok. "But the Captain's looking for them, too," was all she could say. Her thoughts were rushing ahead about this new mission: to rescue Valina and Debian.

"Tell you what," Zedok said, "You'll send a message to your captain. She sounds like a good one, by the way, if I didn't say that before. Anyway, as we leave, you'll send her an encrypted message with the coordinates for where we're headed. Give her a warning about the Radican hideout, too, so she'll take enough firepower and such. That way, if we need it, we'll have some backup. At some point."

Cara looked thoughtful, imagining doing just that. "Barnie can encrypt a message for me. I like that. I mean, of course, I have to let the Captain know."

Zedok leaned towards her and touched her arm. "Listen, the longer we hang about, the greater the risk for 'ya pals." He turned her gently so that she faced him. "Time is running out for them. I can tell ya for sure, the longer they're in the company of the Radicans, the more dangerous it will be for them," he stated.

For a moment, their gaze lingered. Then, biting her lip, Cara took a small step away. "Barnie," she called out, "I need you to prepare an encrypted message and send it to Captain Lydian on my mark." Still in security-mode, Barnie replied on her wrist unit.

Cara quickly composed, double-checked, and encrypted the message. However, she knew they couldn't leave their pre-determined flight plan unless she deactivated the AI again. So she told Barnie to send the message, then distracted him with several mundane tasks before disabling the AI and turning the auto-pilot off.

Zedok was in the second pilot's seat. "Very slick," he said. He tapped the seat next to him and smiled across at her. "Will you be my co-pilot, or shall I be yours?"

Cara hesitated but returned his smile as she sat in the other seat. She knew a smart Listroc like Zedok was a better pilot than she'd ever be. "If we need to get there as fast as possible, I guess that leaves me as your co-pilot."

"Great," he grinned. "Now buckle up, co-pilot Officer Cadet Davis. Time to change course."

"You *can* call me Cara if you like," she said in a small voice.

Chapter 38

Carbonica

Cara had never flown at such a mind-blowing speed. Although Zedok had activated the control that prevented them from losing consciousness, Cara experienced the weirdest sensations. Everything in the cockpit seemed to dissolve into strange shapes with black holes between them. At one point, she tried to yell, "The pod is disintegrating, breaking to pieces. We'll get thrown into space and die!" But her mouth wouldn't open properly, and she couldn't make any sound.

But neither of them got thrown anywhere, and the SP8 kept going. All light and sound seemed to disappear. Cara couldn't even see Zedok beside her but somehow sensed his presence. She felt herself falling as if tumbling headfirst into a great abyss. The falling sensation never seemed to end, and Cara expected to crash or hit the bottom of something solid. She thought – *it isn't possible to fall for so long without slamming into something.*

Her muscles tensed, and her nerves were on edge. She expected, at any minute, to experience a sudden, body-shattering impact. Instead, Cara screwed up her face, terrified at being catapulted through space and darkness. She tried to concentrate on something else, but found it impossible. Cara couldn't see her hand as she lifted it to her face. There was nothing there. *Where's my face? I can't feel my face. There's no light, no sound. Am I breathing? Is my heart still beating? Am I dead? I don't know. I must concentrate on what's happening. I'm not falling. I'm travelling at high speed.*

For Cara, the high-speed travelling sensation ended suddenly. It ended, not with a shattering crash into oblivion but with a whine and a whiff of ozone. She saw with relief that everything in SP8, on all sides, had become solid and visible again.

"Are you ok, Cara?" Zedok said, looking into her eyes. "Are you going to throw up?"

"No," she gasped, 'but I need some water. Barnie, get us some water, will you?"

Of course, Cara had deactivated the AI, and it didn't respond. Zedok stumbled over to get water, and Cara noted how unsteady he was. His blue skin looked a little greenish, his eyes pale and unfocused. He returned with two beakers of water, dripping it everywhere, including over himself and Cara. She wiped it off her face and took a long drink of what remained in the beaker.

After a few minutes of sitting and sipping, Cara turned to look at Zedok. His colour was coming back, and his eyes looked less wild. "Wow!" She said, a little breathless, "That was some journey, Zedok. I hope we're in the right place!"

Zedok took a deep breath and scrubbed his face with his hands before keying in some information to down SP8's power and then turned to Cara. "I've landed the speed pod on the far side of the planet, away from the base. This area ain't under surveillance because the Radicans don't have room to land or take off their bigger craft in these parts. Remember, this is a secret base, only known to Radicans."

Cara unbuckled her seatbelt and stood. Then she immediately sat down again. "I'm all wobbly!" she said.

"You'll live," Zedok assured her. "Travelling at that speed affects your muscles. It'll pass. In the meantime, we'd better work on our plan."

Having made her way to the water, Cara turned back and raised her eyebrows. "Do we have a plan?" She carried water back without spilling much, passing a beaker to Zedok and then sitting down again.

He took a few sips. "How about this: We offer the Power Transmitters to the Radicans in exchange for Valina and Debian. You know, like paying a ransom. Ransom is the language pirates understand."

Cara didn't like the sound of that idea one bit. She was unwillingly responsible for one prisoner and the most potent energy transmitters ever invented. And she'd already let the prisoner loose. So Zedok's suggestion sent an unpleasant tremor of horror and doubt to her bones.

"Aren't you forgetting something?" she said, forcing the words out with difficulty. "If the Radicans get their grubby hands on all those domes and crystals, they could hold an entire universe at ransom. Valina told us criminals could easily transform that power to create deadly weapons and cause the most painful destruction. You even said as much yourself!"

Cara fixed her eyes on the canister holding the Power Transmitters. "Anyway, I'll have to take them with me whatever we plan to do. I can't risk leaving them in the pod – it's my duty now to guard them with my life."

Zedok rubbed his chin in thought and squinted at her. "What if we offered the Grand Master half of the Power Transmitters, and then, once he'd released your crew mates, we could try to steal the PTs back later, and then maybe…?"

"Oh, Zedok!" Cara said, jumping up in frustration but immediately grabbing the back of the seat to steady herself again. She looked down at him. "This is getting us nowhere. We need to act. We need to find out where the Radicans have imprisoned Valina and Debian so we can release them. But, of course, that's assuming they're here and still alive. You've already admitted that we're running out of time."

Zedok huffed out a long breath. "You're right, but if they are still here, I'm sure I can guess where the Radicans are keeping them. So, we'll find them and get 'em out if I'm right."

"Come on then! We can't waste any more time. Let's get some stuff together and start looking for them," Cara said, pacing away.

Zedok stood and moved towards her. "There might be a problem."

"What now?" she huffed.

Zedok leaned toward her. "Not *what*, but *who*! You're the problem, Cara. You, in your blue patrol uniform. Remember, I *am* a Radican!" He indicated his ragged black clothing.

Cara looked back at him with a smirk and said, "An ex-Radican soon, I hope." Zedok's ears twitched with embarrassment. The metal spiral in his earlobe twirled and glinted as it caught the lights.

"And you needn't worry about me getting caught out. I can easily solve this problem," Cara continued as she headed to her cubical. "Wait there, and you'll see!" she called over her shoulder.

Once inside the cubical, Cara reached up to the overhead locker. She dragged her black Radican Pirate outfit, removed her officer's uniform, and replaced it with the costume. Complete with a closed visor and voice modulator.

In less than two minutes, Cara — now a tall figure dressed in black — stood staring at Zedok. Then, in a flash, she grabbed the canister of Power Transmitters, pointed the little laser gun at him, and in a deep and vicious voice, said, "Let's go, fellow Radican. Now!"

She turned off the VM and said in her unaltered voice, "I don't feel comfortable carrying that huge blaster. I — I don't have much weapons training, really."

"Me neither," Zedok agreed. "I'll take the taser if that's alright. These are proper weapons for us. We'd stand out if they saw us with a weapon like that big blaster. They wouldn't allow any slave-level pirate near anything that powerful in case of mutiny. The one I carried on board the Zeg-Mar was a weak fake model, a bit like your tiny lit.."

But Cara shot Zedok such a warning look that he stopped in mid-sentence.

They gathered what little they could carry for the long walk ahead before disembarking from SP8 onto a terrain with black grit and rocks, as far as the eye could see. Well prepared, Cara carried the Power Transmitters in the canister efficiently but thought she might suffocate from the heat, the overwhelming black rocks, and the oppressive grey haze.

"I'm concerned we're not carrying an oxygen supply," she gasped to Zedok standing beside her. Zedok had insisted they didn't need to. But it was not a pleasant sensation inhaling such hot air. It dried her throat, and she coughed. Cara slid open the black visor on her helmet and breathed easier.

"Don't worry! You'll get used to the heat, and we'll shortly be crossing into a cooler area away from the fires." Zedok said as he walked past her.

They were on a slope which led downwards, and when she glanced up, Cara saw flames lapping over the ridges of rock, making the sky glow. "Come on!" he said to her. "We'll get away from here and nearer to the hidden base."

Cara followed him as he turned and made his way down between the craggy rock forms. The black boulders cracked with the heat, and from the cracks, wisps of yellow sulphurous smoke wafted into the air. She saw no vegetation anywhere while feeling a heated wind buffet her face. Sweat crept down her temples, and the pirate suit felt wet and sticky on her back.

"This burning world is giving me a headache," she stated, wiping the moisture from her brow. "Where is the base, anyhow?"

"We need to keep going until we come to some secret tunnels that lead inside," Zedok said over his shoulder as he continued down the slope. "There are three ways to the base. One way is down a chemical river, but we don't have a vessel to navigate it. Even if we did, there are still prominent ridges to scale after that. Those tracks lead to a cavern with steps dropping into one of the vast chambers," he said, looking into the distance.

"Then there's the route that leads to the base's main entrance. That's always heavily patrolled by robotic Radicans. It's also where they lift off and land their spacecraft. The guards there would capture us. So, I'm taking you through a tunnel where we can sneak up on them. It will give us the vital element of surprise."

Without warning, Zedok rushed off into a towering black rock labyrinth surrounding them. As she struggled to keep up, Cara almost veered into him as her feet skidded on the rough path. Once they were through the meandering gaps in the rock walls, the descent rapidly became steeper. There was a track of sorts between tall blocks, and someone had cut simple steps into the rock.

Cara and Zedok descended into hot, reddish smoke. As the visibility grew less and less, she caught her breath and coughed, "Zedok, I think I'm choking, and I can barely make you out through this dense smoke," she said, unclipping her visor and opening her jacket at the collar. "This is not the ideal place to wear a Radican officer's pirate clothes," she said.

Zedok halted momentarily and gestured to her, "Here, give me your arm, and I'll help you down," he reached up to her. "Would you like me to take turns carrying the Power Transmitters?"

"No way! I'll take care of the canister; thank you!" Cara said but grabbed his arm anyway, and they moved on.

Small loose rocks slid from under their boots and tumbled over ledges and through gaps in high rock walls. Finally, after about half an hour of running down slopes, they emerged from the stifling fog. The prominent ridge of rock was now behind them, and Cara was glad to discover the ground here was flatter.

Chunks of black rock cluttered the ground, so Cara chose one and dropped down on it. "Zedok! My throat's parched, and I'm desperate for some water. This place is terrible! How much farther is it before we reach the base?" she grumbled.

"We've almost reached the tunnels which lead into the underground chambers," Zedok said, passing her the drinking tube connected to their water supply. "The tunnels lead to all different areas inside the base, so I'll show you which one you'll need to go along!"

Cara almost spat the water out of her mouth. "Hang on! What do you mean, you'll show *me* which one I need to go along? You can't leave me wandering about down there on my own! So where are you going?" She stiffened and glared at him. "I hope this is not another one of your pranks. Although I don't like to admit it, I was almost starting to trust you!"

Zedock half huffed a laugh in return, "Cara," he said, "stop fretting. I ain't explained the next part of the plan yet. We certainly don't have time for sitting here, squabblin'. Now, if you've quenched your thirst, let's get moving before someone comes along and discovers us," he said, taking back the drinking tube.

Cara blinked at him, shot to her feet, and snapped, "No! I'm not going anywhere until you tell me your idea."

Zedok stretched up on his toes and squinted into the distance. Then, he pointed with one finger, "Look over there, and you'll spot some holes in the rocks. That's where the tunnels begin. Come on, and I'll explain what we can do when we get there," he said.

Retaking Cara's arm, he steered her onto some flatter rocks where it was easier to stand. Cara could barely make out anything Zedok pointed to and had no choice but to do as he told her. The last thing she wanted was for Zedok to leave her behind in such an intolerably fiery place.

She wondered again whether she had used poor judgment by trusting Zedok. After all, here she was in another dangerous situation. Her spirits sank at the thought, and she doubted being able to keep the PTs safe, let alone rescue her friends. Besides that, she'd broken a promise to her grandparents by venturing into the dangerous situation of a destroying planet. They'd probably never know. *Unless I die here,* she thought.

I can't think about family right now; or dying. This situation is not the same as my parents! The Radicans have a base here, and they wouldn't if the planet was dying right now. If it's dying, it's dying sometime in the future.

They made their way down to a lower path which led them through enormous high rocks on both sides. The height of them made the tunnels no longer visible. They hadn't been walking long, but fit as she was, Cara was aware of her aching legs from the effort of trudging through deep mounds of grit that drifted in the hot wind.

Zedok was ahead, and Cara forced herself to go faster, to catch up.

I don't want to get lost. Isn't that what everyone thinks happened to Dad? He got lost on the way back to the ship —

As she reached Zedok, she panted. "I'm sure it's growing hotter by the minute. I'm worried and annoyed at not carrying oxygen. I can hardly breathe!" She didn't mention that her thoughts were torturing her.

Without stopping, Zedok rummaged around in a small pouch attached to his belt and spoke to her over his shoulder, "You're in luck, I always carry a couple of oxygen pills on me, and you can have one if you like," he said passing one back to her.

"Thanks," Cara said gratefully, recognising the pill and immediately swallowing it. After a few seconds, she felt better and listened as Zedok carried on about the horrible planet.

"Carbonica will finally burn up one day. The Radicans are crazy to assume it will be years before it does. I ain't so sure, myself."

Cara came alongside Zedok. "Enough! Enough about the planet," she said harshly. "I can't stand thinking about it! Let's focus on the mission. We have to get in. Get the crew. Get out. Get back to the ship. Leave. Do it all safely, quietly, and fast."

Zedok nodded, laughing. "Yeah. Simple as that."

They tucked down their heads and screwed up their eyes as a sudden hot gust of wind-driven blackish grit blew between the towering boulders. Zedok had to wait for it to die down before he spoke again. "I know how we can get around without being seen much, and we'll blend in pretty well, especially now that your 'Radican uniform' is so scuffed and gritty. With some luck, we can do this."

Cara followed as he walked on. "I'm glad you're with me, Zedok," she said, unsure whether he'd heard her.

They went on farther to where the mounds of grit had become fine grey dunes. They could see they were much closer to the tunnels when they climbed to the top of one. "There are two tunnels," Zedok said as they continued.

They moved faster as the ground became firmer under their feet. But Zedok didn't take a straight path. Instead, he veered off towards some tall rocks for cover. Cara followed close on his heels. "Do both tunnels lead into the base?" she asked quietly, thinking someone might hear her now they were drawing nearer to the base.

"No, I'll show you which one when we arrive." Then, with Cara beside him, Zedok crouched and headed down the last long slope to the mouth of one tunnel. "Come on, it's this one," he said.

Cara glanced at the other, opening a little way off and asked, "Where does that one go?"

Zedok shook his head and chuckled softly. "Ah! That's the thing with humans. So curious. You always want to find out what's around the next corner, don't ya?"

Cara frowned, "Curiosity is a sign of intelligence. And it's a natural human trait."

"Well, I heard the only thing in that other tunnel is a bottomless pit. But I ain't Earthborn, so I didn't check it out myself," Zedok explained.

Cara rolled her eyes. "Very funny," she muttered.

Part FIVE

Chapter 39

Underground

"We'll have to duck," Zedok said as he led the way into the tunnel on the left side, "or we'll bash our heads on the roof."

As they stooped, looking into the darkness, Cara asked quietly, "How far to the base? Can anyone hear us coming in? It's hard to creep on this gravel."

Zedok moved forward a little farther inside. "Not far, and yes," he said, wiping sweat off his brow with his sleeve. "We should be as quiet as we can."

Unfortunately, the crunch of their steps echoed under each footfall as they went along the gritty floor. Any light that had been behind them died to pitch blackness.

"Have you got a head beam on your helmet, Cara?" Zedock asked in a low voice.

Her skin shuddered. "No, don't you have a light? Perhaps we should try a different way into the base," Cara croaked with a dry throat as she tried to focus her brain. "I don't like the darkness nor this heat pressing all around us. And that oily acrid smell. Where's that coming from?" she whispered.

He didn't answer her question. Instead, "I've got this pencil beam I brought from your ship," Zedok said, activating a tiny light on a wristband that shone feebly into the immense darkness. He lifted his arm so that the weak beam lit up their faces. Cara wondered whether she looked as nervous but as steely as he did. "This ain't a place you'd want to get caught in without a light, that's for sure," he said.

"It's not a place I want to get caught in at all. Come on!" Cara added in a loud whisper, giving him a nudge with the back of her hand.

They moved on with speed, deeper into the tunnel that bore through the black rock of the planet. It was slightly cooler down there than on the surface, but a sickly odour of sulphur and burning kept wafting around them. Cara froze.

"What's that?" She cried as something scuttled over her boot. She looked down and kicked out at it. And to her horror, in the feeble light, she saw the shadowy brown shapes of three or four scorpion-like creatures; their tail stings raised.

"Quiet!" Zedok whispered loudly, "We're gettin' nearer to the base, and there might be Radicans about!"

A shiver rippled through her as she steadied herself. Her hand dragged along the wall, knocking off the dust, and bits of the same black grit crunched as they ran. "Well, if there are no Radicans, here there're plenty of nasty little creatures around to make up for it," she whispered. "Ones that scuttle and have stingers!"

Zedok didn't respond as a warm, dry blast of air gusted down the tunnel, picking up the dust that almost choked them. Cara pulled down her visor. But that made visibility worse. Eventually, they came to an archway blocked by a metal door.

Zedok touched a keypad, and the door slid open to reveal another passage. This one was different. The lights embedded in the rock walls cast an ominous glow, an unnatural orange that made the walls look like burning embers.

A little farther along the passage, Zedok veered off to the left. "Now we need to grab ourselves something useful," he whispered.

Cara followed him but couldn't help nervously looking around. "Zedok, I'm not sure this is a good idea. This place looks like a place Radicans might come to often. Someone might catch us here."

"They will," he said rather unkindly, "if you keep yapping!"

Cara glowered at him behind her visor as another door slid open, and they entered a lower ceilinged chamber that contained hundreds of objects and strange pieces of equipment, the likes of which Cara had never seen before. She decided the time wasn't right to ask Zedok many questions about them. Her curiosity would have to wait.

"Stay put while I go get something," Zedok told her. Cara saw the Listroc disappear behind a thick translucent panel. She pushed back her visor to watch him but couldn't see what he was doing. When he finally emerged, he carried two items that dangled from holders. He said, "I take it you've done at least basic weaponry training already at that *elite* Cadet Academy," as he side-glanced at her.

Cara heard his sarcasm again, and though she felt her cheeks flush, she was sure the orange light would hide it well. "I'd hardly call myself a warrior. But, yes, I have done firing practice – not much, though," she answered, trying to quell the irritation in her voice.

"Here you are," he said, handing her the object. "It's a high-calibre laser weapon. Keep it out of sight but handy. You might need to use it before much longer."

Slowly, Cara put down the canister and took the weapon from Zedok. It wasn't small, but not as heavy as she expected. In no time, Zedok had strapped his weapon comfortably over his shoulder and was ready to go. "Come on, Cara; we daren't stay here too long. Like you said, someone is likely to come in. So, strap it on, and let's go!"

Cara looked at Zedok and then at the weapon resting in her hands. "Ah! I see," he said quietly, cocking his head to one side. "Would you like me to help you? And maybe give you a few quick instructions on how to use it?"

Cara nodded. "We never used this type of weapon. It's not a blaster, but I don't recognise it."

Zedok grinned at her. "I think you'll agree it's far more powerful than your teeny 3D model gun but fairly easy to use. Just make sure you ain't pointing it at me when you fire it."

With Zedok's help, Cara soon learned all she needed to know had the weapon strapped on, close at hand but out of sight. "Let's go, " Zedok pointed down the passageway.

Cara hesitated briefly, peering quizzically at the containers and piles of stuff around the chamber and stored on numerous shelves. "Where'd Radicans get so much stuff?" she asked.

Zedok cleared his throat. "It's what they call 'bounty.' Come on," Zedok snapped. "Time to find your crewmates."

Cara nodded and followed without another word. Unfortunately, the second they re-entered the passageway, voices sounded from the opposite end, and for a moment, they both froze. After a second, Zedok gripped Cara's hand and pulled her away from the chamber into an alcove. When two black-clad pirates approached, Cara and Zedok hid in the crevices of the rocky wall. Cara held her breath until they passed by, then waited for Zedok's signal. Finally, she heard him let out a puff, too.

"Phew! That was close," he whispered, still holding Cara's hand. "Come on! It's this way."

Keeping close to the passage walls, they fled as fast as possible to the other end, where more passages led off in various directions. "You can let loose my hand now," Cara smiled. "I think your Radican mates have gone!"

"Oh, sorry," he said, quickly letting go of her hand. Cara noticed his ears twitching, and the spiral earring caught the orange glow. It reminded her of a tiny burning flame.

Cara peered down one passage. "Do we go along here?"

Zedok pointed to the left-hand passage. "No. You go that way, and I'll go straight on with the Power Transmitters."

Cara stopped, narrowed her eyes, clenched her jaw, and grabbed Zedok by the front of his coat. "Just one skagin' minute. Stop right there! First, you'll tell me where this passage goes. And second, why are you trying to send me down it by myself?"

Zedok released himself from her grip, took her arm, and led her nearer the entrance. "That leads to an enormous cage where they keep their captives. I'm sure that's where your crew mates will be." He put his hand out towards the canister. "Now, give me the canister, and I'll—"

She pulled away from him and clutched the canister to her chest as if she were warding off some evil spirit. "Why should I need to give you the Power Transmitters now?"

"Cara, we agreed I would meet Shansa to negotiate the exchange of Power Transmitters for Valina and Debian. You three would join me; between us, we would fight them off and escape back to the SP8 with the Power Transmitters."

Cara's chest tightened, looking at him from beneath her brow. "I don't remember agreeing to anything like that! And while we're about it, who is Shansa again?"

"I told you, Shansa is the Grand Master's second in command. A Human female, like yourself."

In her mind, she could hear Captain Lydian's voice, *"Cara, your greatest weapon is to think clearly."* But, to her dismay, she realised she'd had no clear thoughts about what they should do.

She glared at Zedok. "That's the most stupid plan I've ever heard! Let's not forget that you're still my prisoner. But, by helping me save Valina and Debian, you'll be let off with a much lighter sentence – once we all return safely with the power transmitters."

Still clutching the canister, she said, "I admit, if it hadn't been for you, we wouldn't have got here. And I'm grateful for that. But I have to be careful how I handle things. You see that, don't you? If I lose these, the Galaxy authorities will probably sentence me to life in prison or worse."

Zedok turned away from her and dropped his gaze. "You still don't trust me, do you?" he said.

Cara's brow tightened. "I told you before, Zedok, you must earn trust and respect," she replied rather more sternly than intended. "Everyone must," she added to soften her tone.

Zedok hesitated briefly, leaned in close and, in quick breaths, whispered, "That's what I'm trying to do! I want to earn trust and respect. I want to rid myself of my reputation as a Radican pirate."

They both stared at each other in awkward silence to get their breath, but their gaze seemed to linger a little too long for Cara's comfort. "I know," she said, "but don't gape at me like that!"

As Zedok looked away, they heard a distinct crunching of footsteps from behind them. Cara grabbed Zedok's arm this time and pulled him into the first passage. Again, they hurried along until they could no longer hear footsteps except their own. They slowed to take a breath and stopped to listen. "Can your Listroc ears hear anyone coming up behind us?" Cara whispered, barely making a sound.

Zedok went straight into statue mode and stared at the wall for twenty seconds. "Nothing behind us, that's for sure, but I can hear sound waves vibrating from where we're heading."

Cara shot him a puzzled look. "Even I can hear those." The vibrations were so deep she could feel them in her chest. "But what's making them? Do you think it's anything to do with that disgusting smell?"

Zedok added a confused look to Cara's, "I'm not sure. But the noises ain't voices." He placed two fingers on his forehead and closed his eyes. "It sounds like the vibrations are coming from deep inside the base. Come on!" he said, opening his eyes. "We'll find out soon enough." And with that, they hurried along the glowing orange passageway.

"I can feel the slope of the passage taking us down deeper," Cara whispered between sharp breaths.

"Right," Zedok panted. "we're heading into the depths of the base. It's not far before we reach the cage. We got to be as quiet as possible. Might be guards down there."

Cara nodded in agreement and motioned to him to take the lead. They descended as the passage snaked this way and that. "Are you sure there's an end to this tunnel?" Cara asked as they jogged along, trying not to make too much noise. They both panted as they ran, and Cara felt a pain in her side. "A way back, you said the cage wasn't far. Yet, it seems to go on forever!" she puffed as the acrid smell cut into her lungs.

As they approached a sharp bend, Zedok stretched out a hand behind him – a signal to stop and crouch low. "What is it?" Cara whispered over his shoulder.

Zedok turned his head slightly. "I'm not sure. I picked up a strange sound, but it wasn't a voice. More like a hiss," Zedok whispered back to her. "Maybe some gas is escaping from the rumbling vibrations. Or a machine? Whatever it is, we'll have to go on if you want to reach the cage."

Cara braced herself for the unexpected as they peered cautiously around the bend in the tunnel wall. "There doesn't seem to be anyone around after all," Zedok whispered. They kept low.

"There's the cage," he said, pulling Cara towards him slowly, though not so much as she was entirely out of the shadows. Cara could see two figures huddled together in the far corner of a large cage and thought it rather strange no guards or gaolers were watching over them.

"Are those your crew mates in there?" Zedok asked in a whisper as Cara moved in front of him.

Cara screwed up her eyes. "I think they must be, but the light's poor, and I'm too far away to be certain."

Zedok stuck his head over Cara's shoulder to get a better view. "One of them is a Listroc, a female; I can tell by how still she is."

"Like a statue, yes. That's got to be Valina." Cara peered harder at the figures in the cage. "But I can't recognise the other one. Whoever it is, it doesn't look like Debian," she said.

CHAPTER 40
The Cage

A rank, acrid stench mixed with sulphur fumes hung dankly around the dullness of this other chamber. As Zedok and Cara stood in the shadowy entrance, they saw the dimly lit Cage bars, and when Cara scanned around, she didn't see anyone guarding the prisoners.

"I'm going to the cage door," Cara whispered, leaning into Zedok. "Stay hidden and keep watch! I might need you. If it looks like I'm getting into trouble, come and help." Then, since they had no proper communication system, she added, "I'll call out if I need you."

"What about the PTs?" Zedok asked.

Cara maintained her grip on the canister and looked at him, trying to read his expression. "I don't know," she said at last. "If someone attacks me while I'm over there—"

"If they attack you, they'll take you and the canister," Zedok replied in no uncertain terms and finished what she was about to say.

Cara closed her eyes for a moment, thinking and knowing she had little choice but to leave them with him. When she opened her eyes again, she placed the canister by Zedok's feet and jabbed his shoulder with her finger. "Make sure you keep these safe, Zedok," she hissed with a scowl and a piercing stare. "I'm warning you – No tricks, or you *will* regret it!"

With a grave expression, Zedok returned her glare and nodded tightly.

Then, with the same lowered tone as Cara, "I'll cover you. Don't fear, you can count on me! There's just one other thing you need to know," he added.

Cara straightened at his brief statement. "Go on! What is it?" she asked.

"It's the directions to the main chamber, just in case something goes amiss. You know, like if someone attacks me instead. You might need to save *me*."

Cara pressed her lips tight with an expression of alarm as she hugged herself and thought that getting lost here was probably one of the worst things that could happen. But worse still, if they captured Zedok, she'd need to save him and the Power Transmitters. She tried to concentrate while Zedok explained the directions.

"Take this other passage," he said, pointing to one fork in the tunnel. Then take another left fork, and you'll come to a sliding metal door. You won't need a code to open it but keep your visor closed so no one can recognise you."

Cara only nodded, trying hard to listen and remember.

Zedok continued. "First, go through that door, then to the one that leads to two narrow chambers. Then, go through the next door, into the righthand section," he continued, speaking with his eyes closed, recalling the directions.

He opened his eyes and touched Cara's arm, leaning closer. "Be alert at this place because it takes you to an alcove that leads directly into the central chamber."

Cara took a deep breath and frowned. "Okay. I don't know whether I can remember all that, so make sure you stick around, please!"

"Want me to explain it again?"

"No! There's no time for that. I have to go," Cara said sharply, edging slowly out of the shadows.

Before sliding carefully along the darkened part of the wall, Cara closed her visor, clenched her hand over the weapon, and crept silently towards the large cage. Her eyes darted every which way, and reflexively she occasionally touched the activation clip on the gun at her hip. This powerful weapon was more reassuring than a tiny 3D model laser gun. On full alert, Cara gradually crept closer to the captives, expecting a Radican to run out of the shadows at her every second. She thought it strange that there were no guards.

Though her visor was closed, Cara perceived a terrible odour, like rotting meat – a vile stench – that penetrated her nostrils and coated her throat, making her thoroughly nauseous. A pulsating hissing accompanied it, and she thought it must be foul-smelling gas escaping from the rocks. But she couldn't think of any gas that smelled of slaughter, blood, and rotten flesh. Cara continued moving cautiously, and as she approached the cage, she saw that the figure she had spotted from a distance was indeed Debian. She sat upright, her back to Cara, with Valina's head resting in her lap. Cara saw that Debian's bright orange hair hung untidily in jagged ends, spilling past her shoulders and sticking out at odd angles. Debian's beautiful tight braid was gone. *No wonder I didn't recognise her from a distance,* she thought.

When Cara reached the cage and stood hesitantly by the door, she looked around, still seeing no guard. Then, in a low voice, she called, "Valina, Debian? Are you awake?"

Valina's eyes shot open, and instinctively but wearily, she turned her head so that her sharp hearing picked up the tiniest sounds. Cara noticed confusion in her eyes and guessed that although her voice must have sounded familiar, Valina was perhaps afraid of having a tall Radican Pirate at the Cage door looking straight at her. When Cara saw her confusion turn to disappointment, she closed up nearer to the cage bars and tried to whisper a little louder, "Valina, it's me. It's Cara!" she said, pushing back the visor on her helmet.

By this time, Valina's sudden awakening had alerted Debian, and she turned to stare at Cara. "Debian, is that you? What's happened to your hair? I could hardly recognise you," Cara said, gripping one bar as she peered in.

The two prisoners continued to gape at her but did not speak or approach Cara. Instead, they gazed past her, fixated on the spot like dummies. Finally, in disbelief and running out of patience, Cara said, "Valina, is something wrong? Why haven't you tried to deactivate the cage-locking device? I'm sure it'll be easy for you!"

At that moment, Cara had the sensation of something behind her. It caused her to shiver, and the stench of slaughter became stronger. She didn't know why, but she felt a quick beating in her chest, much like fear, as she heard something again. It was a loud, scuttling noise accompanied by a stomach-turning hiss. Cara was aware the atmosphere had become thicker with that same penetrating sharp stench, and when she turned to discover what had startled her, she went rigid. A dreadful chill from scalp to fingertips left her fixed. It was there. It had been there all along, watching, waiting. There, perched on a ledge just behind her and poised to leap, was a hellish and ferocious Kaligiabeast.

Cara's throat tightened as a memory spiked in her mind. When she had seen the Kaligiabeast emblem on the spider-craft, she'd feared a great horror would come for her. And now it was here, in the flesh. Not an image on the underbelly of a Radican ship. *It's real. It's alive. It's an evil monster waiting to tear me to pieces!*

Its black, preying eyes seized upon her in the dim light, and its lips curled back to expose hundreds of hideous, long-pointed fangs. Cara saw some as long as her leg. It arched its back, and its head swivelled around in short jerky movements as it focused on her face. The giant sting in its tail quivered and pulsated as it drew a lynx-like head back into its shoulders and crouched.

As the beast reared to its great height, she felt the urge to scream to Zedok for help, but she knew there was no time. So instead, with all the force of her will, Cara made herself run towards it, going straight for the tail. She focused on it and saw where the grey, rippled skin joined the massive quivering sting. She smelled its poison, a thick gagging sourness. Her legs tensed to leap away, but there was no safe place to go.

Its hissing and rattling became louder, and Cara went for the weapon at her hip. Her fingers felt stiff and slow, and she fumbled with the activation catch. Her hands shook as she glimpsed the hideous beast edging towards her on the ledge. At last, she flicked off the safety catch and yelled, "Zedok, help! Where are you?" But before the monster could leap, she aimed the weapon and fired.

The powerful laser nudged the weapon away from the target and caught the base of the beast's thick tail. It uttered such a terrifying scream that Cara expected alarmed Radicans to overrun the place. She'd hoped Zedok was ready to defend her. Even so, he did not appear.

Meanwhile, the monster panicked, riled, and moaned in pain. Then, it gave a mighty convulsive jerk that caused it to topple into a gaping aperture on the other side of the ledge. In a few swift moves, Cara gymnastically scaled the ridge and cautiously peered down into the fractured rock. She saw the mutant creature so tightly jammed that it could only hiss and rattle.

She pulled shut her visor as a sickening stench wafted into her face from the oozing yellow puss in its deadly stinger. Again, she called out for Zedok, and again he failed to appear. *Where is he? What the skag's happened to him? Have they captured him, or has he run off with the skagin' canister?* She didn't know which idea was worse.

While her thoughts distracted her, without warning, the vile beast screamed, flicked up its injured tail and thrashed it wildly towards Cara. As it lashed through the air, it caught her leg and threw her entirely off her feet. Shocked but with little hesitation, she clambered back onto the ledge and aimed the weapon at the vicious head of the struggling beast, still wedged down in the crevice.

"It's time you took a long nap, you heinous mutant!" She said, repeatedly firing the weapon at its ugly head until the disgusting creature finally lay silent and still after a few more spasms from its body.

Cara didn't move until she shakily caught her breath and almost stumbled back towards the cage. As she did, she again heard rumbling vibrations around her and decided it was the same sound they'd heard in the passage earlier. *Was that perhaps the cause of Zedok's not coming to help?* She wondered.

She needed to investigate his disappearance, but Cara overjoyed that Valina and Debian had made it closer to the cage bars, sped across to them.

Her eyes sparkled as she leaned forward, her nose almost touching the cage's bars. "Hey, you two!" she said in a loud whisper, grinned and put her hands through the bars to reach them. Her crewmates did the same, and all three clasped hands tightly, blinking back tears.

"I'm going to get you guys out of here!" she told them.

"How did you . . . What are you doing here, Cara?" Debian asked, brushing pieces of loose orange hair out of her face. "And how did you find us?"

"Your suit's distress beacon came through, and of course, I came to save you. There's a guy, a Listroc. He wants to quit the Radicans. It's a long story. Anyway, he brought me here and helped me find you."

"A Listroc? But how? Who?" Valina asked in a weak voice.

"I haven't got time to explain right now. The Listroc – Zedok – is still here with me, I hope. He was supposed to be keeping a lookout while I came over to you, but for some worrying reason, he didn't show up when I needed him. Fortunately, I killed the beast without his help."

Valina and Debian listened to Cara but still didn't say anything, and she guessed they must both be in shock. "What I want to know is, are you both ok? It must have been terrible for you imprisoned in here like this. I hope those sk*agin'* Radicans haven't hurt either of you?" Cara said, screwing up her eyes and looking from one desperate face to another.

Debian said, "I think we're feeling better now that you've got rid of the vile monster." She put her hand to the back of her head, "I'm fine, apart from my hair that some horrible Radican girl, Shansa, viciously slashed off with a knife. She tried to interrogate me about who we were, where we'd come from and how we had arrived here. Then, when I wouldn't cooperate, she took a deadly knife to my plait and hacked it off."

So, Zedok told me the truth. There is a villainous female Radican pirate, after all! Cara thought, her eyes darting around the chamber, watching for intruders.

"Valina, though, is not so good," Debian continued with a tremble in her voice and looked down at her, where she'd slumped to the floor again. This time, Valina didn't even look up and said in a quiet, breathless voice, "The woman attached some device to my neck. Now I – can't think – clearly – I." She closed her eyes and said no more.

"When I refused to answer their questions," Debian continued, "they increased the power to the thing on Valina's neck. She screamed and writhed, then collapsed. I couldn't let them torture her like that!" Debian put her hands over her face and sobbed at the memory.

"In the end, I told them everything. Even about the TTC, which, I think by now, they've probably found. At least, the pieces of it."

"So that's why you haven't been able to deactivate the locking device on the cage door," Cara realised, feeling wrong about how she'd chided her crew mate earlier. Valina didn't respond.

"This thing on her neck gives her a kind of brain fog which stops her working things out," Debian said, wiping away a tear that ran down Valina's pale face.

"I don't know how to help her, Cara. Shansa tried to put a device on me too, but it dropped off, though I'm certain this one in Valina's neck has blocked out my healing energy. As a result, Valina is getting weaker by the minute. I'm afraid she might die if she doesn't get help soon!" she whispered.

Cara gripped and pulled at the cage bars as she peered at each of them. "If I could get you out right now, I would. But I can't. So, listen. The Listroc, Zedok, will come and calculate how to deactivate the lock and release you as soon as possible." She assured them, even though she might give them false hope since he was nowhere around. For a moment, nobody spoke, and in the silence, Cara noticed voices coming from the passageway. However, she didn't recognise Zedok's voice among them. Where was he?

She closed the visor on her helmet and straightened to her full height as two scraggly beings began walking across the chamber. They seemed to be in a great hurry. Cara turned her back on the cage and stood her ground, hoping these raggedy pirates were lowly enslaved people (like Zedok) and would assume she was an elite Radican assigned to the prisoners.

Cara guessed they'd spotted her when she could no longer hear them talking. As she gave them a haughty side-glance, Cara recognised the cube creature as a Gurlap. The other, an unknown skeletal alien, stank profusely of fish even from a distance and with her visor down. Both carried handheld blaster weapons at their hip, just as she did.

"You need to get out, brother!" the Gurlap shouted across to Cara. "This place is going to blow any time soon. It looks like the Kaligiabeast has already got buried by the exploding rock," he said, peering across to where the beast usually perched.

Cara tensed as she slid her finger closer to the blaster's activation key and reminded herself to breathe. Was Zedok nearby, waiting for a chance to pounce on them? *Please don't leave it too late!* She thought.

Fish breath came closer and leered into the cage at Valina and Debian, "Ha! If you're hoping to have a bit of *fun* with those two before you go, you'd better get a move on, boy!" he said to the accompaniment of chattering teeth and clicking bones from his armbands.

"Yeah! It looks like that blue one's already on its way out!" the Gurlap said with a crude laugh as he gawked at Valina.

Another loud rumble resonated through the chamber and startled the two wretches but, unfortunately, not quite enough to get them fleeing for their lives. Cara was going to have to pull rank on them. She turned the voice modulator back on. *If they try to attack me, at least I can defend myself, even if Zedok's not here to help.*

She turned sharply to face the ratty pirates. "You scabby pair have your orders, don't ya? So shut up and get on with it!" she yelled in an angry, deep voice made more menacing and loud by the voice modulator.

Entirely in character now, Cara turned back to face her crew mates. "And I don't want to hear any more from you. Whether we leave you here to die is no business of yours!" Cara laughed the evilest laugh she could manage.

Debian responded by joining in with Cara's playacting. "Ok! We won't make any more noise – we promise!" she said in a loud, shaky voice for anyone around to hear. "Please don't leave us here!"

It worked. Without another word or glance, the pirates turned and dashed away, suddenly intent again on getting across to the other passageway. Those creatures were gone, but in case others were within hearing distance, Cara pointed her finger at the two prisoners and yelled in the disguised voice, "Remember now, I'll be back for you. Or not!!" Followed by more evil laughter.

Reluctant to leave Valina and Debian in such an awful predicament, Cara raised her visor slightly, winked, and smiled at them. Then with her visor shut, she turned and strode out of the chamber towards the passage where she had left Zedok and the canister of power transmitters.

When she arrived, Cara discovered, to her desperation and anger, that Zedok and the canister were gone. Without hesitation, she set off to find him. Either to help him or, more likely, to give him a piece of her mind for leaving her in such a dangerous situation. *And what about the crystals and domes?* She dreaded to think about what might have happened to them.

Chapter 41

Alone

"*Where the skag is he?* Cara wasn't sure whether she was angry at Zedok for leaving her to fight the beast alone or anxious over what might have happened to him. She decided it was both. After all, she'd handled the Kaligiabeast just fine on her own. But whoever Zedok was and whatever he'd done before they'd met, Cara didn't like to think that Radicans might capture and torture him.

Did he try to make a deal with the woman — Shansa — in exchange for Valina and Debian? Or did he hand the PTs over to the Radicans for a reward? The more she thought about it, the more uncertain she felt.

Still, she knew she had to find him. It was her only choice. *How else will I free my crew mates and escape from this place?* She couldn't wonder whether or not to trust him. It was too late for that. *Right now*, she told herself sternly, *I have to remember his directions to the main chamber*. She didn't dare contemplate what she might do if Zedok had abandoned her.

Cara took a settling breath and tried to remember the directions as she moved on, repeating them in her head. First, she took the passage Zedok had shown her. After that, she turned left and approached the sliding door that opened without a code.

Cara ensured her visor was closed and the voice modulator turned on, but there was no sign of anyone. Not at the moment. Yet, as the sliding door opened, the deep rumbling came, and once again, the passageway shook beneath her feet. The farther Cara went, the hotter it became, with the smell of burning surrounding her.

She continued through the door until the passage brought her to the two small chambers. Then, after taking the righthand chamber as Zedok had directed, sure enough, another door awaited her. *So far, so good!* She thought as she went through and into an alcove.

By the time she reached that place, her heart was racing, and every muscle in her body was tense as she remembered Zedok's words: *"Be on the alert at this place – it takes you to an alcove that leads directly into the central chamber."*

Cara held her breath and peered cautiously from the alcove into the chamber. She nearly gasped when she saw its vastness and the many passages that led off in different directions. A small group of figures in the centre caught her eye, and she could see clearly that one of them was Zedok. Standing facing and talking to him was a female Radican pirate.

She must be the human Zedok said is second in command to the Grand Master. Cara remembered Zedok saying the woman was vicious that she was ruthless, and a witch. And now there was Zedok, trying to make a bargain with her.

We should have made a better plan than this! she thought as she kept close to the wall, hidden in the shadows. Cara took care not to hurry. She knew this was not the time for her to take risks. She was moving and breathing slowly and silently, but she was still worried that her pounding heart might be so loud that others would hear it.

Raising her gaze, she saw a line of four or five pirates standing on a slightly higher chamber level. They all watched fervently as Zedok and the woman talked. A high-backed chair resembling an elegant throne stood in the centre of the line of silent Radicans. The shapes of scorpions, pointing their golden stings upwards, were carved into the yellow metalled arms, and small bright spotlights placed all around it made the chair glimmer and shine. Cara silently closed the distance to get a better view. Although she was still not confident enough to trust Zedok, she dared not reveal herself.

Just ahead, a great rock slab jutted out, looking as if it had slid down the wall, perhaps recently. In the safety of the shadows and barely breathing, she crawled watchfully towards it. She felt a taut band of anxiety wrap around her chest, and she wasn't sure she was getting enough air. However, she continued crawling on all fours closer to the rock ledge and the pirates.

Just as she came up even with the slab, Cara's boot crushed a pile of loose grit on the floor, making a noise that carried in the chamber.

For an instant, she froze. *No one but me heard it!* Cara insisted with determination as she slid behind the fallen slab of rock. But then, as she waited, low to the ground and quiet, Cara thought of Listroc hearing.

Zedok probably knows I'm here now. Would he say something? Or was he really on her side?

But there was no time to wonder about that. Cara could now see the figure sitting on the massive throne. It was a giant Radican Pirate, resembling the armoured suit Zedok had dressed in when he tried to steal the Power Transmitters from Gorn's spacecraft. *Is it the Grand Master Radican suit?* she thought, *with that false giant head on top.* Whoever it was inside, she could hear him breathing like he wore a fallout mask. Around his chest, he wore a thick gold chain with a golden scorpion hanging from it.

That has to be the Grand Master Radican, and – partly obscured by the sweeping arm of his chair, she saw another figure who, for all intents and purposes, was trying to keep out of sight.

Tall and straight, the young dark-haired woman stood close to Zedok, and Cara felt the air was thick with a listening silence punctuated only by the ominous rasping from the Grand Master. The young woman's lips parted, and her eyes flashed.

"Well, Zedok, you've escaped after all! And I see you've even brought us the power transmitters. What a surprise! How'd you manage that, you clever boy?" she asked, a self-satisfied smile spreading across her face.

"Turns out I got real good luck," Zedok said, still clutching the PT canister and looking extremely pleased. "*Somebody* stashed these on the GPF space pod they chose for my prison transport. Can ya believe it? Then with very little trouble, I got the girl who was guardin' me to hand them right over."

The woman leaned in closer to him, "Excellent luck. We thought we'd lost you to the GPF prison system," she said, her voice slicing the air.

Cara's attention on the woman suddenly changed as a bellowing voice split the air. "Never give praise, Shansa. He doesn't deserve it! We cannot trust a Radican who gets himself so easily captured." The Grand Master Radican waved a giant hand dismissively at Zedok.

Zedok shuffled his feet and looked from Shansa to the Grand Master. "Grand Master. At last, I've brought the Kwaidem Crystals and Imperium Domes you commanded me to steal," Zedok said and hesitated slightly. "And so I'm here to ask a small favour of you."

Shansa gave a low, menacing laugh. "Ha! Listen to him, Grand Master. Zedok, we Radicans favour no one unless it's to *our* advantage. You should know that."

Zedok composed himself by standing at attention, ignoring Shansa and focusing on the Grand Master. "You have two prisoners held in the cage, sir," Zedok began.

"What of it, boy?" came the grotesque, unnatural voice of the Grand Master.

Zedok cleared his throat and continued. "Well, I've already captured their crew mate on board the SP8 the Galaxy Patrol Force gave me—"

Cara gaped in silence, fists clenched as Zedok bragged about taking her prisoner and hijacking the SP8. She couldn't believe what she was hearing, and *at some point,* she thought, *I'll need to intervene here.* But for the moment, she waited and stayed hidden.

" – and so, since they promised a reward plus a small ship and crew of my own if I stole the PTs, so I'm thinking these three little space cadets ought to do just fine for my first crew."

Shansa put her hands on her hips and made a '*Huh,*' sound in disbelief. The Grand Master only growled in Zedok's direction.

Shansa grabbed Zedok's arm and turned him to face her. "Let me guess what ship you want, Zeddie? That fancy little speed pod?"

Zedok nodded. "It's just about the right size. The girls can take turns bunking with me, right? Of course, I'll have to spend some of my booty gettin' the SP8 armed, but I'll have my well-trained crew to do all the hard work. You'll see, Grand Master, sir. I'll muster them into a right Radican gang and make them do my bidding. They've got useful skills and talents that'll benefit me and you, Grand Master Radican. They'll obey, or I'll force them to!" he said with a devilish grin.

Shansa threw back her head and roared, "Ha! You're a true Radican after all, Zedok. Welcome back to the gang!" she shrieked with laughter.

Heart hammering and still hiding, Cara went rigid with the weapon in her hand. Zedok's story and the plan he'd just revealed were shocking. But seeing him – right at that second – about to hand the PT canister over to Shansa was too much. Cara would not allow that to happen.

How will we ever get them back if he gives them away!? We're so outnumbered we won't even have the slightest chance!

So, keeping low, she inched her way with as much speed as she could manage. The muscles in her legs screamed, but she stayed low until she was close to the ridge where the Grand Master pirate sat on his garish throne.

Cara raised the ballistic weapon, remembering the slow-motion close-up hologram she'd watched of Zedok's helmet when a crewman shot at the suit and cut off his oxygen. Then, aiming carefully, she fired at the Grand Master Radican.

The result was like watching the hologram again. The person in the Grand Master Radican suit was seated this time, but Cara's shot hit the costume and shut off his oxygen just the same. He pulled off the helmet and threw it aside. Time seemed to stand still for seconds as everyone stared at the headless Grand Master, writhing on his throne.

Then something else happened. Like a lightning strike, a massive flame hit the chamber with a flash and a deafening blast. It threw Cara off her feet, and her weapon spun away under the falling rocks. She found herself near Zedok, who turned away from the blinding heat.

From her position on the floor, she saw more tongues of flame. They lapped and crackled around the edge of the chamber. Radicans ran screaming and yelling along the passages. Tongues of flame licked at them wherever they fled. Rocks cracked and sent splinters everywhere. One piece hit the back of Cara's shoulder. She yelled out in pain as another splinter pierced the leg of her trousers. A shard nicked Zedok's head, and a smear of blue Listroc blood trickled down his face. "We have to get out of here!" He stood up and offered her a hand.

But Cara was mad. She hadn't finished with him. As another flame leapt between a massive crack in the rocks, she yelled, "You left me to fight the Kaligiabeast alone!" and kicked out at Zedok's legs, which brought him down next to her. She reached out as if to hit him, but Zedok ducked away. He was back on his feet at once, and as she yelled at him for losing the power transmitters, he pulled her to him. "Be quiet, Cara!" Zedok said as he grabbed her around her waist and propelled her to the edge of the chamber.

Cara could still hear screaming and shouting as tongues of flame licked the walls, causing more Radicans to flee in all directions. Together now, Zedok and Cara dived under a jutting crag. Fortunately, they made it just in time to see the ceiling of the chamber crack. In trepidation, they reflexively ducked as the tremendous weight of the rocks brought the centre of the roof cascading down in front of them. When Cara peered through the overhanging rock, she saw it had protected them from the masses of falling debris.

Flames cut their way along the passageways and towards the chamber floor. More lumps of rock and black splinters crashed down. The whole chamber shuddered under its force, and Cara felt the searing heat as another enormous tongue of flame lashed in through the hole in the ceiling and shot to the ground.

The impact of the falling rocks sent shock waves through the chamber that knocked out almost all the lighting. In the dimness and growing heat, Cara imagined her clothes were baking to her skin and screamed as more stone cracked and began breaking apart. Following that, she heard an ear-splitting, rending groan, and they both ducked, trying to avoid being hit by more debris flying in every direction.

Cara saw, over Zedok's shoulder, two figures escaping in the flashes of bursting flame, running along a tiny smoking passage that was clear of fire. To her dismay, one clutched what looked like the canister of Power Transmitters. She wasn't sure, but for an instant, the way the one moved – incredibly and unnaturally fast because of artificial legs. *She thought that has to be Lieutenant CyJay, but who was that other person with him?*

Cara pulled roughly at Zedok's jacket, "Look!" she yelled over the noise, pointing to the vanishing figures. "Over there!"

"Come on! Zedok hollered, "They're getting away with the PTs!" For a moment, Cara hesitated.

"Come on! What's wrong?" he urged.

"I'm considering if I should trust you after everything you said," she replied over the din.

"I told lies to pirates! Just like we planned. Besides, you've already trusted me, Cara, so what have you to lose?" Zedok replied and grabbed her hand to pull her along. Cara didn't resist. What choice did she have?

As they raced towards the fleeing figures, without warning and to her horror, she saw a vast crack appear in the centre of the chamber floor. Cara tightened her grip on Zedok's hand and cried, "Jump!" With one mighty leap over the gaping crack, they tried to land on the only ledge of rock that stuck out from the wall in front of them. But unfortunately, as her feet hit the rock shelf, Cara's boot skidded on the gritty surface, and she felt herself falling back toward the fiery pit.

At first, Zedok gripped her hands tightly, but Cara could feel the heat under her feet as her right hand slipped free. Pieces of rock nearby broke away and crashed into the flames below, one after the other.

"Cara!" Zedok yelled with a gasp, "I'll pull you up! Keep hold of my hand!"

"I don't think I can much longer," she cried, casting a terrified look below.

"You can do this, Cara. You're strong! And I won't let you go. Now reach up and grab my other hand. Come on!" Zedok stretched out his hand as far as he dared, and Cara lunged at it. An unbearable pain went through her as her hand hit the ledge too far from Zedok's, and more grit fell and plummeted below. With a scream, she tried to grip the edge. When Zedok finally grabbed her hand, he held on tight. And then the Listroc went entirely motionless – he closed his eyes, and they both hung there, dangling over the fire.

Black terror was rising in Cara's brain. "Zedok!" she screamed, "Zedok! Please! Wake up and help me! What's wrong? Are you hurt? Please, I don't want to die like this! Help!"

She couldn't understand what was happening. *Has he fainted? Is he in a trance or something? Has something hit him in the head?* She held her breath and felt her hands beginning to slip, little by little.

Oh, Grandma, I'm sorry! I didn't think I'd die here. I guess nobody ever thinks they'll die, maybe. I didn't mean to lie to you!

Cara gave up hope when, to her amazement and with an unexpected force, Zedok suddenly leapt to his feet, pulling her along with him. Suddenly, Cara found they were standing cheek-to-cheek on the ledge, his arms wrapped around her, holding her safe.

They stood like that for a few seconds until he blinked and spoke slowly, like someone waking from a long dream. "Oh. Good. You made it. Wasn't sure that would work," he said, stepping back to look directly into Cara's eyes.

CHAPTER 42
The Bottomless Pit

As Cara and Zedok clung to each other on the ridge, boulders twisted apart and fell below with creaks, thuds, and thunderous crashes. There was no sign of Shansa or any other Radican pirates, everyone having run for safety.

"We need to move fast, or we'll lose sight of them," Cara sounded as shaky as she felt, but all she knew was to keep moving. "Hurry! Have you still got your wrist beam?" Cara unclipped her Radican helmet with shaking hands and dropped it into the fiery pit. "Give me the light," she held out her hand.

As soon as Zedok gave her the wrist band she stretched and altered it enough to attach it around her head. She switched on the light, and the weak beam faintly lit up the ledge. "That's better. Now we'll have both hands free to grab onto the rock face if needed," she said.

They moved faster and soon stood on solid ground at the passage entrance, but the disaster of the collapsing chamber had made Cara lose all sense of direction. "I can't work out where we are. Was this the entrance to the chamber?" Cara asked as they entered the remains of the alcove.

"Yes," Zedok answered. He didn't say more, but Cara followed, grateful he was there. Without him, she would have been nothing more than a cinder.

In the ever-increasing heat of the tunnel, sweat glistened on their faces as they hurried toward a sliding metal door. As they approached, Cara worried it might not open. And then what would they do? Would the sliding metal door trap them in here? Was there even another way out?

When the door slid open, it was an immense relief. The lights were still working, and the air felt cooler as they ran through the door, and it closed behind them. But there was no time to celebrate.

"This is where we split up," Cara said, turning to Zedok, who shot her a shocked and desperate look.

He jabbed a thumb over his shoulder toward the room with the cage. "Remember? Friends to rescue!"

Cara wiped the sweat off her brow with the back of her hand. "That's going to be your job, Zedok. Remember, you're the one who can work out how to deactivate the cage's lock mechanism. Am I right, or am I right?"

Zedok's brow creased. "And you?"

Cara's lips thinned into a small smile. "I will do what I set out to do on my original mission. Recover those skagin' domes and crystals. Now go!" she said, giving him a gentle push. "Get that cage open, and don't even think about turning my friends into Radican pirates! Meet me at the SP8."

As she moved off, she heard him say, "Cara, be careful!"

At first, Cara *was* careful, knowing this was the main way out of the base and that every pirate was running for their lives. But she didn't see anyone except the thieves in the distance carrying the power transmitters. They weren't running anymore, as if they had no reason to hurry.

They don't even know I'm after them. Cara hoped that gave her some slight advantage. Of course, it would be better if she hadn't lost her weapon. Still, as long as she had them within sight, Cara wouldn't give up.

Soon she picked up speed and ran as fast as she could manage, closing the distance. Then, panting and sweating, Cara came to the exit of the first tunnel and found herself out in the open again. She hesitated for seconds, struggling to catch her breath and watching as the pair disappeared into the second tunnel.

Carbonica continued to crack up and explode around her, and she heard equally loud noises overhead. She looked at the sky and saw a roaring cacophony of Radican spacecraft fleeing their crumbling world while the rumblings of the planet continued like an angry, dying beast. Cara spotted a huge battle craft arriving and realised the GPF had joined the action. It was firing its weapons and heading off the Radicans' ships.

According to Zedok, the second entrance led only to a bottomless pit. *So why are they running down there rather than to some ship to escape?* She wondered. Cara hurried forward and peered into the dimness, saw only more rocks and the sight of the thieves disappearing into the dimly lit tunnel. *Well, so much for that being a bottomless pit,* she thought.

But if those thieves were down that tunnel, bottomless pit or not, Cara was going down after them. Her weak light flickered as she ran, and the path was, at first, a much steeper drop than the first tunnel. Conscious of her boots crunching the grit beneath her feet, Cara slowed down, hoping nobody would hear her coming. Then, at the last second, the tiny light she wore showed Cara that she was about to step off an edge and into thin air!

She stood, wavering momentarily, adjusting her light and squinting down. *Steps*, she realised. *Steps into the bottomless pit.* She felt with one foot, found the first step, and then another. She took them slowly, one by one, trying not to imagine what might have happened had she not seen that first step.

Eventually, the steps ended in a path and opened out into another vast chamber lit again by orange light. Cara crept around the corner, staying close to the wall as she entered. The room was too dark to see much, except at the far end, where she could make out the shape of a large cylindrical object. Standing next to it was the figure of a tall man with his back to her.

Cara crept along the wall and then, keeping as silent as possible, moved slowly up behind the man. She watched his movements, and it looked like he wore a uniform or protective clothing. But then she saw the canister of power transmitters right next to him.

Without thinking about what might happen, she shouted, "Hey! Who are you? What are you doing? That is stolen property!" But when he turned to face her, the shock almost overcame her. "You!" she said in a gasping breath. "Commander Predaton!"

His expression as he recognised Cara was one of unprepared surprise, and at first, Cara was more curious than afraid. Yet as she watched him, she saw the familiar flash of fury in those stone-grey eyes that seemed to pierce right into her. His brow narrowed as he glared at her. "Oh, you'll not get in my way again, Cadet! I have possession of the Kwaidem crystals and Imperium domes now. Their power is my power, and it is not for such as you to question what I am doing."

He took a stride towards her, and Cara's courage diminished as his voice sliced the air and he glared at her. "Ha! A little wretch like you cannot stand against me. What I desire, I will achieve. Not only shall I be the Grand Master of the Radicans, but I shall be Grand Master of every living creature, planet, and galaxy in this universe."

Around Predaton's neck, Cara saw the golden scorpion catch what light there was, and she felt herself tremble at the sight. It seemed the gas in the chamber had thickened, and she gasped for breath. Though she tried to be brave, Cara knew it was a hopeless situation for her. She saw no mercy in Predaton's eyes and had no way to defend herself.

Cara gathered her courage and held out her empty hands. Then, in a clear, unwavering voice, she said, "Commander Predaton, sir. I have no weapon against you. It hardly seems a fair battle, you, a renowned leader, against an unarmed cadet. I've read about your amazing victories and achievements. You're already an admired and powerful leader, famous throughout the galaxy. So why would you need so much more power? You have everything," she said, hoping to soften him.

For a second, Cara thought he would explain the reason for taking them. He looked almost thoughtful when he cocked his head, became still, and looked at her. But then his wary eyes quickly transformed into narrowing brows. "You dare to ask me that? Nothing has changed between you and me. As of now, your career and your life end right here."

Then, without taking his eyes from her face, he yelled, "Lieutenant CyJay! Finish the job!"

In a flash, Cara saw Predaton head to the far end of the vast chamber and disappear into the dim distance. CyJay appeared just as quickly, a short way from her. He carried a powerful hand weapon in one hand and grabbed the canister of power transmitters in the other.

"My pleasure, Grand Master!" he called so loud that his voice echoed around the chamber.

Cara stood frozen in the open chamber with nowhere to hide, waiting for what she knew would come next. When CyJay raised the weapon and aimed it straight at her head, she closed her eyes. She wanted to scream, to cry, to run away! But what good would any of that do? She'd still be dead.

Cara heard the squeal of the laser beam as it left the weapon. She saw the bright deadly flash through her closed eyelids, ducked reflexively and covered her head with her arms. So, sobbing silently, she waited alone to suffer the final pain.

*

There was no pain.

The time stood still for Cara until she opened her eyes a crack. Squinting through half-closed eyes, she saw a black-gloved hand a few inches from her face that she recognised immediately. The deadly beam deflected away from her and back to its source. CyJay's weapon abruptly burst and exploded loudly into dust.

For seconds, he stood looking bewildered at the explosion's shock, and his cyborg arm seemed to smoke, possibly on fire. The Captain took aim at the little traitor, but CyJay saw her, turned, and fled into the shadows with quick but staggering steps.

Cara straightened, opened her eyes wide and reached for the bionic hand. "Captain Lydian! You saved me. You deflected the beam with your hand! How did you know I was here?" she sobbed.

Captain Lydian clasped her hand around Cara's for a second, then pulled it away. She took a small hand weapon from a sleeve holster and handed it to Cara. "Never mind that! Here, take this; you'll need it! There's no time to explain or to break down. Collect yourself now, Cadet Davis. You must save the PTs while I take my robotroop to sort out our Commander or, should I say, *the Grand Master Radican.*"

Cara hesitated. "Go, Cara!" the Captain said, gently slapping Cara's arm. "There's no time to lose. You can do this!"

Cadet and Captain broke apart, and Cara dashed after CyJay and the canister of crystals and domes. She raced out of the chamber and down another tunnel, almost catching up with him when she turned a slight bend. As he staggered and swayed along, Cara saw distinctly that his arm was still smoking.

This looks encouraging, she thought. *The Captain damaged CyJay more than I thought.* The Lieutenant visibly slowed as she closed the distance between them. And it was pretty clear what she needed to do.

Cara reached out an arm, hooked it around his neck, and then yanked it to pull him to a stop. His head jerked back, and Cyjay dropped to the ground, landing awkwardly on his back. Though Cara kept him on the floor with one foot on his chest, he kept an annoyingly fierce grip on the canister of power transmitters.

She pointed Captain Lydian's hand weapon at his face. "Let go of the canister!" she demanded. He moved his hands as if to let go, but as she bent to take it, CyJay twisted himself around unexpectedly. He landed a powerful kick straight into the small of Cara's back. She staggered forward and fell to her knees. Meanwhile, CyJay scrambled to his feet and away with the canister.

Cara stood unsteadily and attempted to go after him. He might be strong, but even now, Cara was faster. They were at the end of the tunnel when she caught up with him again. Cara grabbed him by the arm this time, spun him around, and smashed him in the face with a flying kick. Amazingly, it seemed to have little effect, but she yelled at him anyway.

"You will hand over the canister—" Cara began but was interrupted by a loud explosion on the right side of her head.

She couldn't understand what had happened, what the noise meant for a moment. Then she felt a blinding shaft of pain and realised CyJay had struck her with the canister. The severe pain in her head sickened her, and she clenched her jaw, which made the pain worse. But even as queasy black exhaustion flushed over her, Cara willed hard to stay conscious.

Large crimson spots dripped, spattered over her boots, and with each one, her senses faded. Cara watched dimly as the lieutenant, who still gripped the canister, hurried past her and back towards the chamber from where they had come. Everything else became a blur of hazy shapes as she staggered to the tunnel wall and vomited bile and saliva. Darkness threatened again, and she collapsed to the floor.

A sudden, loud cracking of rocks from somewhere nearby sent a piercing thought through her mind, bringing her awake. *Clear thinking will be the most potent weapon you will ever have.*

Cara was sickened with pain and the fear of failing, but she couldn't allow herself to be defeated. She turned, leaned on the wall and inhaled deeply. Clear thinking was, for the moment, impossible. She could still see CyJay gradually moving away, back into the chamber. "He's certainly not thinking too clearly," she said aloud, wondering, "Why's he going back in there?"

However, she knew she would go after him because even now, Cara's most apparent thought was to stop the Grand Master. But first, she had to finish off his minion, CyJay, and get those power transmitters back.

That clear and positive thought drove her on, and with adrenaline easing the pain a little, Cara's spirits rallied. Her heart raced in her ears, and with some difficulty, she raised her head and stood to her full height. Clutching up the hand weapon from where it dropped, she stumbled forward and stumbled after CyJay.

She thought *I should have shot him when I had the chance.*

CHAPTER 43

Battle for the Power Transmitters

As Cara approached the 'bottomless pit' entrance again, she kept at a low crouch, cautiously peering through a thin haze of yellow-tinged gas. She felt it catch in her throat and swallowed hard to prevent herself from coughing.

The gas wasn't so dense that Cara couldn't see through it, and from where she crouched, she could scan the entire length of the chamber without being seen. She noticed there was now no sign of Predaton. *So, why aren't they leaving on a ship? And why were they in this gas-filled cavern?* Cara wondered as her head throbbed with pain.

Advancing cautiously farther in, accompanied by the constant noise of explosions and eruptions, she caught sight of two GPF robo-troops strategically placed behind rock crags. Their positions suggested to Cara that Captain Lydian had ordered them to guard the entrance to prevent pirates from escaping.

Cara, reluctant to approach the armed robots, stayed hidden. She knew they were programmed to be alert to enemies approaching. But, while still in her black pirate costume, Cara thought they might mistake her for a Radican and capture (or kill) her. So, leaning back on the chamber wall, she stayed out of their sight for the moment.

As she glanced around, Cara noticed that the little wrist light Zedok had thought to bring was still functioning. Dim but functioning. This one small thing conveyed a bit of normality and hope to her otherwise utterly insane situation and revitalised her spirit. *I have to keep going. I just have to,* she thought.

Discreetly moving away from the wall, she kept low to the ground and well away from Captain Lydian's guards. She ventured out until she could see the Grand Master and CyJay at the chamber's far end. What she saw mystified her.

What the skag!?

Cara screwed up her eyes to focus better, but it hurt her face too much, and for a few moments, staring hard into the distant section of the chamber, she couldn't work out what she saw. A cylinder-like contraption stood on a raised block of solid rock, pulsating with blue light constantly encircling it. The size of it was much bigger than her canoe back home on Earth, but for her life, she couldn't work out what the cylinder machine was.

Realising she was probably not safe where she stood, she slowly moved to conceal herself behind some nearby rocks. As she ducked behind them, Captain Lydian came into view. Energised from the relief of seeing the Captain, Cara quickly crept closer. In a low whisper, she called out, "Captain!"

Cara came to an abrupt halt when Captain Lydian, whose reflexes were on a high taut, swung around with such speed that Cara immediately stared into the connector of an extremely powerful blaster weapon. She stopped breathing until the Captain lowered the weapon and exhaled a long breath of relief. Lydian's brow creased, and with thinned lips, she groaned, "You never do that! Creeping up on us. I might have killed you!"

Cara's throat tightened as she held back tears. "Sorry, ma'am, I have no communication tech in this disguise," she replied.

A laser blast hit the top of the rock where they were shielding, and they dropped to the floor for cover as the robo-troops regrouped. They stayed low, kneeling behind the boulders.

"Well, next time, Davis remember tha – what's that dreadful gash across your cheekbone?" the Captain said all in one breath.

"A present from CyJay. When I tried to grab the PT canister, he hit me with it!" Cara said. "And escaped again," she added in a deflated murmur.

"Well, I think it's time we taught the Commander and his nasty little lieutenant that we're not giving up! Don't you?" the Captain said in a firm tone. Cara nodded her agreement. Even that hurt, and she winced.

"But first, we must do something about your injury. Come here!" Captain Lydian said and raised her bionic hand toward Cara's face.

Not knowing what to expect, Cara recoiled from it and cried in an anxious tone, "What are you going to do?"

"Don't be afraid. I'm tending to your wound. I'll program my hand to direct regenerating stimuli beams into your injury. It often comes in useful to be a little bit cyborg. Now sit still!" Captain Lydian replied assertively. Cara went rigid and shut her eyes as the Captain's bionic hand gently touched the gaping wound, and for a moment, she felt something like a cool, soothing breeze brushing her cheek.

"There! All done!" Captain Lydian said.

The pain was gone. Cara put her hand up to her face to touch the healed skin of her cheek. "How did you…?

"There's no time. We have a battle to win and a Grand Master Radican to capture! Come on!" the Captain started forward, moving among the standing rocks to get closer to Predaton, CyJay and the power transmitters.

Cara followed, and when the thing she'd seen before came back into view, she pointed, whispering, "What's that enormous cylinder thing over there?"

The Captain looked in the same direction and said, "It's the experimental Time Travel Capsule. Recognise it now? It's the same one that Valina and Debian travelled in to save you. When it crash landed here, the Radicans were no doubt eager to capture and restore it. Hopefully, they've failed to repair it properly."

As she followed the Captain, Cara heard the loud sounds of rumbling and cracking rocks around them. She felt the heat building by the minute, and the ever-increasing smoke and gases engulfing the chamber made her cough. "We must capture and arrest Predaton," the Captain said. "After all he's done, I cannot allow him to escape."

Some movement caught the corner of Cara's eye, followed by a loud rending sound. An enormous black rock came crashing down from one side of the ceiling, followed by a ferocious flame lapping across the chamber. Like the others, this chamber was collapsing. Carbonica was well on its way to destruction.

It was a fearful reminder that their time was limited, and she wondered whether Zedok and her two crew mates had successfully escaped yet.

Cara heard a resonant humming above the turmoil and looked to see what it was. Strange bands of bright blue beams encircled the large cylinder from one end to the other as though the contraption was coming to life. "Oh no!" Cara cried, pointing in the humming tube's direction.

"Fire! " Captain Lydian called to her robotic squad. "Fire at it now! Don't let it take off!"

Although holding a hand weapon, Cara stood there, watching and feeling helpless. Her weapon hadn't the range to hit the TTC. Then she spotted Predaton sneaking up behind the Time Travel Capsule, followed by Shansa.

"Commander Predaton and that Radican woman! There!" Cara yelled. Captain Lydian dashed forward to intercept the traitorous commander, with Cara following.

More debris fell from the ceiling, and everyone scrambled to avoid rock shards hitting them. In doing so, Cara and the Captain were now close enough to the TTC to glimpse Predaton's face. As he peered out from behind, narrowed eyes, his dark, murderous gaze focused on Captain Lydian. His whole countenance had morphed into a grotesque, evil being. In a perverse, manic voice, he screamed, "You'll never capture me, Sarah Lydian. You're as useless and weak as ever. Here's a shot to take off your other hand!" He paused and aimed at the Captain.

Before Predaton took his shot, several things happened. First, the injured cyborg Lieutenant came staggering out of hiding, following his Grand Master. Cara immediately noticed that CyJay was still carrying the canister of power transmitters. In his confusion, CyJay moved directly into Predaton's line of fire. The shot meant for Captain Lydian took the lieutenant's arm off at the shoulder, causing the canister to jump wildly across the chamber floor as he screamed.

Cara leapt immediately to snatch up the canister while staying low to dodge the crossfire as best she could. She grabbed at it, but the canister slid away until it became wedged between two large pieces of black, burning rock.

Only a few inches away from it, Cara stretched out to reach the canister's handle. "Got you at last!" she cried, clasping her hand around it. But before Cara could get to her feet, she heard the most spine-chilling scream and felt roughly tackled from behind. She held desperately onto the canister as whatever had jumped on her screamed and pinched at her back. "I'm not letting go. I have them at last, and I'm not letting go!" she yelled, flipping herself violently, then scrabbling to her feet and dodging away.

Although dazed, she steadied herself and, to her horror, realised that what had grabbed her was CyJay. Or what was left of him. He struggled to reach his feet, with only half a cyborg arm remaining. Besides that, he'd gone mad, judging by the crazed expression on his face. His red uniform was blackened, in tatters, and an utter mess.

CyJay lunged toward her with another horrible inhuman scream and began snapping his jaws as he came closer. Cara realised then what the pinching had been. *He was biting me!* It was also apparent that he wouldn't stop attacking as he got to his feet and came closer, still ready to bite.

Cara, already stable on her feet, yelled a warning and fired her weapon to stop him as he rushed toward her. The squealing beam hit him at blank range, and she felt the tension in her body uncoil as it stopped him dead in his tracks.

Cara couldn't resist giving him a hard shove with her foot as she ran by. *Just making sure he's dead,* she thought. *Not going to jump me again, are you, Lieutenant?*

A great blast of hot air shot through the chamber and flung Cara off her feet while more small splinters of sharp jagged rock sprayed down onto her. She fell backwards, still gripping the canister, then scrabbled to her feet, knowing she could *not* risk losing them again. Through the chaos, she looked for Predaton and Shansa near the Time Travel Capsule. But to her dismay, there was no sign of them. Worse, the TTC had gone too.

"Captain!" Cara cried, "Captain, where are you?" The rumblings and blasts continued, but no one answered as she searched the rubble. Pieces of some destroyed robo-troops lay scattered all around, and, to Cara's horror, next to them lay a motionless Captain Lydian.

Chapter 44

Race to Escape Carbonica

Cara shot over to where Captain Lydian lay face down. She knelt beside her but could find no sign of a wound from Predaton's weapon. Instead, Cara noticed that tiny shards of sharp rock had littered the Captain's shoulders, and when Cara touched her head, the warm sticky substance that matted her blond hair smeared her fingertips. She gently rolled the Captain onto her back and supported her head. Cara did not know how she or anyone else could escape this turmoil.

"Captain! Captain!" she cried frantically, "Please wake up. We must get out before this planet kills us." Anxiously, Cara pressed two fingers to the Captain's neck and found a pulse. She breathed a sigh of relief. The Captain was alive!

Even though Cara was sturdy and athletic, she was thinking clearly now. She knew she could not safely carry the Captain and the PT canister out of the collapsing chamber. Most of the Captain's robotic personnel lay buried beneath rocks, broken or powerless, unable to be of any help. She stroked the Captain's forehead and tried again to bring her back to consciousness. The chamber's insides were like a furnace, and Cara was desperate. Finally, she choked back tears, placed her hands on the Captain's shoulders and cried, "Sarah, Sarah! Oh, please wake up, Sarah!"

For a moment, Cara closed her eyes, bowed her head near Sarah Lydian's face and felt short, thin breaths touch her cheeks. Although the Captain lived, Cara was powerless to help her. "I don't want to leave you here," she said as tears ran down her cheeks. "But I have to save the crystals and domes. Please, wake up, Sarah!"

Another loud blast made Cara cringe and lean over the Captain's body protectively. Then, in the brief silence that followed, a sophisticated voice whispered, "Davis, is that you?" Cara sat back, opened her eyes, and looked down to find Captain Lydian's eyelids flickering open.

"Oh, Captain, thank goodness you're awake. We must get out of here. Do you think you can stand? Come on, I'll help you, and then you can lean on me." Cara put her arms under the Captain's shoulders, and they both got to their feet with a bit of a struggle. Then she placed one of the Captain's arms around her shoulder for her to lean on.

Although Captain Lydian was in pain, she gave Cara one of her beautiful smiles and said, "I see you've got the PTs safely in hand. Well done, Officer Davis! Now please help me out of this awful place, will you? It's becoming hotter than Venus by the minute."

As they set off, two figures emerged from the thickening smoke as Cara and the Captain approached the tunnel's opening. But, unfortunately, the fumes were so dense neither of them could make out who the people were.

"I sincerely hope those are not Radicans waiting to ambush us," Captain Lydian said in a low voice. "Give me your weapon, Cara. I'll still need to lean on you for support, but I have more firearms accuracy than you have."

Cara gladly handed the weapon over to her commanding officer, and they cautiously approached the figures. However, as they moved closer, the figures turned towards Cara and the Captain, who raised the weapon in her bionic hand and pointed it at them.

When the distance closed between them and the group, Cara saw one of them levitate slightly. "Don't shoot, Captain," she said, "It's Debian!"

Cara smiled when she saw it was Zedok next to Debian, carrying Valina over his shoulder. "And that's Zedok – my prisoner – carrying Valina."

The Captain lowered her weapon as Zedok peered back with wary eyes and said, "Listen, Valina here is very sick. They put this sonic gewgaw on her, and we Listrocs can't stand direct contact with that sort of sonic weapon. That's what the device is on her neck, but I ain't got the medical tools to get it off. She'll die if we don't get help for her soon."

Though Cara was relieved to see them all safe, and concern for Valina overwhelmed her, there was no time for greetings and questions. They all needed to get off this planet.

"Maybe you can heal Valina, Captain," Cara suggested, "with your hand."

Captain Lydian shook her head. "No. I can't risk directing regenerating beams into her while she still has that device attached. They could collide with the sonic wavelengths and probably stop her heart. So, in the meantime, we must all do our best to get her to the nearest ship and medics."

Cara realised their situation was worsening every minute they remained on Carbonica. In her unconscious state, Valina could not even sip water. Zedok would have to carry Valina's dead weight to the battle craft, and the Captain was still in pain. One thing Cara hoped for, more than anything, was that she could trust Zedok not to escape.

They all took a slug of water and prepared to move on. As the group emerged into the open terrain, Cara felt a certain pang of something tighten her throat. The familiar stab of fear grew, knowing the planet was seriously on the verge of blowing up and taking them all with it. Then, alarmed at how quickly the destruction of Carbonica was catching up with them, she exhaled a panting breath and turned to the Captain, "May I ask you, ma'am, where are we heading?"

Captain Lydian screwed up her pallid face and, in shallow breaths, said, "Mr Gorn landed his Zeg-Mar down in the same quadrant as the SP8. We have to get to Battlecraft 24 as quickly as possible, but it is in orbit by now."

The Captain closed her eyes for a moment, and Cara waited for her to continue. "But if the destruction worsens, Gorn can't stay much longer. And now I'm afraid none of us has any functioning communication to inform him of our position," she said.

Cara knew that only too well. She'd had no communication right from when she and Zedok left SP8. *Having no means of communication was another one of my stupid mistakes!* she thought with embarrassment.

Before Captain Lydian gave the order to move off, she gripped Cara's arm tightly, showing either that she was in pain or shock, and Cara felt helpless towards her. She was even more perturbed when they finally emerged into an area where several solar vehicles lay strewn across the ground in shattered pieces. The Radicans must have destroyed them from the sky, and Zedok concluded in a grim tone to her they were entirely irreparable. So, like the rest of the group, Cara had to face that the only way back to Gorn's ship was on foot.

As they set off across the hot and gritty landscape, they all struggled, including herself, who supported Captain Lydian while carrying the precious canister of crystals and domes. "Would you like me to carry the canister for you, Cara? I can still carry Valina and hold it in my other hand," Zedok ventured to ask.

"No way!" Cara said in a thin-edged tone, staring straight at him. "Now that I have them at long last, no one is carrying them except me until we've locked them safely on the ship! Besides, it's not exactly protocol, you know."

Zedok sighed. "I guess, after everything, I forgot about being a prisoner. Just wanted to help."

"Well, you are helping. You're carrying Valina and saving both her and

Debian's lives. So you've helped a lot!" Cara said with a huff as they all trudged along. But she frowned and stared ahead, cutting off any further talk. The last thing she needed just then was a discussion in front of the Captain about all the responsibilities she'd assigned to the Radican pirate who was supposed to be her prisoner! She'd prefer the Captain didn't know about Zedok's programming and then piloting the SP8 independently. Or how he'd run off with the PTs to offer them as a bribe to the Radicans, to name a few.

A weariness crept over Cara, but fear drove her on. It could be touch and go by the time they reached the ship. Already she saw that vast chunks of the planet were exploding and catapulting away into space. Soon, the whole thing might spin into the atmosphere and burn up, or worse, destroy itself in one almighty humongous explosion, taking everyone and everything with it, including the precious Kwaidem crystals and Imperium domes. Cara knew in her heart that she had not entirely completed her mission.

CHAPTER 45
A Deal's a Deal

Cara squinted across the blackened vastness of what remained of Carbonica's foreboding terrain and glimpsed a speck on the horizon that looked like a vehicle advancing with speed towards them. Its image grew as it closed the distance between herself and the exhausted group. She had never been so glad to see a solar truck, especially as it had taken them over an hour to get this close to the Zeg-Mar5. Gradually, they all slowed down to watch the truck approach.

"Who do you think sent it for us?" Cara asked the Captain.

"Golbat Gorn, I suppose. They must have detected our images as we came into range. Now come on, let's go! Gorn's not likely to sit around waiting much longer before the whole place explodes," Captain Lydian said, wiping sweat off her face and moving haltingly towards the truck as it stopped. Cara could see she was in pain.

A member of Gorn's crew assisted them aboard, and they finally set off for the ship. Captain Lydian, who had maintained the weapon on Zedok the whole time, handed the gun to Cara and ordered her to guard the prisoner in the back of the vehicle. They road in silence, now approaching the Zeg-Mar5 at speed. Debian supported Valina in the middle seat, and the Captain sat in the front with the driver. All they could do was hope that the medics on Gorn's ship would stabilise Valina and transport her to the sickbay on the battle craft in time.

Cara felt a strong urge to thank Zedok, for he had been a lot of help up to now. Of course, it wasn't her place to say (or probably even to think), but she felt the Captain owed Zedok thanks and an apology, too, at the very least.

And now I have to sit here and hold a blaster on him. If only there were time to explain everything to the Captain. Maybe she'd see that Zedok could be trusted. But can he really be? He saved my life. All our lives, in a way. But he's also a criminal, and I can't forget that. If he could have got away, he would have taken the PTs when he invaded Gorn's ship, and Predaton would have them now.

But her thoughts were short-lived when the Captain turned to her and said precisely, "Cadet Davis, once we arrive at the Zeg-Mar5, Zedok will still be your prisoner. Let us not forget his crimes, even if he did help us, and we are all grateful for that. Your orders are still to return to HQ with him and hand him over to Galaxy Law Enforcement. The rest of us will return to New Dawn Space Station as soon as we're all well enough. I want you to await further orders from me once you have confirmed the GLE has taken Zedok into custody."

Cara didn't respond. She risked a glance at Zedok, who sat at the back, hugging his knees. When he saw Cara looking at him, he turned his gaze to the floor.

*

As they arrived at Gorn's ship, Cara watched the portal open so that the truck drove straight in as the portal closed right behind it. When they boarded, Gorn arrived to relieve Cara of the canister personally.

"I will take these and secure them myself, Cadet Davis," he said. Cara was surprised to see that he smiled at her.

"I happily give them to you, Mr Gorn. And I thank you, sir, for taking them." He smiled wider when she added, "I hope I never see them again!"

Stretchers and medics arrived to take Captain Lydian and Valina. While the crew made final preparations to take off immediately, Cara wearily took up the blaster and a wrist communicator before turning to power-cuff Zedok, ready for the brief journey to SP8. She noticed how woeful he looked as he kept his eyes down.

"The solar vehicle's power is now too depleted," Gorn explained as Cara and Zedok prepared to be lowered back to the surface. "And at this point, it is slightly safer to walk. But don't take too long. There isn't much time left. Maybe only hours. Get to your ship and contact me from there if there's any problem. And to you, Radican, I hope you are as rehabilitated as you seem. I assure you that some of us will speak up on your behalf because of what you've done today. Good luck, Officer Cadet Davis."

They began walking toward the SP8 while the Zeg-Mar5's thrusters began to fire behind them.

"I . . . I'll bet we're the last ones on the planet," Cara said. Zedok looked down at the power-cuffs as he walked quickly beside her. He didn't reply.

She wanted to apologise to him but said uncertainly, "I – I have to do this, Zedok. It's my duty. I'm an Officer Cadet and must obey orders."

Zedok's lilac eyes grew dark. "Do you still think you need to point a high-powered blaster at me? You have serious trust issues, don't you? I mean – Skag you, Cara! After everything we've gone through together?"

To her dismay, Cara found her eyes beginning to sting. She couldn't remember hearing Zedok swear before, especially not at her. On turning to study him, a flicker of uncertainty touched her, and a faint warmth rose to her cheeks. The only thing Cara could think to say to him was, "We have to hurry," but she tucked the weapon into her holster.

She felt awkward that she was alone again in Zedok's company, and some of what they'd both been through seemed almost unreal to her. Even after all they'd survived together, Cara was wrestling with doubt. After the swearing incident, they walked in silence. Cara kept her eyes on the SP8 up ahead. How she was going to cope with the long flight back to HQ together, she didn't know.

Perhaps she wouldn't have to. A seed of an idea was already growing in Cara's mind. But would it work? She puzzled over details as they grew closer to the speed pod. When they had almost reached the pod, Cara stopped walking. Zedok stopped after a minute and turned. "What?"

But Cara ignored his remark. "Wait. Come here," she ordered. He stared at her, not moving.

"Come on," she said. "If we get any closer to the SP8, its automatic security will start recording us. Come back here so it can't see us."

Zedok paused for another few seconds, then walked back to where Cara stood. "What?" he repeated.

Moving in closer to him and screwing up her face, Cara said, "I just can't make out which part of you is telling the truth or even which side you're on. Did you mean what you said about forcing Valina, Debian and me to become Radicans and use our unique skills to work for you?"

Though Zedok opened his mouth to speak, she didn't let him and continued, "Or did you mean it when you said that you don't want to be a Radican and you only wish to escape from them?" Cara glanced sideways at him and narrowed her eyes. "I still can't make you out, Zedok! I'm not completely convinced that I should trust you."

Zedok levelled and stared into Cara's eyes, "Cara, I'm tellin' you! I had no mind at all of usin' you, Valina, or Debian to do bad stuff for me. But I needed to play for time until you got to the chamber, so I lied to Shansa that

I was still a loyal gang member coming back with the PTs and bargaining for my reward, see?"

"Then what?" Cara asked with knitted brows.

"Then what? *Then what?*" Zedok paused, dark blue with anger, before answering almost all in one breath: "Then I would have released your crew mates. Then helped them to safety! Then I'd have helped you, your Captain, and crew get to the nearest ship. Then apparently, I'd get sent off with you to get locked in your prison system. Then – Well, then I suppose I'll rot there. Never mind that we made a deal, and I stuck to my part of it in every way. And then more!"

Cara stared at him wide-eyed and slowly shook her head. Her emotions were dangerously near to the surface again. She couldn't even imagine how Zedok had managed to save her friends and escape from all those Radicans. With a pang, she realised she'd never be able to hear him tell how he'd done it. *Not without it being part of 'official questioning.'*

From what she'd heard about it, Cara felt her scalp prickle at the thought of spending any time locked away on Canton. She hated the idea of anyone spending a moment on that prison planet, least of all Zedok. And there wasn't much time to think, but Cara understood what she needed to do.

She took a step back and looked Zedok in the eyes. "You're still my prisoner, so *I* decide what to do, right?"

"Yes, Officer Cadet Davis," he said, glaring back into her eyes. His expression changed then, and he became less angry and more serious. Before Cara could blurt out her idea, Zedok suddenly said, "But. What do you think about us changing places?"

It threw Cara off guard. Her brow tightened, "Changing places? What are you talking about?"

"What if you became my prisoner instead? You said you wanted adventure. So, what's say we take the SP8 and get out of here together! We could make everyone think I'd kidnapped you." Zedok's voice rose excitedly, "We could find our own adventures! As long as we never reactivate ole Barnie the AI, they'll never find us. I know how to fix that pod up so nobody'll identify it as GPF." He leaned in closer to her, "What ya" say, Cara?"

Cara studied his face and considered his idea for a minute. His words half convinced her, and when she thought about it, she knew that Zedok would be a good travelling companion. For a few seconds, she found the idea almost irresistible.

She would be free to explore the galaxies, see new planets, discover unique creatures, and meet new beings. She and Zedok together. Away from the dull routines of New Dawn Space Station. Away from her friends, Valina and Debian, who had risked their lives to venture out and save her. And she thought of her grandparents. You can't steal a Galaxy Patrol Force speed pod and then 'pop back home' to Earth to visit the folks. – *Which life should she choose?*

Cara smiled, then rolled her eyes at him. "Ha! Trade places. What kind of crazy idea is that?" she asked. Then she paused and became serious again. "No, Zedok, I will not be your prisoner, and you will not be mine. You saved my life back there in that fiery pit. And you saved my crew mates, and whether she'll admit it or not, also my Captain. So the least I can do is set you free, as I promised. After all, a deal's a deal."

Zedok's brow creased, and then his eyes and mouth opened wide in surprise. As he struggled to speak, the planet's surface rumbling in the near distance sounded again, and the ground shook ominously.

Cara put up her hand and became stern. "But, promise me something. You promise that as a free man, you will endeavour to make something of yourself – something good, something honourable. I've seen that, deep down, you're brilliant and also good. Maybe you can do something that helps others. I don't know."

"B-but, Cara. How will you—?"

"They may catch you someday, but I'm willing to give you a second chance, Zedok," Cara said as she deactivated the power cuffs on his wrists. "But we've got to hurry. I have to run back to Gorn's ship before they take off. Otherwise, they'll leave me behind.

Zedok hesitantly took Cara's hand and, with a quiet gasp, said, "I don't know how to thank you, Cara. But I tell ya' what! I *will* make something better of myself. I promise. I might even make you proud."

After a pause, she released his hand and unstrapped her weapon. "Here, take this," she said, passing it to him. "It has to appear that you attacked me so that you could escape."

Furrows creased Zedok's brow, "I think I know what you mean, Cara. But I don't think I'm gonna like this part one bit," he said, faltering as Cara pushed the weapon into his hands and took a few steps back.

"Okay, hit me. Then move back a little, adjust the power to the smallest micro setting and shoot me in the arm," Cara said flatly.

"I don't . . . I can't even – ." Zedok's protest was cut short by a tremendous explosion. It lit up the sky and set the ground under them to rumble more fiercely.

"Do it!' she yelled, "before we're blown into the next galaxy!"

Zedok swallowed hard, screwed up his face and looked at her. Cara took a deep breath and said, "Make it look real, please."

He pulled his arm back and punched her in the jaw hard. Cara's head jerked back, and as she rubbed the sore spot, Zedok looked at the weapon in his hands, carefully checked the gun's power control and adjusted it to the lowest possible setting. Then he stepped back and aimed it at Cara's upper left arm.

"Are you sure about this?" he said in a shaky voice.

"If you don't hurry, Zedok, I'll jump into the SP8 myself and leave you on this crumbling hellscape to fend for yourself!" she shrieked.

It surprised Cara when the sharp blue pencil beam hit her, though the actual pain was no more severe than a few nasty bee stings all at the same time. "*Ouch!*" she cried and clutched the top of her arm, where she felt a tiny hole in the fabric and a slight burn on her skin.

"Cara, are you ok?" the young Listroc said as he dashed up to her. "Can you get back to the Zeg-Mar5? Are you sure you won't come with me?" he urged.

"No, I'm fine. Go! And don't forget, don't ever reactivate Barnie unless you want him to phone home and set the GPF after you!"

Zedok's face was tense, uncertain. Cara smiled at him, though it was more of a grimace as the pain throbbed in her arm. "You'll get by without the dumplings and puddings!" she laughed.

Suddenly, Zedok darted forwards, caught Cara and pulled her to him." Thank you," he said and planted a kiss lightly on her lips. "You're my first true friend, Officer Cadet Cara Davis!"

They gazed at each other for a few seconds, and then with flushed cheeks, Cara took a step away and flapped her hands. "Go!" she told him.

Before I change my mind, Cara thought. She didn't wait for him to go but turned to run back toward the area where the Zeg-Mar5 landed.

Please don't take off without me! She begged as she ran. *I don't want to die on this horrendous planet!*

Chapter 46
Getting Away

Cara touched her wrist communicator as she ran, and it lit up. "Calling Zeg-Mar5! This is Officer Cadet Davis. Zeg-Mar5, do you copy? Emergency!" she cried over the ear-splitting booms and blasts. There was no answer except for a constant interference of buzzing.

"Skag it!" she cried. But she kept running, hoping to make it before they took off. What else could she do?

The laser wound, she noticed, had begun to bleed, and the pain in her arm increased at every step. Soon, Cara's athletic running dropped to a clumsy jog. Then, like a tremendous invisible force, she felt hot winds whipping her body. It hurled clouds of grey grit into her eyes and throat. Explosions from the crumbling Carbonica became ever more frequent. Cara thought she might not have the strength to endure such unbearable conditions but hoped with all her heart that Gorn's ship had not yet taken off.

With the lack of communication, she now wished she had taken the chance to escape in the SP8 with Zedok. It had been a tough decision to make, and she feared that, once again, she had made the wrong one. Now, she might not make it back in time. And she might end up dying here, alone.

In a feverish state, a tragic thought whispered through her head. *It doesn't matter if I don't make it back. I've accomplished my mission. The Kwaidem crystals and Imperium domes are safe. My crew mates are safe. But there'll be no trace left of me, that's for sure.*

Unexpectedly then, the light on her communicator lit up, and without slowing down but breathing in quick gasps, she put it up to her mouth and yelled frantically, "Hello, hello! This is Officer Cadet Davis. Do you read? Copy."

In reply, she heard a familiar, rasping voice. "Officer Cadet Davis, this is Golbat Gorn. Do you copy?"

"Yes, sir! I Copy!" Cara answered eagerly.

"We've been trying to contact you to confirm that you and the prisoner have boarded the SP8. Unfortunately, it's fallen off our grid, and we can't locate the ship – only your wrist communicator. Is there a problem? Copy."

"Mr Gorn, sir, I'm…." Cara tried to cut in, but he didn't hear her.

"Zeg-Mar5 is preparing to take off within the next few minutes, and if you haven't already, I suggest you do the same. Copy?"

"Copy! I hear you. Do you copy?"

"Cadet Davis! We have only a few minutes before the whole planet destroys itself and everyone on it! So, you must take off immediately! Copy and out."

Cara shouted into her communicator as she ran, refusing to give up. "Mr Gorn, please listen! Zeg-Mar, do you hear me? Copy!" But no one replied.

She wondered how far Zedok had made it and if he'd taken off yet. But that was the least of her worries. *I have to reach the skagin' Zeg-Mar5 before it takes off!*

When Cara saw that Gorn's ship was not too far ahead, her sensations felt surreal. Her chest was heaving with exhaustion. Her legs felt like heavy lumps of lead, as though she were morphing into an old rusty robot that would soon stop and never move again. She left her communicator switched on in the hope Gorn would contact her again, but what she heard from his ship now sent her mind spiralling into terror.

Resuming countdown for take-off in sixty seconds…59…58…57

Cara summoned every ounce of energy she had left in her body as she tried to pick up speed, but her body seemed to waver.

30…29…28…27…26… Activating elevator for clearance…25… 24

"No! *No*, wait! Mr Gorn, it's Cara Davis! Please don't leave without me!" she struggled to yell into the communicator, still running, gasping for breath in the oppressive heat.

As she reached the base of the Zeg-Mar5, the elevator began to ascend. Then a deafening klaxon sounded, nearly knocking her off her feet. The elevator stopped and then quickly descended again. The door slid open for Cara.

Covered in sooty grit and gasping shallow, coughing breaths, Cara stumbled forward and lurched through the open door. It took five seconds for the elevator to ascend and enter the spacecraft.

As the door slid open again, Cara clutched her painful arm. She meant to take a step forward, but her legs gave out, and she collapsed at the feet of Mr Golbat Gorn.

He called for medics and began shouting orders to resume take off. When he finally knelt down and asked Cara what had happened, she broke down and cried. "I'm sorry. – Prisoner. – Escaped. – He took the SP8. I'm sorry, sir! He took my blaster. He sh-shot me! He's gone. Tried to stop him . . ."

"*Ready for lift-off,*" were the last words Cara heard before passing out.

Chapter 47
A Change of Heart?

Almost four weeks later, Cara, Valina, and Debian had returned to New Dawn Space Station after recuperating and debriefing at an HQ medical station. Fortunately, the Galaxy Patrol lost no lives during the Battle of Carbonica, only weapons and equipment. Those losses were extensive, though, and included the precious SP8. So far, every investigation of the series of events had cleared the members of New Dawn's crew of any serious or criminal actions. The team didn't feel they were entirely in the clear yet, though, and they couldn't help worrying. After all, losing the SP8 and the TTC were no small matters.

"Predaton is the one responsible for everything!" Cara often ranted when the three spent rec/rel time wondering about their fates. "He only sent Gorn to get the crystals and domes when he did because he had Zedo – a desperate enslaved Radican – lined up to raid the Zeg-Mar5 and take them. He knew the Radican would never get past the security on New Dawn! So, we were right to be suspicious!"

If Valina or Debian added anything about any of their personal actions being possibly impetuous or poorly thought out, Cara always quoted the psych counsellor from HQ who'd told her: "A good officer listens to their instincts and acts to protect their crew and mission." It was her new personal motto.

"That's done, and great job!" Cara proclaimed aloud as she closed the cover on the tracker system. She'd just completed another successful repair job on a highly intricate thermal panel. "Guylo, will you run diagnostics now?"

She carefully replaced the delicate micro-tools in their case and used a tiny vacuum to clean up any lingering dust microbes. After learning so much from Barnie on their journey together, Cara was now a much better Officer Cadet. She knew she'd never have the skills of a Listroc, like Valina or Zedok, who could read the workings of a machine by staring at it, but she was more confident and eager now to learn about the many technological energies on New

Dawn. Valina, delighted at Cara's enthusiasm and pleased with her improved skills, reported as much to Captain Lydian. But so far, the Captain hadn't commented about Cara's improvements.

She sighed as she put everything away. If only Captain Lydian would offer some recognition or encouragement for her work. *It can't be that she hasn't noticed. I don't know what else I can do to impress her.*

Despite all the terrifying risks Cara had taken and how she almost lost her life many times, she dreamed now more than ever of being a warrior in the Galaxy Patrol Force. She hoped one day she could put herself forward for that duty. But, in the meantime, all she could do was strive to be the best Officer Cadet she could be and await the consequences of her actions.

She was thinking about having a coffee break and wondering what Zedok was doing and where he was now when Guylo's voice startled her from her thoughts.

"Cadet Davis, you have an important message on your compad. The Captain has asked me to alert you," the AI said. Cara swore quietly under her breath, then glanced guiltily over her shoulder. Captain Lydian had warned her that she would not tolerate swearing on New Dawn Space Station.

"Oh – *er* – ok. Yes, Guylo," Cara replied. "Now, where'd I leave my compad?" she mumbled to herself. As she looked around for it, she wondered why the Captain would ask Guylo to alert her rather than just waiting for her to find the message on her own. This worried Cara because her grandmother had not been well for the last two weeks. Had Granny become worse? Since her grandparents were her only living family, she'd tried to keep in better touch with them recently. They were so proud when Cara told them how she'd rescued the top-secret but highly important power transmitters. Of course, she'd left out details about the rules she'd broken and the silly mistakes she'd made that had almost led to her death (several times).

The compad was nowhere to be seen, and she was now nervous about the message's contents. "I give up. Guylo, could you locate…"

"Your compad is on the shelf next to your workstation, on the viewing deck, Cara. Remember to respond immediately," Guylo cut in at once.

Cara tutted and rolled her eyes. *"Thank you!"* she muttered, annoyed at herself for constantly misplacing it. But, as usual, Guylo was right, and as she entered the viewing deck and approached her workstation, she could see it flashing. But, to her surprise, Cara saw no image of her grandparents on the screen. Instead, it was only the Captain's name and the words 'Personal and Confidential.'

Why would Captain Lydian send me a personal and confidential message? Cara wondered. She felt afraid to read it. Could it be bad news about her grandparents? Or bad news about her future in the GPS? It could be either, but whatever it was, she doubted it was good news. Finally, after hesitating until she couldn't stand the suspense any longer, Cara tapped the screen and read it.

The message from the Captain troubled Cara and left her with a tightness in her stomach. And worse, it left her with questions and more dread than before. She stared blankly at nothing and was hardly aware of the quiet hum of the space station or the chattering voices of Valina and Debian as they descended the gantry steps.

"Your neck looks as though it's completely healed, Valina. I thought it might leave a scar, but it hasn't."

"Yes, the nanosurgeon said she thought it would heal clean," Valina replied. "And luckily for me, it didn't permanently damage my brain or nervous system."

"I wonder if …" Debian tailed off and said, "Oh, hello, Cara, I didn't realise you were in here. What's up?"

Cara didn't look up or acknowledge either of her crew mates. Instead, she sat motionless at her workstation, leaning her head on her hands and staring at her compad blankly.

"Cara! Are you ok?" Valina asked.

Cara felt Debian touch her shoulder tentatively. "What's the matter, Cara? Is your arm still hurting from the laser gun wound? Has something happened?"

Cara lifted her gaze, revealing her tear-stained face. "Sh-she said she wouldn't! B-b-but she . . . She's . . . "

"What, Cara? What's happened?" Valina said.

Cara held up her compad, tapped the screen, and the message appeared. In a tearful voice, she said, "I got a message . . . " before dissolving into tears again.

"Is it from your grandma?" Debian cut in. Then she gasped, "Oh no! Is it *about* your grandma?"

Cara handed the compad up to them. "She said she would n-not put me in front of a Martial Court. But look!" She cried as she watched them read the Captain's brief message.

Valina returned the pad and folded her arms but didn't immediately speak. Then, after exchanging a look with Debian, she said, "Cara, unless Captain Lydian has stated that the meeting is an actual Court Martial, it probably is not."

"Oh no, Valina, I've failed in my duty on all counts," Cara sobbed. "Remember? I even let a Radican prisoner escape. With valuable GPF property!"

Cara shut her eyes to keep the tears in and let her head fall back into her hand. Debian floated to the other side of Cara's seat and gently swivelled it around, taking Cara's chin in her hand and tilting her face up. Looking into Cara's eyes, Debian said, "But that prisoner Zedok attacked you. He could have killed you! So, it wasn't your fault he escaped, was it?" She produced a handkerchief and lightly dabbed at Cara's tears.

But it was my fault, Cara thought. *I let him go. And what if the Captain has somehow found out about it?* She blinked hard, trying to control herself. Although she didn't like telling lies, she would probably get quite good at telling this one because she'd never be able to tell anyone what she'd done. Although she suspected Debian and maybe even Valina might have done the same thing in her position, she could never tell them the truth.

Debian handed Cara the handkerchief, and she blew her nose, her sobs subsiding a little. "Don't worry, Cara!" Debian continued, "I'm certain the Captain wouldn't go back on her word."

Valina stood motionless and staring at them. She seemed to be deep in thought. Then, in a second, she blinked, and her trance was gone. "Cara, I agree with Debian. Captain Lydian is an honourable officer."

She gave both Cara and Debian a stern look. "But don't forget. We lost a highly experimental, one-of-a-kind Time Travel Capsule. Of course, the GPS can replace the pod you lost, but our loss was invaluable and irreplaceable. And worse yet, the head of all the Radicans got his hands on the TTC because of us. Mostly because of me, honestly."

Debian looked uncomfortable and worried. "When and where is the meeting scheduled again?" she asked.

"Here, on New Dawn, in twenty-four hours," Cara said, wiping away more tears. "Which means the Captain will return to the station sometime soon."

Valina took a step towards them. "In that case, Cara, as First Officer, I'm ordering you to get some rest."

"Oh, I won't be able to sleep! I'll be dreading this meeting!" Cara wailed.

Debian touched Cara's cheek and smiled, "Valina's right, Cara. And I can make sure you get a sound and healthy sleep."

Valina picked up her compad from the control desk and called, "Guylo, activate nocturnal mode for six hours." At once, the lights dimmed to a calming green, and all noise silenced.

*

When Debian and Cara had gone, Valina spotted a message alert on the screen of her compad too. *Sender: Captain S Lydian. Personal and confidential.* It was the same order to attend the same important meeting as Cara. Surprised by the message, Valina pondered for a moment, then realised Debian was back and hovering nearby, waiting to say something.

"Valina, I've received a message from Captain Lydian. She has ordered me to attend that meeting. Have you received it, too?" Debian said in a quavering voice. Valina looked at her and nodded.

Without another word, the two cadets wandered onto the viewing platform. They stared at the sky as two or three comets dashed across the darkness. Debian broke the silence. "Maybe the meeting is about something far more serious than we imagined," she said.

Valina continued to observe the void and its multitude of stars. The constellations dipped and wheeled, yet they always seemed so ordered, always in the right place. She narrowed her eyes. "Are you thinking what I'm thinking?" she asked.

Debian murmured, "The TTC?"

Valina nodded. "If that's the reason . . . Well, it looks like it's not just Cara who's in serious trouble, is it?"

Chapter 48

Together

The next day, feeling nervous, Cara proceeded to Captain Lydian's meeting with Debian and Valina along New Dawn's gantry. Their light blue uniforms were pristine, including Cara's. It astounded Cara to learn that Captain Lydian had ordered Valina and Debian to attend the same meeting. Convinced it was her fault that they were in trouble, too, Cara felt guilty.

They waited outside the Captain's Command Station door; Cara, fidgeting with her hands, felt familiar anxiety boiling in her gut. "I wonder if they've decided our fate yet. Will they dismiss us, do you think?" she whispered. Neither of the other two officer cadets answered her and looked away. Cara clasped her hands, thinking the prospect of 'dismissal' was the least of her worries. But, for all she knew, they might charge her with treason and imprison her for life in Canton.

Startled by the door sliding open with a swish, Cara heard Guylo's voice say, "You may enter."

To Cara's surprise, there were no other officers in the room. Alone, Captain Lydian stood with her back to them, one gloved hand behind her, staring out of a viewing window. When the officer cadets entered, she turned to them with an unsmiling but not harsh expression, and all three stiffened to attention and saluted her.

She returned the salute and said, "Take a seat, all of you," gesturing to three seats around her desk. They did as the Captain ordered. Cara felt numb.

Captain Lydian sat in a high-backed chair on the opposite side of her large desk and fixed her gaze on all three. When she placed her hands on the desk, Cara noticed, with some relief, that her gloved hand appeared relaxed.

A promising sign, she thought.

Without hesitation, the Captain moved her eyes and scrutinised Cara's face. "Well, Cadet Davis, that was quite a show you were involved in."

"Yes, ma'am," Cara said, knowing full well that Captain Lydian was referring to everything that had happened since she dressed as a Radican and gone after Golbat Gorn and the power transmitters.

"Is there anything you want to say about it?" the Captain asked.

"Only that I'm sorry, ma'am," Cara said.

"Sorry for what, exactly?" the Captain responded.

Cara hesitated, taking time to consider before answering. "I should never have doubted Mr Gorn's integrity without first talking to you, Captain. I should not have been *er*-afraid to contact you. I know now that I wasn't wrong to go after the power transmitters, but I was wrong to take so much upon myself, Ma'am."

"Anything else you'd like to add?"

After taking a breath, Cara looked down in shame. "Ma'am, I should never have allowed myself to have trusted the Radican prisoner Zedok."

"Why did you, Officer Cadet?"

Cara was glad to tell the truth about this part. "The prisoner offered to help me find Carbonica. He knew that was where Valina and Debian's distress signal came from. And he *did* rescue them from the Radicans, all by himself. So that I could go after the power transmitters," she said in one breath.

"And this Zedok? Did he ask you for anything in exchange?"

At this, Cara lied, knowing full well he'd asked for his freedom from the Radicans and the GPS Law Enforcers. "No, Captain. He said he'd 'settle up with the big brass after becoming a hero.' And I foolishly believed him. I, I guess I wanted to believe him. And I needed his help."

Captain Lydian tilted her head and gave Cara a side glance. "Are you sure about that?"

Cara swallowed hard and tried a different tack. "Well, on one occasion, he disclosed that the Radicans enslaved him, and so he'd lost all hope of ever escaping them. So, I guess I believed he'd stay with me and go to HQ. I thought he'd ask for mercy. And Mr Gorn told him he'd speak up for him when the time came. So, I thought …"

Cara was squirming at the way she was answering the questions. She needed to convince Captain Lydian why she'd allowed Zedok to help her. She hoped the Captain wouldn't ask for details about his escape. Finally, Cara breathed, straightened in her seat, and regained her courage. "In my defence, Captain, I was desperate to rescue Valina and Debian and determined to recover the power transmitters."

When the Captain only looked at her in silence, Cara went on. "Zedok, as you know, is a Listroc. With his advanced abilities, knowledge of the Radican base, and piloting skills, he located where the distress beacon originated and transported us both with warp speed to Carbonica." Cara stopped, hoping it was enough to satisfy Captain Lydian and the official file.

Captain Lydian looked at her with half a smile and said, "In your defence, Officer Cadet Davis, I don't think you had much choice, did you?"

She opened her bionic hand and placed the palm downwards on the desk. "I realise you made the right decision this time because we're all here, safe. And we have the power transmitters back in a secure place, where they belong. What's more," she continued, "you alone eventually prevented them from falling into the hands of Predaton, who we now know is a traitorous, power-mad tyrant."

Captain Lydian paused, leaned back in her seat, and stared hard at Cara. "It's just unfortunate, isn't it, that you – how shall I put it – 'dropped your guard' and allowed prisoner Zedok to escape?"

Cara swallowed hard and nodded. She felt the heat rise in her neck and continued to hold the Captain's gaze but couldn't speak. She thought, *I'm getting uncomfortably good at lying, but not that good.* Cara couldn't read the expression in Captain Lydian's eyes, and the uncomfortable silence seemed to go on far too long. Until, to Cara's relief, Valina broke it.

"Permission to speak, ma'am?" Valina said.

"Permission granted," Captain Lydian answered, breaking her steely gaze from Cara and turning to Valina.

"Do we know where Commander Predaton is?"

Captain Lydian frowned and sighed. "No, and we have little hope of finding him. So, we must assume he is still gadding about in that time travel capsule. Therefore, we may never find him."

The Captain shook her head with a doubtful expression on her face. "He might have easily perished while attempting to travel in the damaged machine. Frankly, your description of the crash landing and your journey on Carbonica made most of us doubt that those pirates could have successfully repaired the TTC so quickly."

Cara noticed Debian drop her gaze to concentrate on her hands clasped in front of her. *Valina needs to change the conversation!* Cara thought.

The first officer cleared her throat, and her lilac eyes became keen again. "May I ask, Captain, for what purpose will the scientists use the power transmitters in the future?"

Captain Lydian leaned in and looked from one to another. "Now that is a much better topic. As you all know, many dead and dying planets exist in this part of the universe. Once the PTs have reached their maximum strength, we shall deploy them to help revive those planets. We hope their power can save every failing world and every dying ecosystem our teams of investigative scientists can find."

That last statement of the Captain's jolted Cara's attention. *And that's what Mom and Dad were. Investigative scientists. That's how they got killed.* She wondered if Captain Lydian knew anything about them.

The Captain earnestly continued, "Thanks to these power transmitters, life will flourish on many worlds of death and destruction."

Again, there was a pause in the discussion until Debian shuffled to the edge of the seat, and Cara heard her say in a small voice, "Captain, what's happening to us?"

"Well, now you've mentioned it!" Captain Lydian said.

Cara, all eyes and ears, watched the Captain rise from her seat and take a few paces away before turning to face them again. Her expression was serious, almost severe. Cara was dreading what the Captain was about to say.

"Now listen!" the Captain began again. "The three of you have to make a choice." she paused, giving each of them a quizzical look. Cara realised she was clutching the arms of her chair as if it was about to be ejected from the station. She closed her eyes.

"Do you all want to stay here on New Dawn Space Station, or," she paused, "do you want to come with me?"

Cara gaped at the Captain in surprise. She glanced at Valina and Debian and saw they looked the same. Captain Lydian smiled and stood to her full height. "Did you wonder why the Galactic Council called me away yesterday?"

Cara nodded, held her breath, and waited for an answer.

"Well, to be brief," Captain Lydian said, "they offered me a promotion, and I've accepted it." She paused and said, almost giddy with excitement. "I'm to replace Predaton as Commander!"

There was a perceptible collective gasp from the cadets. Cara couldn't stop herself from leaping to her feet. "Captain, you mean you're now *Commander* Lydian?"

"Not yet, Davis, but soon. The Galactic Council has created a new Enforcement Section to prevent criminals like the Radican Pirates from forming armies and committing more terrible crimes. I shall be in command of that section, and I'll need a dependable team to help me," she said, emphasising 'dependable'.

The three officer cadets gave each other excited glances, but Cara couldn't stop yelling earnestly, "When do we need to say? I mean, whether we want to be part of your squad?"

"Cara! Don't go on so!" Valina scolded while trying to hide a grin.

Cara remembered the dynamic feeling when she was part of all the action – speeding through space, destroying the Kaligiabeast, battling Predaton and the Radicans, and retrieving the power transmitters at the last possible second. At times, it was terrifying, but despite all of that, it was precisely the excitement she craved.

"No, wait, wait! I mean, IF. I mean, suppose we want to join you, Captain, sir. Uh, *ma'am*," Cara chattered on. "Because nothing is certain – obviously. But how long until we should—?"

Captain Lydian shook her head and gestured for Cara to stop. 'You three have just a few weeks to complete your training programme. Then, after you've graduated and become full officers, you will need to decide."

Cara cut straight in again. "If we join you, will we be on another space station? A bigger one?" she gasped, her pulse quickening with the thrill of it all.

The Captain threw back her head and laughed. "No, no, no!" she said. "I have a brand-new starship called *The Endeavour* waiting for me, for *us* – if you decide to join me, that is!"

Cara smiled at Valina's and Debian's knowing glances and the look the two of them exchanged. *Yes, my friends, you're right. I've already decided,* she thought with a grin.

Captain Lydian became formal again. "There is much for you to think about. I'm ending the meeting now so you can resume your duties."

They stood and saluted the Captain before turning to leave the meeting.

"Carry on!" Captain Lydian ordered, returning their salute. Then, as all three turned to go, she called, "And Davis. Make sure you achieve your Flying Pass this time!"

Cara turned back with sparkling eyes and smiled. "Oh, I'm confident I'll pass it. Don't you worry about that, ma'am. After all, I've had plenty of practice. I'm sure my piloting and navigating skills are now super accurate." Her beaming smile shone briefly on them all. Then, as she turned confidently to go, Cara heard a chorus of, "Look out!"

It came too late. "*OW!* Skag me!" Cara yelped as she crashed into the closed door, and her hand flew to her nose. Bright drops of blood dribbled down onto her pristine uniform jacket.

Stained again, she thought, looking down. *Well, so what? I'll keep things interesting around here, that's for sure!*

Cara smiled and dabbed at her nose with her handkerchief. She heard them tut-tutting behind her and suspected their heads were shaking at her. But Cara didn't mind. Her unwavering confidence was back, and she knew she could look forward to an exciting future.

There'll be a realm of electrifying and infinite possibilities awaiting me. This time I'll have every opportunity of making my family and everyone proud of me. I won't let them down. Just wait and see!

The End

Also by Diane Pike

Bleak Trail

It is 1880, and Canada is a vast, wild
country where pioneers have started
to build a railroad from east to west.
Edward, a wealthy family teenager
in England, leaves home to meet
his brother in Jasper, a ramshackle
town in western Canada. On arrival,
Edward finds to his great dismay
his brother, George, a rail company
surveyor, is no longer there. Edward
is left all alone to fend for himself
in the wilds.

Can the seventeen-year-old Edward
survive the terrible bad luck,
treacherous weather conditions
and life-threatening challenges that
await him ...?

Milton Keynes UK
Ingram Content Group UK Ltd.
UKHW020720230823
427276UK00006B/117